SHADOW KNIGHTS

KNIGHTS OF THE REALM, BOOK 2

JENNIFER ANNE DAVIS

REIGN PUBLISHING

Published by Reign Publishing

Cover Design by KimG-Design
Editing by Cynthia Shepp

ISBN (paperback): 978-1-7323661-8-3
ISBN (ebook): 978-1-73233661-7-6

Library of Congress Control Number: 1-8062216010

OTHER BOOKS BY JENNIFER ANNE DAVIS

True Reign:

The Key

Red

War

Reign of Secrets:

Cage of Deceit

Cage of Darkness

Cage of Destiny

Oath of Deception

Oath of Destruction

The Order of the Krigers:

Rise

Burning Shadows

Conquering Fate

Knights of the Realm:

Realm of Knights

Shadow Knights

Hidden Knights

Single Titles:

The Voice

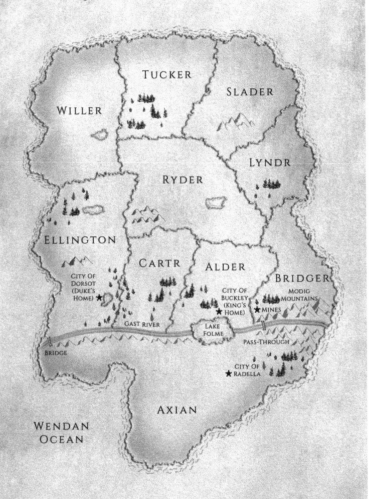

CHAPTER ONE

Reid clutched the soldier's hand as she climbed out of the boat. The strong wind twisted the dress around her legs, almost tripping her. She wanted to punch Idina for insisting she travel in this ridiculous attire. At least now that Reid was officially in Axian, she could wear whatever the hell she wanted.

"This way, Lady Reid," the Axian soldier said.

She slung the strap of her bag over her head and onto her shoulder, following the man along the dock toward the shoreline. Reid couldn't believe she was about to come face to face with her fiancé. The thought made her skin crawl. She didn't know who to be mad at—King Eldon for insisting on the match in the first place or her father for agreeing to it. Or maybe Prince Ackley? Her eyes narrowed. Somehow, Ackley had his hand in this. She was certain of it.

Reid took in the sight of her fiancé, Prince Dexter. He stood at the end of the dock with his legs shoulder-width apart and his hands clasped behind his back. Dressed in solid black—including his ominous cape—he reeked of intimidation. Reid glared at him. Did he normally dress in black? Or had he done so to let Reid know what he thought of their union? It wasn't like she wanted to be here. Although, she *did* want to be in Axian. But she definitely didn't want to be engaged. Especially to Dexter. She would much rather be engaged to his younger brother, Colbert. At least he seemed human.

The only good thing to come out of this disastrous mess was her family's safety. Not only had her father been pardoned for his crimes, but he was also now able to deed his land to anyone of his choosing, male or otherwise. He'd probably pick Reid's sister, Ainsley, since she was the oldest of the five siblings.

Stepping off the dock, Reid stood before Dexter, her head held high. She still couldn't believe she'd fought him. He was a good foot taller than her and twice as wide.

"Lady Reid," the soldier said, "may I present to you our esteemed commander, Prince Dexter."

Reid inclined her head. She would not curtsy before this man who'd treated her so rudely the last time she'd seen him.

"This is Captain Gytha," the soldier said, indicating the woman on Dexter's right. "And this is Captain Essie." He gestured to the woman on his left.

"Nice to meet you," Reid said. It was refreshing to meet two formidable women who were also soldiers. Both wore slim black pants and form-fitting shirts topped with leather armor. Each also had a sword strapped to her waist. Maybe Reid could become a soldier.

However, as much as she might want to join the army, she couldn't. She was a Knight—and she had a job to do. Her fingers tightened around the strap of her bag, remembering the letter from Ackley hidden inside. It contained her next assignment. As soon as she was alone, she needed to read it.

Neither woman responded. They were as welcoming and cordial as Dexter. Reid couldn't help but smirk. If no one was in favor of this union, maybe it didn't have to take place.

"Why are you smiling?" Gytha asked, wrinkling her nose in

apparent disgust. "I wouldn't be happy if I were sold off to a man like cattle. I'd be ashamed."

Heat creeped up Reid's neck and face, and she knew her skin had turned bright red. She focused on Dexter, but he wasn't even looking at her. His attention was on the water behind her, as if she didn't even exist.

The other woman snorted. "You don't know the meaning of the word *ashamed*. You'd chop off his balls then send him back home."

Gytha burst out laughing. "Yes, that sounds like something I would do." A single brown braid hung to the middle of her back. The dark makeup around her eyes enhanced the sharp features of her face, making her appear fierce and intimidating.

"You don't have to worry about being sold off," Essie said. "Your father wouldn't degrade you like that."

"No, he would not."

"And you're already attached to someone." The corners of Essie's lips curved into a sly smile.

"Not anymore." Gytha's brown eyes darkened.

Dexter abruptly turned and stalked away, his cape rippling behind him in the gusty wind.

"I guess that's the only welcome you're getting from our prince," Essie said.

"It was more than she deserved," Gytha replied.

Both women followed Dexter.

Reid watched them go. Although Dexter had been rude, not even bothering to utter a single word, she couldn't help but admire the fact that he had two female captains. Not wanting to scurry after them like a dog, Reid started walking along the shore in the opposite direction.

"Where are you going?" the Axian soldier who'd introduced her asked.

Pausing, she fiddled with the strap of her bag. She felt out of place, and not because she was in a foreign county, but because she wasn't herself. She'd spent so long pretending to be a man, her father's heir, and someone she wasn't. Now, she didn't know who to be or how to act. Maybe it was time for her to step out of her own shadow to finally learn who she was and what she was capable of.

"What's your name?" she asked.

"Lieutenant Gilbert."

"Well, Gilbert, I'm heading west." She resumed her path.

"Um, why are you going that way? Everyone else is gathering east of the dock."

"That is precisely why I've chosen to go west."

"You need to come with us," he said, jogging after her.

"Why is that?"

"Because Prince Henrick and Princess Nara wish to speak with you."

"Okay." She kept walking. The clouds rolled in, concealing the sun and making it difficult to tell the time of day.

"Why are you still going the wrong way?"

"Who says this is the wrong way? There are many ways to get to the palace, and this is the way I am choosing to go. You're not coming with me, are you? I'd rather travel alone."

He stopped, then mumbled something she couldn't understand.

"Lady Reid," Gytha barked. "You're coming with us. Now." Her commanding voice left no room for argument.

Reid whirled to face Gytha, who stood about forty feet away with her hands on her hips. While Reid did not care to be ordered around by this brusque woman, she didn't want to come across like a spoiled, stubborn brat. Her goal was to reach the palace to speak to Henrick and Nara. Even though Reid didn't care for or like Dexter, she was curious to learn more about the Axian army and the soldiers within it. It was also advantageous to travel with people who had the necessary supplies to make such a journey. Without saying a word, she headed back toward the soldiers.

When she joined them, Dexter raised his hand, and everyone fell into three lines. They headed south, no one speaking. Reid joined a row, keeping her eyes open for a place that would afford her the privacy to change into pants. After two miles, Dexter halted, then started splitting the soldiers into groups of ten.

Reid stepped out of line, examining the area. There was a forest to the east, fields to the south, and wild vegetation to the west. She still couldn't get over how green everything was on this side of the Gast River.

"I recognize you," a deep voice said, startling Reid.

She turned to see a familiar face. It was the man from the festival—the one who'd been in charge of the archery competition. Somewhere in his mid-twenties, he had close-cropped brown hair. He'd slung a bow and quiver over his wide shoulders. While his face was pleasant, it was a bit plain. Reid realized she liked that about him.

"You look different without your cart of bows and arrows," she said by way of greeting.

He chuckled. "And you look different in a dress."

She was attempting to rectify that situation. Sighing, she wondered how much time she had before they set out again. "Do you know what's going on?" She nodded to where Dexter spoke with a handful of soldiers.

"The commander just put us into smaller groups. Each one has a different task to complete."

"What are you supposed to do?"

"Accompany the commander and his fiancée to the palace." He raised his eyebrows, almost as if waiting for an explanation.

Reid didn't have one.

"I assume you're the fiancée?"

"I am Lady Reid Ellington, but you can call me Reid."

"I'm Markis." The corners of his lips twitched as he fought a smile. "Everyone has been talking about you."

Several people blatantly watched her. "I have no doubt. Tell me, will we be walking the entire way to the palace?"

"I don't know what the commander has planned."

Besides desperately wanting to change, Reid needed to read the note Ackley had slipped in her bag. She was eager to know her next assignment. Unfortunately, she didn't see a place nearby where she could do either.

A whistle rang out. "That's our cue." Markis led Reid over to where Dexter stood with Gytha and eight other soldiers.

Dexter didn't spare Reid a glance as he addressed the group. "There are horses five miles south of here. Once we reach them, we'll stop for the night. Then, at first light, we ride." He started walking, Gytha beside him.

They fell into two lines behind the commander and the captain. The others set out as well, each heading in a different direction. Reid wondered about each group's destination.

Dexter set a relentless pace, and they reached the horses in under two hours. After traveling five miles on a dirt road, Reid's shoes and the bottom of her dress were filthy. She scanned the area, not seeing a lake or stream in sight. Erected in a semi-circle on the thick green grass were six tents.

"Lady Reid," Gytha said, "you're with me."

Gytha escorted Reid to a tent situated toward the middle. Exhausted, Reid crawled inside. There were two bedrolls, and Gytha plopped on the left one. Reid sat on the right one, wishing she could have a moment alone to read Ackley's note. Her stomach growled. "Will we be eating supper soon?"

"They need time to cook it, princess." Gytha leaned back on her elbows, crossing her ankles.

"I'm not a princess."

"Yet."

Reid let the comment slide. She carefully opened her bag, making sure the note remained at the bottom along with that blasted pawn from her chess set. Really, what had Ackley been thinking? She went to pull out her pants and tunic, only she couldn't find either. "I'm going to kill him."

"Now you're speaking my language," Gytha said. "Who are we going to kill?"

Annoyed, Reid set her bag aside. "No one." She rubbed her face, wondering when Ackley had managed to remove the pants from her bag. All that she had in there was another ridiculous dress. Did he have any idea how hard it was to travel in something so impractical?

"Too bad. I would have enjoyed that." Gytha knelt on her bedroll. "It's probably time to eat."

"I'll be there shortly. I need a moment alone."

"Whatever." Gytha left the tent.

Grabbing her bag, Reid opened it again and pulled out the note from Ackley. On the outside, he'd written—*Your next assignment.* She unfolded the paper, her hands shaking as she did.

Gain Prince Dexter's trust. Find out where he goes at night. Discover who Henrick has declared his heir. All correspondence is to go through the bookstore where you bought the map.

Well, her assignment certainly wasn't what she'd thought it would be. The first part—gaining Dexter's trust—would be impossible. But the rest shouldn't be too hard. Reid refolded the paper, needing to get rid of it. A thought suddenly occurred to her. Who was in charge of the Knights? She'd assumed Ackley was the leader of the elusive group. However, he'd told her he was *part* of the group. He'd even revealed he'd been recruited. So, who was in charge? Who determined her assignments?

Her stomach rumbled, reminding her that she needed to eat. Rising, she shoved the paper down the front of her dress, hiding it below her bosom before she exited the tent. At least she had boots on. Otherwise, she would have murdered Ackley.

Outside, the soldiers sat around a fire, eating. She scanned their faces, noting the absence of Dexter and Gytha.

"I wasn't sure if you'd be joining us," Markis said, approaching Reid with a plate of food.

He offered it to her, and she took it with a murmured thanks. "I was hoping to change."

"Why didn't you?" He glanced at her dress, making a strange face.

When he sat, she knelt beside him. Instead of answering his question, she took a bite of the meat on her plate.

"Aren't you going to ask where the commander is?" Markis whispered.

She narrowed her eyes. "No."

"You're not curious where your fiancé is?"

"He is not my fiancé by choice."

Markis smiled. "That's what I thought. Prince Dexter and Gytha have been pretty cozy with one another for over a year. We expected them to announce their engagement. I was shocked when he told me we were coming here to fetch his fiancée. I was even more surprised when I recognized you."

She had a suspicion about Dexter and Gytha being romantically involved. However, to have it confirmed disturbed her. No wonder they both hated her so much.

"You're Duke Ellington's daughter, yet I saw you in the City of Radella by yourself."

He was fishing for information, but she had no intention of giving him any. "I think I'll turn in for the night." With a nod at him, Reid stood and headed toward her tent. Instead of going inside, she glanced at the fire, making sure everyone was still there. When she didn't see anyone paying her any attention, she went around to the backside of her tent. No one called out or came running after her, so she headed toward the cover of the trees.

Reid had two goals in mind—to relieve herself and to destroy the paper outlining her assignment. Tossing it in the fire would have been ideal. However, she hadn't wanted anyone to see her do so. Someone might have asked questions she couldn't answer. Not wanting to stray too deep into the forest since it was dark and she didn't want to get lost, she headed parallel to the tree line. There had to be a water source nearby. Otherwise, Dexter wouldn't have chosen to set up camp here with the horses.

"Where are you going?" a voice demanded, startling Reid.

"None of your business," Reid replied, discreetly making sure the note was still hidden in her bosom before turning to face Gytha.

"You are my responsibility. Go back to camp. Now."

"Do not order me about. You'd do well to watch your tone as well. I outrank you." It was better to put Gytha in her place now, so Reid wouldn't have to keep dealing with her.

Gytha bristled. She stood there for a long, uncomfortable minute before responding. "I apologize, Lady Reid." Sarcasm oozed through her tone. "Our wise and competent Princess Nara asked me to watch out for and take care of you on our journey."

That surprised Reid. "Listen, Gytha, I think we got off on the wrong foot." She didn't want to fight with this woman.

"Since you insist on being overly formal, it's Captain Gytha."

"Fine, Captain Gytha." Reid took a deep breath. "Thank you for watching over me. As soon as I relieve myself, I'll return to camp."

"I'll wait." Folding her arms, Gytha started tapping her foot.

Reid sighed, knowing she'd lost the opportunity to destroy the letter. After she ducked behind a tree to quickly relieve herself, she said, "Let's go back."

Gytha led Reid to their tent. "In you go."

"Aren't you joining me?"

"I'm on watch. Once my shift is over, I'll sleep."

That explained why Gytha hadn't been eating with everyone else. Reid suspected Dexter was also on watch. Not that it mattered. But she did file that information away for later. It revealed a lot about the type of leader and person he was.

She stretched out on her bedroll, mulling over her life-changing day. She still couldn't fathom she was engaged. Not wanting to think about it right now, she focused on her assignment. The Knights wanted her to get close to Dexter and gain his trust. But why? What did they suspect he was doing? She also needed to discover who Henrik had declared his heir, though she assumed it was Dexter. However, it could be Eldon since he was the firstborn. At least Reid understood why that mattered, since title and land could only pass from father to son in the kingdom.

Rubbing her face, she remembered what the king wanted her to do—find the letters proving he was Henrick's son. She knew he would destroy them the moment he got ahold of them. The problem was she'd already found the letters. Somehow Ackley had stolen them. She didn't have any proof, but it was the only thing that made sense. When Nara had opened the box, the letters were in it. Then, she'd closed and locked the box right in front of Reid, who then took it and returned home. She hid the box in her room, then Ackley showed up. When she retrieved the box, she'd heard it rattle. Ackley had even made a comment about the chess set in her room. When the king opened the box, one of Reid's chess pieces—the queen—was inside, but the letters were not.

Ackley had to be responsible for the swap. Although how he'd managed to open the box, Reid didn't know. Leigh, his mother, had a key, which she'd given to the king so he could open the box. Could Leigh have given one to Ackley as well? Reid had no idea where Leigh stood on the matter. Both Eldon and Gordon were her sons, even if they had different fathers. Both had a legitimate claim to the throne. Which of her sons had her support?

Reid rolled onto her side, recalling a conversation she'd had with Idina. Something about whether Reid could get close to a man in order to gain information. Surely the Knights hadn't masterminded her engagement to Dexter. That seemed like too big of a stretch. She just happened to be in the perfect situation to find out what he was up to. It was a coincidence. It had to be. Too bad Dexter disliked her as much as she did him. It would make getting close to him impossible.

CHAPTER TWO

Reid refused to ride to the City of Radella while sitting sideways on a horse. Besides it being uncomfortable, she feared she'd fall. And it was embarrassing being the only one in a garment that limited her movements. Not wanting to ask one of the female soldiers if she could borrow a spare uniform, she decided to alter her dresses. Luckily, she had two to work with.

When she exited her tent the next morning, everyone stared. Reid had on both dresses. It made her look silly, but she didn't care. She'd ripped the bottom skirt up the center in both the front and back, allowing her legs to fit on either side of the saddle. Not wanting her bottom exposed, she'd torn the top skirt up the sides, then tied the fabric between her legs.

Ignoring the stares and whispers, Reid tried to walk normally as she joined everyone near the dying fire. She ate a quick breakfast of boiled oats, thankful to have something warm since the ground was damp from the thick morning fog. When she finished, she helped Gytha pack their bedrolls and tent. After, Markis brought over a saddled horse. He laced his hands together, offering her a leg up, and she stepped on them, hoisting herself onto the saddle. As she settled, she made a few adjustments to ensure she'd adequately covered her legs. Satisfied, she looked up, realizing everyone had already mounted and were waiting on her.

Pinching his lips together, Markis averted his gaze. Reid suspected he was on the verge of laughter. Gytha, on the other hand, had her eyebrows scrunched, as if trying to understand the rules of a game she'd never played before.

"Now that we're *finally* ready," Dexter said, "let's get moving." Nudging his horse into a trot, he led the way, Gytha at his side. Everyone else fell in line behind them.

Markis rode alongside Reid. "Nice getup," he said with a smirk.

"Thank you." Holding her head high, she refrained from commenting.

"You know," he said, lowering his voice to a whisper, "you could go up there and ride next to the commander."

"Why would I do that?" she asked, trying to decipher his motives.

He shrugged. "To make a statement."

This was a small, intimate group of only a dozen people. Was it necessary to assert her position as Dexter's fiancée? Did she have something to prove to these soldiers? To Gytha? Dexter? Maybe even to herself? "I'm not ready." Reid needed to get her bearings first. Since the king had announced her engagement, she'd felt as if someone had tossed her in a lake, leaving her unable to determine which way was up. Until she felt righted, she would stand down.

Besides, forcing herself on Dexter wasn't the best way to gain his trust. And, frankly, she didn't want to spend time with a man who intimidated her.

"At some point, you will need to assert your position in Axian."

"I understand." And she would when she was ready. "Why don't you tell me about the army and how it's structured?"

She'd expected him to talk nonstop, leaving her to observe her surroundings without having to contribute much. However, he didn't say a word. "What's your rank in the army?" she asked.

He shrugged, still not speaking.

Reid narrowed her eyes. "Did Prince Dexter order you not to discuss any aspects of the army with me?"

He shot her a smile. "You're quick."

What were they supposed to talk about then? Obviously, Dexter didn't want her to gain any knowledge about his army, but what about those around him? "Can you tell me about Gytha?"

Markis chuckled. "That I can do." He reached over his left shoulder, adjusting the bow slung across his back. "Captain Gytha grew up in the City of Radella. Her parents are blacksmiths. She joined the army when she was only fifteen."

"Why so young?" Reid thought she remembered Nara saying people had to be eighteen to join. Anyone younger required parental permission.

"Dexter recruited her."

"How come?" What qualities had Gytha possessed at such an early age that caught Dexter's interest?

Markis smiled. "If you ever have the privilege of seeing Captain Gytha fight, you'll understand."

Jealousy started to worm its way into Reid, which she didn't like. It was an unfamiliar feeling. Shoving it aside, she asked, "Prince Dexter and Captain Gytha have been courting for about a year?"

"Officially, they are nothing more than friends," Markis said. "Unofficially, they've been sneaking around for years. However, they became pretty serious over this past year."

"Why have they been sneaking around?" Was it because Gytha wasn't well-born and therefore not considered suitable for a prince?

"That's a complicated, loaded question, which I'm not comfortable answering. You'd have to ask them."

"In Ellington, where I'm from, parents decide who their children will marry. If two people fall in love, they cannot marry unless both sets of parents agree to the match. Is it the same here in Axian?"

He eyed something up ahead and to the left. "If I'm not careful around you, I'm going to say something I shouldn't." He slung his bow off his shoulder, placing it across his lap. "In Axian, people are free to marry whoever they choose. That's not to say parents don't encourage or discourage certain matches."

Before Reid could ask another question, Gytha dropped back to ride alongside Markis.

"Are you even paying attention?" Gytha hissed.

"I am," Markis replied. "I was just about to take care of it."

Gytha glared at Reid before nudging her horse and returning to Dexter's side at the front.

Curious, Reid watched Markis raise his bow, grab an arrow, and nock it. He aimed to the left, past Reid. They'd been traveling alongside a dense forest. She squinted, but she didn't see an animal lurking in the shadows of the trees.

Markis's eyes narrowed as he took a steadying breath and released his arrow. It whizzed by Reid, flying straight into a tree. When Reid peered closer, she realized he'd impaled a six-foot-long brown snake that matched the coloring of the tree trunk.

Blinking, she gaped at Markis as he calmly slung his bow back over his shoulder. "You just shot a snake."

"It was venomous."

Her question wasn't *why* he'd done it, but *how* he'd managed to hit a small target that completely blended in with its surroundings.

He must have sensed her curiosity. "Since I was a boy of only five, I've had a bow in hand. My grandpa taught me to shoot. I took to it naturally. Because I'm so good at it, I try to find ways to challenge myself—like striking moving objects or trying to hit something with my eyes closed. That's why Prince Dexter recruited me."

"He saw you shoot?"

Markis nodded. "My village has a fair every year. The year I turned seventeen, I was showing off for money." Almost preening, he grinned. "People were placing bets on what I could or couldn't hit. Unbeknownst to me, the prince was in the crowd. A seven-year-old girl had run out into an open field to set up targets for me. I don't know what made me look, but I sensed something was amiss. Maybe it was the way the forest surrounding the field stilled or the unnatural sway of the tall grass. Regardless, I nocked my arrow and shot before I even knew what I was doing. Just as a mountain cat leapt for the girl, my arrow struck it. It landed right next to her, dead before it even hit the ground. If I'd hesitated for even a second, it would have killed her."

"And Prince Dexter saw this?"

"He did. Recruited me right there on the spot. Said he needed a man like me in his army."

Reid mulled over this information. Had the prince wanted Markis because of his skill with the bow or because he hadn't hesitated when he saved the girl? Both said a lot about the type of man Markis was. Begrudgingly, she admitted it said something about the man Dexter was, too.

When the sun started to set, Dexter called a halt for the day. Reid realized they were heading east instead of south. "Where are we going?" she asked as she dismounted.

"To the City of Radella." Yawning, Markis stretched his arms over his head.

Reid's right thigh ached, a trickle of blood sliding down it. Rubbing against the saddle all day must have chafed her skin. Since the material of her dress wasn't nearly as thick as pants, it offered less protection. She'd have to be more careful tomorrow.

She surveyed the soldiers as they unloaded supplies and set up camp. "Where is our detour taking us?"

"Why do you think we're taking a detour?" Markis asked.

"We're not heading south like we should be."

"I don't know." Two soldiers gathered the horses, then led them to a nearby stream to drink. "We should help. Otherwise, we'll be stuck with the last watch of the night."

Reid agreed, heading over to help Gytha erect their tent. Once they finished, they joined the other soldiers sitting around the fire, eating. Reid carefully sat on the ground, making sure her skirt covered her legs. Markis handed her a steaming bowl of soup. As she took a sip, she scanned the people near her. "Where's Gytha?" The woman had been right there a second ago.

"I think she has the first watch," someone answered.

At that precise moment, Reid realized Dexter was missing as well. Presumably, he had first watch, too. Reid's face flushed for a multitude of reasons—one being she had no desire for people to believe she was jealous. While she might feel a bit envious over Gytha's position of captain in the army and her reputation as an excellent fighter, Reid was not upset over the woman's relationship with Dexter. Besides, Reid had no idea if Gytha and Dexter were actually on watch or if they'd used it as an excuse to have some...private time. Reid's face burned hotter at the thought. Taking another sip of the soup, she hoped anyone who noticed would think her flush was a result of the hot food.

Frustrated, Reid had no idea how she was supposed to gain Dexter's trust. Since the moment they'd met in Prince Henrick's bedchamber, he'd despised her. Now, he was being forced to marry her. To complicate matters even more, he was in love with another woman. Instead of Axian being the freedom Reid had hoped for, it was turning out to be one big complicated mess.

One by one, the soldiers went to their tents for the night. Now that the sun had set, the stars were out. The air had started to turn chilly, too. Holding her palms out, Reid pretended to enjoy the heat from the fire.

"Allow me to escort you to your tent," Markis said as he stood.

"It's twenty feet from here. I think I can manage on my own." She kept her focus on the flames, hoping he wouldn't see the lie.

"Suit yourself," he said with a shrug before he left.

Only two women remained outside. As the wood burned down, the flames slowly lost their luster. Before long, both women rose, bid Reid goodnight, and ducked into their tents.

Now was her chance. Furtively, she withdrew Ackley's letter from her bosom and quickly tossed it into the fire. The edges curled and blackened before it disintegrated into ashes. What felt like a huge weight lifted from Reid, allowing her to breathe easier.

"What was that?" Gytha demanded from behind Reid, startling her.

Not wanting to lie, Reid decided to tell a version of the truth. "Not that it concerns you, but it was a letter." Maybe the way to gain Dexter's trust was through gaining Gytha's.

"A letter from your king?" Gytha moved into sight, towering over Reid.

It didn't escape Reid's notice that Gytha had said *your king* instead of *our king*. "No, from a friend."

"A male friend?" she asked, too much interest apparent in the question.

"Yes."

Gytha sat beside Reid, her focus on the dying fire. "Are you sad to leave him behind?" She seemed to sincerely want to know.

Reid studied the warrior woman, realizing she had a unique opportunity here. She could lie by pretending she'd had to leave a lover back home. Maybe it would be something they could bond over, a way to gain Gytha's trust. But Reid was tired of lying. Even though she had no problem stepping into a role and playing a part when needed, she had a tough time hiding her emotions. In the end, she decided to go with honesty. "While the letter was from a man, he is only a friend, nothing more."

Gytha tilted her head, gazing candidly at Reid. "Are you romantically involved with anyone?"

Out here under the night sky, with this woman's attention directly on her, Reid felt exposed. "No. What about you? Do you have a romantic relationship with anyone?" Would Gytha admit she had feelings for Dexter?

"Not anymore." The answer was spit out, clipped and sharp.

Well then—that said it all. For whatever reason, Dexter and Gytha had severed their relationship. Had it been because of Reid? Had the roles been reversed, would she have done the same? Picking up a small pebble from the ground, she rolled it between her fingers. She needed to start gaining allies. "I was raised as a boy." It was hard to open up to someone like Gytha. Someone who clearly didn't want to be Reid's friend.

Gytha snorted. "What does that even mean?"

Keeping her eyes focused on the pebble, Reid attempted to explain her childhood. "My mother died while giving birth to me. I was the fifth child—and the fifth girl. Without a son and heir, my father stood to lose his land and title. In desperation, he made the announcement that my mother had borne a son instead."

"Why didn't he just remarry?"

Reid rolled her eyes. *Because that would have been too simple.* "On my mother's deathbed, he swore to her that he wouldn't remarry." Reid tossed the pebble into the flames. It hit a log, sending a few sparks into the air.

"How did he foresee that working out?"

"Apparently, my father assumed one of my sisters would marry and have a son. Once that happened, he would change his heir from me to his grandson. Except, somehow, my sisters only gave birth to girls." Reid wrapped her arms around her legs, pulling her knees to her chest.

"What changed?" Gytha's brows crinkled as she observed Reid, as if seeing her for the first time. "How did you go from being raised as a boy to being here, dressed as a woman, about to marry Prince Dexter?"

It was a good question. Reid had pondered that very thing

19

since the king announced her engagement. "My life took a drastic turn on my eighteenth birthday." She explained how Prince Gordon and Prince Ackley had shown up at her house to recruit her father's soldiers only to discover Reid wasn't a man at all, then about the bargain she'd struck with Ackley.

"I take it things did not go as planned."

"No, they did not. After I was taken to the City of Buckley and introduced to the court as Lady Reid, the king sent me on an errand. He told me that if I snuck into Axian and stole a box for him, he would not only pardon my father from treason, but he would also grant a proclamation which allowed him to choose either a male or female heir to inherit his title and land."

"Did you do this errand?"

"I did."

"Then why are you here?"

Again, another good question. Reid squeezed her knees tighter. "Because the king did not find what he'd expected in the box. The next thing I know, King Eldon said he and my father had come to an arrangement. He pardoned my father, allowing him to pass his land and title to anyone in his family, regardless of gender. In return, my father signed a contract agreeing to a marriage between Prince Dexter and me."

The fire crackled as they each sat there, lost in her own thoughts.

After a moment of silence, Gytha asked, "The king sent you back here to find the missing item, didn't he?"

"He did."

"Do you plan to steal it from the royal family?"

"No, I do not." Because Reid had already stolen the letters once. They'd just somehow managed to disappear in the process. Although, she was fairly certain Ackley had them. As to what he planned to do with them, she couldn't say.

"If you harm the Axian royal family in any way, I'll kill you."

Reid chuckled.

"Why are you laughing at me? Do you think I'm lying?"

"No, not at all. I'm laughing because you think I *could* harm them. They know more than I do. I think they know exactly why I'm here. And I believe they are already a step ahead of me. You have nothing to fear." Abruptly, Reid stood and headed toward her tent.

"I'll be watching you, Lady Reid," Gytha called after her.

"I'd be disappointed if you weren't." Reid could have sworn she heard the warrior woman chuckle.

CHAPTER THREE

Dexter raised his hand, halting their group on the dirt road. After he gave a command Reid didn't understand, the soldiers maneuvered into a single line. She wanted to ask what they were doing. However, since no one spoke, she figured it was appropriate to keep her mouth shut. When Markis waved for her to fall into line behind him, she did so without question.

Gytha moved to the front, leading the group into the dark forest on the left side of the road. The trees were close together, the dense foliage blocking out most of the sun. The temperature dropped, making Reid shiver. Her horse whinnied, pulling to the right. Unease filled her as she reined her horse back in line.

They traveled through the forest, no one speaking, for almost an hour. Finally, Gytha pulled her horse to a halt. Towering trees surrounded them, the tangy scent of pine heady in the cool air. Dexter dismounted before walking to the front. He paused there as if waiting for someone or something. Markis's hand rested casually on his bow, an arrow already nocked.

A minute later, an elderly man wearing brown pants and a

tunic emerged from the forest. "That you, Prince Dexter?" He limped, one leg slightly shorter than the other.

"It is, Seb."

"To what do we owe this honor?" Seb asked as he shook the prince's proffered hand.

"We need to talk. Unofficially. Do you have a minute to spare?"

"For you, I always have time." The lines around Seb's eyes deepened. "Leave the horses here so they won't trample on anything."

The soldiers dismounted. Reid followed suit, tying her horse to a nearby tree. Gytha ordered Markis and two female soldiers to accompany her and Dexter. The remaining soldiers were to stay with the horses.

Dexter leaned toward Gytha, speaking close to her ear. When she nodded, he stepped away. "Lady Reid," Gytha called, her voice clipped. "You're with us."

Reid joined the small group as they followed Seb. He took them another hundred yards to the east, winding between trees and stepping over fallen branches. An eerie sensation made Reid's skin prickle. She scanned the trees above, searching for the source of her unease.

"There are three men tracking us," Markis whispered. "But it's nothing to worry about."

She raised her eyebrows in a silent question.

"They belong to Seb's tribe," he explained.

A twenty-foot wall made entirely of logs loomed before them. At Seb's shout, a narrow door opened, granting them entrance.

"It surrounds their entire village," Markis said before he passed through the entrance.

Sharp spears jutted from the top of the wall. Etched into the wood above the door were words in an unfamiliar language. She followed Markis, entering the village.

In an area cleared of trees were fifty or so wooden homes, smoke rising from a handful of the chimneys. Children ran about underfoot, and people worked in a vegetable garden off to the side. Seb escorted them between the homes toward the center of the village. When they reached a circle of tables situated around a fire pit, Dexter, Gytha, and Seb sat.

"Come on," Markis told Reid, leading her and the other two soldiers over to a well about thirty feet away. He proceeded to pull up a bucket filled with water. After taking a drink, he offered it to Reid.

She shook her head, too busy observing the sight before her. On the other side of the fire pit, four kids stood side by side. They faced a tree stump with a potato set on top. The girl on the end lifted a small bow, nocked an arrow, pointed it at the potato, and then shot. It nicked the top of the vegetable. The kids laughed while the girl stomped her foot. A boy raised his bow next. He took a steadying breath, then released the bowstring. The arrow sliced straight through the potato.

"That was impressive," Reid mumbled. None of the children appeared to be more than six or seven years old.

"Come on," Markis said. The four of them went to an empty table and sat.

"Why are you here?" Seb asked, his voice loud enough for Reid to hear.

"I fear war is coming," Dexter answered. "I want to make sure you and your people are prepared."

"We're pretty secluded here." Seb rubbed his gray beard. "Is it those ignorant northerners?"

"They're more backward than ignorant," Dexter said with a grin. "But yes, I fear King Eldon is going to invade Axian. If my information is correct, he'll lead in a force of five thousand strong."

Seb whistled. "That's a lot of soldiers. If that many come here, they'll trample our lands and destroy our fields."

"I know. Which is why we need to be prepared."

"Do you plan to stop them at the border?"

Dexter clenched his hands into fists. "My father gave me a direct order to stand down."

Reid wondered why Dexter bothered to tell Seb any of this. Like Seb had said, they were relatively out of the way. The chances of soldiers overrunning this village were slim.

"Well, your father isn't a king—he's only a prince. Like everyone else, he falls under the king's jurisdiction. If the king wants to march into Axian with his soldiers, he can." Seb leaned forward on his elbows, clearly challenging Dexter.

Sighing, the prince rubbed his face. "You're right."

"Then why are you here?"

"I'd like to make a deal."

"I'm retired."

"What if I promise it'll be worth your time?"

"I'll listen to your offer, but I won't guarantee anything."

When Dexter started discussing numbers and locations, Reid turned to Markis. "What exactly are they negotiating?"

"Weapons. Seb is a master crafter of bows and arrows. Plus, Seb was the commander of the Marsden army under King Broc."

Gytha glared over her shoulder at Markis. "Lady Reid doesn't need to know our business."

"Then maybe you shouldn't have brought her," Markis mumbled.

"Lady Reid?" Seb asked, sitting up straighter. "Where have I heard that name before?"

"This is my fiancée, Lady Reid Ellington," Dexter said, his lips twitching as he fought a smile. "Duke Ellington's daughter."

A grin spread across Seb's face. "It is a pleasure to meet you, Lady Reid."

Reid had the distinct impression he knew her father. She couldn't say from where or how, but recognition had dawned in Seb's eyes at the mention of the duke.

Seb turned back to Dexter. "I'll take you up on that deal."

Dexter slid a piece of paper across the table to Seb.

"Lady Reid," Gytha said, rising abruptly. "Come with me."

Reid joined Gytha, allowing the woman to lead her away from the village center.

Once Dexter returned with Markis and the two soldiers, their group set out. Instead of traveling back the way they'd come, they continued east, through the forest. Curious to see what Dexter was up to now, Reid refrained from asking any questions. A day later, they entered a small town near the coast.

"Same as before," Dexter ordered.

Reid dismounted, then handed her horse's reins over to another soldier. She joined Markis, Gytha, and two female soldiers. They followed Dexter along the main road that cut straight through the seaside town. Waves crashed in the distance, creating a soothing background noise. The wind blew, the smell of salt heavy in the air.

A sign reading *Maiden Voyage* hung above a door, creaking as it teetered in the wind. Dexter shoved the door open, then entered the tavern.

"You armed?" Markis whispered to Reid.

She shook her head.

Gytha handed Reid a small dagger. She took it, tucking it in the folds of her dress.

Dexter sat at a round table before the fireplace while the others went to another not far away. Drinks and stew were ordered all around.

"What are we doing here?" Reid asked after their food arrived.

"No idea." Markis shrugged.

"Didn't the commander tell you?" How could these soldiers blindly follow Dexter without having any information at all? Did he demand total and complete loyalty and obedience? Or had he earned it?

"He did not tell us what we are doing here," Gytha replied. Instead of eating, the warrior woman kept her focus on Dexter.

Reid took a bite of her stew, surprised at the tastiness. "How can you be prepared for an attack if you don't know who it's coming from?" She couldn't imagine trying to protect the prince when he didn't give any details about their location or who he planned to meet with.

"I'm always prepared," Gytha answered with a huff.

The two female soldiers chuckled, but they didn't say anything.

The door squeaked as it opened. A large man entered, his dark skin weathered from the sun. He made a beeline for Dexter, taking the seat across from him.

Since it was the afternoon, the tavern only had a handful of people in it. Reid took another bite of her stew, watching the commander greet the man.

After shaking hands, Dexter pulled out a piece of paper and slid it across the table. "Is this your ship?" the prince asked.

"Aye."

"I have questions for you." Dexter withdrew a money bag, pushing it across the table. Then he placed a well-worn leather book in front of himself. Tapping the cover, he said, "This is your ship's log. What were you doing in the kingdom of Melenia?"

Reid had never heard of such a place before.

The sailor warily eyed the book. "Trading."

"Trading what?"

"I sold jewelry in exchange for leather armor, spices, and money."

"Jewelry from where?"

"From Bridger," the sailor replied. "Mostly silver necklaces, bracelets, and trinkets. The women over there love that stuff."

"Why leather armor?"

"There are rumors of a war."

Dexter leaned back, observing the man. "Where did you hear that?"

The sailor shrugged. "A friend of mine in Bridger was commissioned to make a thousand swords. In one day, I sold all the leather armor I acquired in Melenia to the citizens of Bridger."

Dexter scratched his chin just below his ear. "How often do you sail to Melenia?"

"Once every two to three months. Takes about a fortnight to get there."

"What about other counties here in Marsden?" Dexter asked. "Do you trade with any of them?"

The sailor's face paled.

Dexter tossed him a second bag of money. "You won't be in trouble either way," he said. "All I seek is the truth."

"I only trade with counties in northern Marsden. Never Axian."

"Then why are you in Axian?" Dexter asked, drumming his fingers on the ship's log.

"They won't let me leave port until I have your permission," the sailor explained. "The soldiers at the dock said I had to come here to meet with you. Once you return my ship's log, I can set sail."

Dexter shook his head. "What I want to know is how did you come to be in an Axian port in the first place?" His right hand slid to his thigh, forming a fist, the muscles along his forearm bulging. Even though he managed to maintain an even voice as he spoke to the sailor, Reid could tell he was restraining himself.

"Oh, funny you should ask." The man shifted in his chair. "There was a storm. I meant to enter a port in southern Bridger. The sea was rough, and we got blown a bit off course. We ended up here by accident. That's when the Axian soldiers closed the port and wouldn't let us leave."

"And who is *us*?"

"Me and my crew."

"Did you bring anyone from Melenia here with you?"

The sailor wiped his hands on his pants. "Yes."

"Explain."

"Some men paid me mighty handsomely for passage to Marsden. I didn't ask any questions though. Just brought them here." He swallowed.

"Thank you for your time," Dexter said as he shoved his chair back and stood. "Here's your ship's log. I'll escort you back to port, so you don't get off course again." When they exited the tavern, Gytha silently followed them.

Reid rose and went to the table, examining the discarded paper on top. It had a sketch of a ship with the name *Widow Maker* on it. Running her fingers along the drawing, Reid wondered if it was a coincidence that it was a Bridger ship. The men who'd attempted to assassinate the royal family in northern Marsden had claimed they were from Axian. However, when she'd stumbled upon the mines in Bridger, those men had resembled the assassins. She suspected the king had hired the miners to assassinate his siblings in order to eliminate any contenders for the throne. If that was the case, then how did this ship fit into everything? Maybe Reid was simply overthinking it by trying to find a connection where there wasn't one.

"Let's go," Markis said, tossing some money on the table to pay for their food and drinks. The other two soldiers had already exited the tavern.

Reid grabbed the paper, shoving it beside the dagger hidden in her dress.

They rode until it was too dark to travel, then set up camp for the night. The following morning, they set out before the sun had even risen. They repeated this pattern for two days, the commander keeping a relentless pace. Reid had heard someone say they were making up ground so no one would question where they'd been.

Late one afternoon, Dexter halted them. Glancing at the sky, Reid wondered why they were stopping when the sun wouldn't set for another two hours. The soldiers dismounted, but no one moved to set up camp.

"What's going on?" Reid asked as she climbed off her horse.

Markis adjusted the bow across his back. "We're only a short distance away from the City of Radella."

A sigh of relief escaped Reid's lips. She could use a bath and a soft bed to sleep in. But then a new fear crept in. Would those luxuries even be afforded to her or did the royal family plan to keep her locked up somewhere?

"Lady Reid," Gytha said as she approached.

"Yes?"

"Come with me." She led Reid away from everyone else.

"Where are we going?"

"This way."

Well, yes, Reid knew which direction they were going, but she wanted to know why they were headed this way. Instead of arguing, she followed Gytha over a small hill and down into a narrow valley. A stream rushed through it. Maybe the warrior woman needed help getting water. At the edge of the stream, they stopped.

Behind her, Reid felt a strong presence approach. She tensed, knowing without looking that it was Dexter.

"Your Highness," Gytha said, her words tight.

"Thank you, Captain. You can return to the others."

Gytha glared at Reid before stomping up the hill and out of sight.

Turning to face the prince, Reid shoved her panic down. Since arriving in Axian, this was the first time she'd been alone with him. She suspected he wanted nothing to do with her—at least they had *that* in common. However, since they were about to reach the palace, he probably needed to prepare her for what was to come.

With his feet shoulder-width apart, he folded his arms, his biceps bulging. The leather armor he wore made him look like a fierce warrior rather than a prince. "Do women normally wear two dresses like that in northern Marsden?" His voice came out low, rumbling like the stream.

"No."

His brows pinched. "You look ridiculous."

She shrugged, not really caring. "I wasn't about to ride sideways on a horse. This solved the problem." Granted, she'd ruined both dresses, but they'd served their purpose.

"One of my soldiers would have loaned you pants."

Ignoring his comment, she said, "I assume we're here for a reason?" Reid wanted to return to the safety of the group. She didn't trust Dexter.

"You don't like to rely on others or ask for help."

She wasn't sure if that was a question or a statement, so she kept her mouth shut, waiting for him to get to the reason behind their clandestine meeting.

"The king sent you here to spy on us."

"He did."

"Your father sent you here to keep you safe."

He had? Why couldn't he keep Reid safe in Ellington? She twisted the ring around her finger—the one her father had bestowed to her. It allowed Reid the duke's rights and protection as if she were Duke Ellington himself. If any harm came to her, Duke Ellington could call upon the other dukes of Marsden to right the wrong. It was one of the reasons the king hadn't already killed or imprisoned her. Why did her father think she would be safer in Axian? "Why did your father agree to our match?"

"To avoid a war with King Eldon."

"Yet, we both know we're headed in that direction anyway."

"He is a new king. My father thinks Eldon is testing our loyalty to him."

"Are you?" She knew Axian didn't follow all the laws of northern Marsden.

"We have functioned as our own kingdom for twenty-five years. Not once has the king demanded we pay taxes, provide soldiers, or even spoken to us. We have lived on our own and in peace."

That didn't answer her question. "Are you aware of Eldon's lineage?"

Dexter's eyes narrowed. "I am." He took a step closer, towering over her.

Reid didn't back away. "Are you aware your father wrote to all the dukes and said if any had a daughter of marriageable age, he'd marry you off to her to show he didn't want to go to war? He also said he'd send you to live in that county as a show of good faith." Suddenly, it became clear why the Knights wanted to know who Henrick's heir was. If Dexter were the heir, Henrick would have never offered to send him to another county. But if he declared Eldon—his firstborn son—as his heir, then it made sense to offer Dexter.

"What is it?" the prince demanded.

"Nothing." Reid worked to erase the shock from her face. If Henrick declared Eldon his heir, then a war between northern Marsden and Axian was pointless. Even if Henrick was the rightful king of Marsden, Eldon would eventually inherit the title and throne. Where did the Knights stand in this? The law stated a son couldn't hold his father's title until the father died. Which meant Eldon couldn't inherit until Henrick passed. However, was it worth inciting a civil war when the outcome would be the same no matter who the victor was? Wouldn't it be better to let Eldon remain on the throne? Reid's head started to pound.

"It's not nothing," Dexter said. "You just figured something out, and you don't want to tell me what it is."

"How can you expect me to confide in you when you don't even trust me?"

"Of course I don't trust you. You broke into my home. Twice. And you work for the king."

"I don't work for the king."

"Who do you work for, then?"

She shook her head, refusing to answer. How could she gain this man's trust when he was determined to hate her?

Reaching out, he grabbed her hands. She yelped in surprise, trying to yank away, but he shoved her sleeves up, examining her wrists.

Her heart pounded. Was he looking for the mark of a Knight? If so, how did he know about the Knights? From his father? Thankfully, her tattoo wasn't in the same place as other Knights. Since she was a woman, Ackley had her tattoo placed higher up, near her elbow, so it would be less visible.

She used the opportunity to glance at Dexter's arms. Each of his inner wrists was tattooed with odd writing she couldn't decipher.

When he released her, they stared at one another, both wary.

Dexter shoved his chin to the side, cracking his neck. "Your response to my grabbing you wasn't what I expected it to be." He examined her from head to toe, eyes assessing. "It's almost as if you knew what I was doing and why."

Reid tried not to flinch under his scrutiny. Somehow, he knew about the Knights—she was sure of it. "When I broke into your parents' bedchamber, your mother took my hands and examined them, just like you did. She said she was searching for evidence of poison. I assumed you were doing the same." In hindsight, she should have protested when he grabbed her wrists. However, she'd been too shocked at the realization of why he was doing it.

He took a slow, menacing step toward her, invading her personal space. "Tell me, Lady Reid, how did you come to be the king's only female employee and personal lackey?"

CHAPTER FOUR

Reid took an involuntary step away from Dexter, his words ringing in her head. What was he implying? As soon as she arrived at the palace, she planned to send her father a strongly worded letter asking why he'd agreed to this absurd match. But she already knew. Besides this union being used to keep her safe and out of the king's clutches, Duke Ellington had been granted his pardon and deed. And most people in northern Marsden had arranged marriages.

Her heart ached. Her father had consented to this marriage without asking what Reid wanted, which was typical of how her entire life had been up to this point. It was all about doing what was best for the family. Not once had Reid done anything for herself. Why did the men in her life assume they could make decisions for her? Why had no one ever asked what she wanted?

Tears threatened. Reid blinked them away, not wanting to cry in front of Dexter. She wouldn't give him the satisfaction of knowing he intimidated her. Shifting away from him, she focused on the stream. *I will not cry,* she ordered herself, blinking to clear her suddenly hazy vision. "Is there anything else? If not, I'd like for you to leave me alone."

"Gladly." He stomped away, mumbling as he went.

Reid knelt, taking in a deep, steadying breath. Her fingers twined in the grass. She held on, trying to calm herself. Everything felt wrong. It was like someone had tossed her from a boat, leaving her to thrash about in the water as she tried to figure out which way was up.

"Lady Reid," Gytha called from the top of the rise. "Let's go."

"I'll be right there." Reid's voice shook. She couldn't believe she was on the verge of having a breakdown. Her sisters all had the occasional crying fit for no apparent reason, but not her. At least not until now. But she had a reason. *Reasons.* However, being raised as a boy had taught Reid not to show any emotions. After taking another deep breath, she stood.

"The commander can be a little intimidating," Gytha said as Reid walked up the hill to join her. "It's one of the traits I admire most about him."

Was Gytha trying to console or discourage Reid?

"You'll get used to it." Gytha smirked. "Eventually."

While Reid loved Axian and all it had to offer, she did not appreciate being sold off like a piece of property, and she refused to be treated as such. Purposefully stepping around Gytha without acknowledging her, Reid joined the others. "Well?" she asked the group before her. "Are we going to head out?" Her words came out sharper than she'd intended, her irritation seeping through her voice.

"First, we'll eat," a soldier answered. "Then we'll travel into the city once it's dark."

"Why?"

"Because that's what the commander wants," another answered.

A fire already roared, and two soldiers began preparing a meal.

Reid shrugged, then plopped on the ground next to Markis. "Where are you stationed at? The City of Radella or somewhere else?"

"Why do you ask?"

"I'm just curious." Seriously, why wouldn't anyone give her a straight answer? Did they all assume she was a spy? "When I get to the palace, am I free to do as I wish?"

"Pardon?"

"Am I allowed to join the army? Can I have a job? Will I even be allowed to roam free?"

"I have no idea." Markis scratched his head. "I guess so?"

If the kingdom of Axian treated women as equals, then she should be able to do as she wished without needing her future husband's permission. When she'd met Nara, the princess had on leather armor. Reid doubted the warrior woman sat around the palace knitting all day.

"Why are you smiling?" Markis asked. "Am I missing something?"

"I'm going to be able to be a woman in public, dress as I want, and work." The part about her having to marry—especially a man she didn't care for—she'd locked in a box to be dealt with at another time. For now, she would focus on the positive.

He leaned back, his hands hitting his bow.

"Can you teach me to shoot?" Her father had taught her years ago. However, she'd never taken to the bow and much preferred swords.

"Once you're settled in, come find me at the military compound. I'll take you to the range there to practice."

"Couldn't you teach me now?"

"Oh." He glanced around. "Sure."

Reid jumped to her feet, pulling Markis up alongside her.

He picked up his bow and quiver. "Let's move farther away from everyone." A cluster of boulders stood about fifty yards to the east. They headed that way. "We'll use the moss on that boulder as our target," he said, handing Reid the bow.

She observed the mossy mound, about a foot in diameter, which clung to the side of the boulder.

"Here's an arrow. Do you know how to nock it?"

"Yes." She took it, placed it in the bow, and aimed.

"Don't release the arrow," he warned. "I just want you to get a feel for holding the bow and aiming it correctly."

The bowstring was tighter than she remembered, and she had difficulty drawing it.

"It's a little big for you," Markis said as he adjusted her arm a little higher.

Someone approached them. However, Reid kept her focus on the moss, not caring to talk to anyone besides Markis at the moment.

"The commander wants you two to remain with everyone else," Gytha called from where she'd stopped about twenty feet away.

"We'll be right there," Markis responded.

He put his right hand on Reid's back, then placed his left hand under her elbow, adjusting the bow slightly. "You want to make sure your dominant eye is aligned with your arrow."

While it felt as if he'd raised her left arm too high, when she looked down the arrow at the target, she could see it was aimed at the center of the moss. "Got it."

He let his hands drop to his sides. "When we're at the palace, you can join me at the archery range to practice."

"I'd like that." She lowered the bow, then handed it back to him.

He slung it over his shoulder, and they returned to the group. Food was distributed, so Reid took a bowl and sat near the fire, sipping her soup. Glancing up, she noticed Markis was no longer there. He'd been beside her only a moment ago. After a minute, she found him. He stood off to the side, speaking quietly with Gytha. They kept glancing in Reid's direction, so she assumed they were talking about her. Gytha was probably scolding Markis for teaching Reid how to shoot. After all, Reid was a spy.

Markis nodded, then went over and claimed his bowl of soup.

Without looking in Reid's direction, he sat across from her, on the other side of the fire. Since no one else had befriended her, she had no one to talk to as she ate. Sadness crept its way into Reid. Instead of dwelling on her loneliness, she tried to focus on the positive. They'd almost reached the palace. Maybe, just maybe, she could get to know Nara better. That prospect immediately lightened her somber mood.

Once the sky turned dark, Dexter gave the order to pack up. Reid mounted her horse, making sure to tuck the material of her dresses around her skin. A few spots on her legs had been chafed raw. While it hurt, there wasn't much she could do about it. At least she'd be at the palace in a few hours. Hopefully, she'd have the opportunity to bathe then.

They set out in their usual formation. However, instead of Markis riding alongside Reid as he had the entire journey, a female soldier took his place. Markis now rode at the back. It was obvious they'd been purposefully separated, and that infuriated her. Was she not allowed to have a single friend in Axian?

When they finally reached the city, Reid estimated it was well past midnight. Most buildings were dark, and no one was out and about. The only sound was the clicking of the horses' hooves. Dexter had them swing around and approach the palace from the west since the stables were located there. When they entered the building, the sweet smell of hay reminded Reid of home. She dismounted, then untied her bag from the horse. A stable hand rushed over, taking the reins from her before leading the horse into an empty stall.

She caught a glimpse of Markis unpacking his supplies from his saddlebag, seeming to purposefully avoid looking her way.

"Lady Reid?" a young woman asked.

"Yes?"

"My name is Joce. I'll be your lady's maid."

Reid blinked. She'd never had a personal servant before. She was accustomed to taking care of herself. Maybe the royal family wanted to have someone in Reid's room to watch her. A spy for the spy. If she weren't so exhausted, she might have laughed.

"This way," Joce said.

Reid followed her out of the stables and into the palace. At this late hour, most hallways were dark, lit only by the moon shining in the windows. Joce took Reid up to the fourth floor, which surprised her. The royal family's rooms were located on this level. She'd assumed she would be on a lower floor where the guest suites were. Joce turned down another corridor. Since it was dark and they'd taken the main staircase, Reid wasn't sure where she was in relation to the prince and princess's bedchamber.

"This will be your suite until the wedding," Joce said, opening a door and ushering Reid inside.

The wedding. Reid had been careful not to think about that upcoming event. "Do you know when it is set to take place?" Hopefully, it wouldn't be for a few weeks. She needed time to get her bearings.

"The engagement hasn't been announced, so you have some time."

Relief filled her.

"The bedchamber is the room on the left, the bathing chamber to the right. This is the sitting room. Would you like me to light a few candles so you can see everything?"

"That won't be necessary," Reid replied. "However, I would like to bathe if it's not too much trouble."

"No trouble at all, my lady." Joce curtsied, then went into the bathing chamber.

Just enough moonlight filtered in to reveal two sofas and a low table situated in the center. A desk was off to the side. Reid peeked into the bedchamber, but the curtains were drawn, blocking out the light.

"Do you need help undressing?" Joce asked from behind Reid.

"No, I'm good. I would like something to sleep in, though," she said, dropping her bag just inside the bedchamber.

"I'll light a candle or two so you can see." Joce stepped around Reid to enter the bedchamber. "When it became clear you'd arrive before your personal items, Princess Nara made sure to supply you with everything you'll need." Joce lit a handful of candles, then faced Reid. "Your sleeping clothes are in the armoire. Will you require anything else before I retire for the night?"

"No, that will be all. Thank you."

Joce curtsied, then left.

Not wanting to get her bedchamber dirty, Reid went straight to her bathing chamber. She peeled off the filthy, tattered dresses, leaving them on the floor, then stepped into the blessedly hot water, sinking down into the tub. She'd never felt anything quite so wonderful. Knowing she was on the verge of falling asleep, she quickly washed herself before getting out. After drying off, she hurried to her bedchamber.

With the candles lit, she could see the deep blue curtains at the head of the four-poster bed, an armoire set next to it. A closet on the opposite wall caught her eye. Excitement coursed through her. Nara had picked out Reid's wardrobe.

She rushed over to the closet, throwing open the door, then coming to an abrupt halt. Instead of the sleek Axian warrior clothing she'd expected, the inside held only dresses. *Dresses!* What had Nara been thinking? The princess knew Reid had been raised as a boy. Had she assumed because Reid had grown up wearing pants that she wanted to wear dresses now? Frustrated, Reid growled. Why was nothing going her way?

Exiting the closet, she went over to the armoire. After she found a nightdress and pulled it on, she climbed into bed, not even bothering to get under the blankets. She fell asleep in seconds.

Reid awoke, stretching her arms above her head. After spending so many nights on the ground, the bed felt wonderful. Since the curtains were drawn, she had no idea what time it was. She crawled out of bed, then pushed the curtains aside. Bright light burst into the room.

"You're awake," Joce said, coming into the bedchamber.

Now that it was daylight, Reid could see her lady's maid better. With her silky blonde hair twisted into a bun, she wore a short-sleeved dress of navy blue, revealing her willowy arms. However, her most striking feature was her large blue eyes, which seemed to glow.

"I'm starving." Reid hoped Joce could bring food to the room. Dining with the royal family wasn't something she was ready to face yet.

"I've been sent to help you dress."

Reid groaned.

"Is there a problem?"

"No. I'm just not sure what's expected of me in Axian." Running her fingers through her tangled hair, she sighed.

"You're our future princess," Joce said, her smile lighting up her face. "Prince Dexter is the most sought-after bachelor in the county. Once your engagement is announced, everyone will be wildly jealous of you. The upcoming wedding will be all anyone talks about." She glided into the dressing closet. A moment later, she exited, a pale purple dress in hand.

"I'm not wearing that."

"What color would you prefer then?"

Reid opened her mouth, intent on explaining she had no intention of wearing a dress and that she planned to don pants and a tunic in Axian. However, before she could say anything, someone knocked.

Joce left to answer it. A moment later, she returned with Nara in tow. "Lady Reid, allow me to present Princess Nara. I'll give you two a moment alone." Joce set the dress on the bed before hurrying from the room.

"We meet again," Nara said by way of greeting.

"I can honestly say I never thought that would happen."

Nara approached Reid. "I had a feeling our paths would cross again. However, I didn't think it would be under these circumstances." She glanced outside, then focused on Reid. The morning sun highlighted the brown in Nara's single braid. Similar to the last time Reid had seen her, the princess wore slender pants and a form-fitting shirt. Her boots went up to her knees, and she'd strapped a dagger to her waist. "I'm sure you understand the precarious position we are in."

Reid thought she did, so she nodded.

"I need you to play your part flawlessly."

"And what part is that, exactly?" Tired of pretending to be someone she wasn't, Reid had hoped she could be herself in Axian. While she understood a war brewed, she didn't know how she fit into the equation.

"You are a refined lady from northern Marsden."

Reid snorted. She'd dressed up a few times at the king's castle to act as a lady. However, she disliked having to play that part.

Ignoring Reid's snort, Nara said, "Your engagement will be announced at the end of the week. It will be followed by a small celebration. The wedding will take place next month." Folding her arms, she leaned against the window ledge.

"You can't be serious."

"About which part?"

"All of it." Reid went around to the side of the bed. In order to have something to do, she straightened the blankets while she tried to organize her thoughts. "I can't believe my father signed a marriage contract on my behalf just to retain his title and land." She rubbed her forehead. "There has to be more to it than that." What was she missing?

"He told the entire kingdom you were a boy. He raised you as a boy. Surely you, of all people, realized he would marry you off to retain what is most precious to him."

It felt as if Nara had punched Reid in the stomach. Sinking onto the bed, Reid understood why the statement hurt. Her father had sacrificed Reid's future and happiness for his. She wasn't his most precious possession—his land and title were.

She pushed off the bed, facing Nara. "The king expects me to spy on you."

"I figured as much."

"Then why did you allow me to come here? Why sign the marriage contract?" What Reid genuinely wanted to know was why the Axian people treated her so nicely. Why were they helping her? What did they hope to gain from this asinine marriage?

"My husband is trying to prevent a nasty civil war."

War was imminent. Instead of voicing that, Reid said, "Why do I have to dress as a refined lady?"

"You are a lady, are you not?"

"I am." *Technically speaking, anyway.*

"Then you will dress and act as one because that is what Axians expect of a woman from northern Marsden."

"But that's not who I am."

"I know that. However, the truth is too complicated to explain. I need you to play the part, at least until everything is sorted out." Nara moved away from the window, her smile kind. "Besides, the people want a fairy-tale romance. They weren't given that when I married Henrick, so I intend to give it to them with you."

Nara wasn't the one who had to wear the dumb dress. Reid muttered, "Fine."

"I expected more of a fight from you."

"I'm too hungry to argue. I just traveled from the City of Buckley while wearing two dresses. At the same time. What's one more?"

Nara chuckled. "I'll meet you in our family's private dining room," she said before exiting the bedchamber.

Joce returned, once again picking up the pale purple dress.

Without arguing, Reid accepted her help putting it on. After Joce tied the back, she combed and braided Reid's hair. There was a vanity in the corner—somehow, Reid hadn't noticed the vile thing until now—so she sat there while Joce applied dusting powder to her face.

Once Joce deemed Reid presentable, she led her from the suite, down the hall, and to the first floor. She pushed open a door, ushering Reid into a quaint room that contained only a long table and a few chairs.

Nara waited for Reid, already seated. "This is where the family eats," she explained.

Joce went over to the corner and rang a bell before she exited, leaving the two women alone.

A servant entered, carrying several plates of food. She set the plates on the table and left.

Reid sat across from Nara, observing her meal options.

"Have whatever you like," Nara said.

Reid grabbed two pieces of bread, a bowl of oatmeal, and an apple. Her stomach growled. Taking a large bite of bread, she moaned. It was still warm.

Nara chuckled. "You weren't kidding when you said you were hungry."

The door flew open. Dexter entered the room, dressed in gray trousers and a loose tunic. He'd only taken three steps when he froze, his focus zeroing in on Reid. "What are you doing in here?"

"Son, that is hardly the way to treat your fiancée."

Glaring at Reid, he sat next to Nara. He'd pulled his hair back at the base of his neck, emphasizing his strong jawline. "Actually, Mother, why don't you explain why you and Father agreed to this marriage in the first place?" Still scowling, he piled food on his plate.

Reid took a bite of her oatmeal, wanting to hear the answer but not wanting to have to partake in the conversation.

"You know your father received a request from the king."

"He just wants a spy embedded in the palace." Dexter piled more food on his plate.

"Yes, I agree. But there's more to it than that."

"I know. That's why I'm asking," he said, sounding exasperated, before he shoved a bite of oatmeal in his mouth.

Nara glanced at Reid. "I'll explain everything later," she mumbled to Dexter.

"I'd like to know," Reid said. "After I finish eating, I'm going to write to my father to ask why he agreed to the match."

"You already know," Nara said. "Land and title."

"Why did you agree?" Reid asked. "I don't understand how Axian benefits from the union."

"I'll explain it to you both over supper tonight when Prince Henrick is present. Is that all right?"

They nodded.

"Excellent. Until then, I have some business to attend to." She stood, then left them alone in the room.

Reid swallowed the lump of oatmeal in her mouth, observing Dexter across the table.

He set his spoon down, the expression on his clean-shaven face wary. "I know my father wants me to marry you to stop a war, but I don't want to wed you."

She chuckled, the sound hollow and humorless. "Don't worry. I don't want to marry you either." Shoving her chair away from the table, she stood. "You should have married Gytha when you had the chance. Then we wouldn't be in this disastrous mess." Turning, she swept out of the room without a backward glance.

CHAPTER FIVE

A nger coursed through Reid as she aimlessly stomped along the corridor, not paying attention to where she was going. How was she supposed to marry a man who didn't want to marry her? What sort of marriage would they have when neither could stand the other? And why were other people always dictating her life? Frustrated, she stopped before two open doors. Inside, books filled the four-story room from floor to ceiling. She recalled the tour she'd taken the last time she'd been here. The guide had said scholars from all over Axian had the privilege of using the library whenever they wanted. The county encouraged reading, studying, and the pursuit of knowledge.

Which meant Reid should be able to peruse the hundreds of books in the library. Particularly, books relating the history of Marsden written by Axian authors—not the history books from a northerner's point of view she'd already read.

Inside, a dozen tables were situated in the front section. Several people sat around them, most reading or writing. Men *and* women, which was something King Eldon would never allow. He wouldn't understand or value women studying to gain knowledge.

She couldn't even imagine him opening his home to others like this.

With her hands clasped behind her back, Reid decided to examine the books along the eastern wall. When she reached the halfway point, she noticed shelves containing even more books filled the entire middle section of the room. Curious, she continued along the east wall to see what the back section of the library held. When she reached it, she found several couches, presumably for reading. Along the north wall were three evenly spaced arched doorways. Reid peered into one. It was a small room. Each wall had floor-to-ceiling shelves piled with papers. Most likely, they were unbound manuscripts. Going to the next arched doorway, she saw a long table with chairs. Probably a meeting room. She strolled over to the last doorway, then peeked inside. A large desk littered with papers, bookshelves on all the walls, and a sofa with blankets strewn over it, as if someone had slept there, filled it. However, none of that fascinated Reid as much as what was curled up on the floor in front of the desk.

The hound raised its head, inspecting her.

Smiling, Reid dropped to her knees. The dog wagged its tail. "Why, hello there," she cooed. "What's your name?"

"His name's Finn," someone said from behind her.

Reid jumped, startled. "Sorry," she murmured, glancing over her shoulder. "I didn't mean to intrude."

Prince Colbert stepped into the office, holding two books. "You're not intruding." He went over to the desk and sat, placing the books on top of a stack of papers.

Reid stood. "I'll let you get back to work."

"I think it's time for you and me to have a chat. Close the door and take a seat."

She'd never spoken to Colbert before. When she'd fought Dexter that one time, Colbert had snuck up behind her, striking her down and tying her wrists together. But other than that, she'd had no contact with him.

Finn nudged Reid's legs, begging for more attention. Her smile returned as she reached down to scratch his head. She used the distraction to consider her options. Colbert didn't scare her like Dexter did. However, that didn't mean he wasn't dangerous. There was only one way to find out what sort of man he was. After extricating herself from the dog, Reid closed the door and sat on the chair across from the prince.

Colbert's shoulder-length hair looked longer than she remembered, and darker with more curls. Like the last time, he wore black pants and a black shirt, the top two buttons open to reveal the intricate tattoo along his collarbone. While Colbert was half the size of his brother, he was by no means slight.

"You're going to marry my brother." He leaned back in his chair, steepling his hands together as he observed her with keen eyes.

While Dexter exuded strength, Colbert radiated shrewd intelligence. Reid needed to be careful what she said around him. "That's what I've been told."

"And I've been told you were residing in the king's castle when your father signed the marriage contract."

What was he getting at?

"Did you know," he continued, "that your father entered into negotiations with my father *before* the king became involved in the matter?"

No, Reid did not know that. However, she didn't want to discuss the matter with Colbert. Nara had said she and Henrick would explain everything tonight. Wanting to change the subject, she said, "You must spend a lot of time in this room." She pointed at the sofa with the rumpled pillow and blankets. "Too bad there isn't a window to let the sunlight in."

"I prefer the quiet darkness."

"And Finn?" She reached down, petting the top of his head.

"He doesn't care so long as he's with me." Colbert smiled. "But enough about me. I want to discuss you."

"I'm not sure there's anything to discuss. I haven't led an overly exciting life." At least up until the two northern princes had arrived at Duke Ellington's castle.

"I find that hard to believe. A woman raised as a man is anything but ordinary."

She didn't feel like talking about herself. "I understand your brother is the commander of the army. What about you? What do you do?"

Lowering his arms, he drummed his fingers on his desk. "The better question to ask is once you marry my brother and become a part of this family, what is your role going to be?"

An incredibly good question indeed. Once Reid married Dexter —which she still couldn't fathom doing—she would no longer be a Knight. Ackley had made it clear that once a Knight married, that person severed ties with the secret organization. Did that mean Prince Henrick was no longer an active member?

Colbert stood. "How about I give you a tour of the palace?" Finn jumped to his feet, wagging his tail and pawing at the door.

Reid eyed the prince. Giving her a tour meant spending time together. Something his brother had refused to do.

"You're going to be my sister-in-law," he explained as he strode to the door. "I'd like to know what sort of person you are. Plus, there's that saying about keeping your friends close but your enemies closer."

Reid joined him. "Which one am I? Friend or enemy?"

"That is the question, Lady Reid, and one I intend to answer." He exited the room, Finn at his heels.

Wanting to see more of the palace, to understand its rich history, and to get to know this prince better, Reid followed as he made his way out of the library at a leisurely pace. Everyone they passed greeted him. Smiling, he returned each greeting using the person's name. While several glanced her way as if waiting for an introduction, the prince simply ignored their silent inquiries, taking Reid through a maze of hallways before opening a door and ushering her outside.

"Where are we going?" she asked. Finn shoved past her legs, then bolted down the grassy hill toward the lake.

"I gathered from your earlier comment you'd rather be outdoors than indoors."

She added *observant* to the prince's list of traits. The only thing she'd said was it was too bad his office didn't have a window. The fact he'd deduced her love of the outdoors from her statement said a lot about his character. "True," she replied, walking alongside him. "But I thought the point of our excursion was to see the palace."

A grin stretched his cheeks. "It is."

They continued across the lawn, skirting around the small lake. The city buildings started about a half mile from the backside of the palace. With the sun shining overhead, the entire city practically glowed. Reid closed her eyes, feeling the warmth on her face and breathing in the sweet smell of cut grass. When she opened them, she caught Colbert watching her, one of his eyebrows raised.

Instead of saying anything, he stopped near the lake, shoving his hands in his pockets.

"This is the most beautiful city I've ever seen," Reid mumbled.

"I'd have to agree with you." He faced south, his back to the palace. "The entire block over there is Dexter's domain. We refer to it as the military compound."

"You mean that's where the army is stationed?"

Colbert nodded.

Like most buildings in the city, the compound was ornate and appeared hundreds of years old. If Colbert hadn't told her it belonged to the army, she never would have guessed since it fit in so seamlessly with the buildings surrounding it.

"Offices are in the first building on the right. The others contain apartments and indoor training facilities. In the middle, there's a large sparring area. However, when Dexter wants to gather all his soldiers together, they convene at the southern end of the city where there's an open field." Colbert turned to face the palace. "Stables are on that end." He pointed west. "This is the back of the palace. On the top floor, dead center, are the royal family's bedchambers. Our private sitting rooms are on the northern side. Third floor is where the guest suites are located. Our servants are housed on the second. On the first, you will find the kitchen, great hall, throne room, meeting rooms, and other rooms of that nature." He folded his arms. "Sometimes, it helps seeing it from this angle to understand the layout better."

Finn started barking at something in the lake.

"It's probably a fish." Colbert chuckled.

A frog jumped at Finn's face. The dog yelped, then ran at Colbert, sprinting around him excitedly.

"Calm down, Finn. It's just a frog."

Finn jumped, his front paws landing right below Colbert's chest while his back paws remained on the ground. He licked the prince's chin.

Colbert hissed, shoving Finn away from him. "Lady Reid, I must ask something of you. Lend me your arm." His voice sounded strained.

Immediately, Reid gave him her arm to lean on even though he stood a foot taller than her. His face had drained of all color. "Are you okay?" she asked, worried.

"I'm fine."

"You don't look it." She put her hand on his, feeling his clammy skin. "Shall we return to your office in the library?" she asked, recalling the sofa and blankets she'd seen in there.

"Where's Finn?"

"He's right behind us," she assured him.

With his free hand, he touched the spot where Finn had pawed him. When he pulled his hand away, blood covered it. "Please escort me to my suite."

"Did Finn do that?" His nails didn't look sharp enough to break skin through a shirt.

"Just help me to my bedchamber."

"Very well. And then I'll fetch a healer to take a look at that."

"No. Just get me upstairs. No one can know."

If Reid aided him in his time of need, maybe she'd gain his trust and respect. "Let's go." She tried to steady him as she helped him into the palace, Finn following right behind.

He told her which way to go to reach the stairs. Clutching onto the banister, he helped her hoist him up the three flights as quickly as possible. At the fourth, he leaned against the wall, breathing heavily. His forehead beaded with sweat.

Reid grabbed his arm. "Come on." She headed toward Prince Henrick and Princess Nara's suite, knowing Dexter and Colbert's bedchambers would be located nearby.

"This one here," he mumbled, his voice weak.

Reid opened the door, practically dragging him into a sitting room. A doorway on either side made her pause.

"Left," he murmured.

She ushered him through the doorway, noting they'd entered his bedchamber. When he sagged against the bed, Reid hoisted his feet onto the mattress so he could stretch out.

"I want to see." She needed to make sure he didn't have a wound serious enough to warrant disregarding his request not to send for a healer.

Colbert peeled his shirt up, revealing a nasty red line near his rib cage. Thick blood oozed from it.

"That's a knife wound."

"How do you know?"

She didn't bother to answer. "It needs to be stitched."

"I had stitches. They must have broken when Finn jumped on me."

Hurrying to the bathing chamber, she searched around until she found a bucket. She filled it with water, then grabbed two towels. Rushing back to the bedchamber, she shoved one of the towels in the bucket and sat next to Colbert on the bed. Wringing out the wet cloth, she carefully cleaned around the wound, trying to better assess the situation. There weren't any lines indicating an infection. "How deep is the wound?"

"Deep."

As she suspected. "Has it been treated?"

"Yes."

Now that she'd cleaned the area, she took the dry towel and pressed it against the wound, trying to stop the bleeding. "Since Finn caused the stitches to open, you should have another dose of medicine for infection."

He nodded.

"And it needs to be stitched again."

He closed his eyes, clearly frustrated.

"Tell me where I can find a healer."

Reaching out, he grabbed her hand. "I told you no one can know about this."

She opened her mouth to argue, but he squeezed her hand, silencing her.

"Get Dexter. He'll know what to do." He opened his eyes, pleading with her.

Not wanting to waste time arguing with him, she asked, "Where is he?"

Face drawn in pain, he still managed to smirk. "Where do you think?"

"The military compound?"

"Correct. Look at you...already knowing so much about your fiancé."

If he could tease at a time like this, he should be okay while she retrieved Dexter. Reid squeezed his hand in reassurance before hurrying from the room.

After exiting the palace, she sprinted across the lawn, past the lake, and to the building of offices Colbert had pointed out earlier.

No one stood guard outside the main entrance, so she threw the door open and rushed inside.

A man sitting behind a desk peered up at her.

Before he had a chance to say anything, she blurted out, "I must speak with Commander Dexter. Immediately."

"He's in the training yard running drills."

"Is it that way?" She pointed down the hallway straight ahead.

"Jem," he called.

A young man stepped into the hallway. "Yes?"

"Can you please escort…" The man glanced at her for a name. When she didn't give him one, he continued, "Please escort this visitor to the training yard."

"Yes, sir."

Reid followed Jem down the hallway. He shoved open a large door, revealing a training yard with fifty or so men and women running through a series of movements. Each person held a sword in his or her right hand. At the front of the group, a man dressed the same as everyone else—in gray pants and a matching gray tunic—led the drills. When he turned to the side, she realized it was Dexter.

Jem stood next to the door. Seeing as how he wouldn't be any help, Reid ignored him and headed directly to Dexter, stopping in front of him. "I'm sorry to interrupt," she said nervously, low enough so only he could hear, "but there's a situation with your brother that needs your immediate attention."

Dexter's sword faltered, his eyes flashing with worry. It was the first time he'd looked human. "Captain!"

From the front row, Gytha stepped forward.

"Take over." Without another word, he exited the training yard. In the hallway, he stopped. "What happened?" Concern etched his words.

"His wound reopened."

Dexter cursed and then sprinted down the hallway, exiting the building. Reid took off after him. She trailed him across the lawn, wondering how someone so large could run so fast. By the time she entered the palace, he was no longer in sight. She headed up to the fourth floor to Colbert's room. When she stepped inside, she found Dexter sitting on the edge of Colbert's bed, examining the wound. Reid hovered in the doorway, watching the brothers.

"I told you to take it easy," Dexter said, his voice low.

"I know. But I was feeling better. I just took Finn outside for a romp around the lake."

"How is the girl involved in this?"

"Do you mean Lady Reid?"

Dexter nodded curtly.

"She's not a girl—she's a woman. And she's your fiancée."

"Nothing has been announced yet."

"Don't be daft," Colbert said.

"Just answer the question."

"We were walking together when Finn jumped on me."

"There's too much blood." Dexter pressed the towel against the wound. "Why were you walking with her?"

"Reid is going to be my sister-in-law. I want to get to know her better. Besides, I find her interesting."

Dexter mumbled something Reid couldn't hear.

Not knowing if the princes were aware of her presence, she cleared her throat before stepping farther into the room. "How can I help?"

"You can help by leaving," Dexter snapped.

"Be nice," Colbert chided his brother.

"I have to stitch this again."

"He also needs a salve applied to prevent infection," Reid said.

"Get out," Dexter barked.

She abruptly turned and went to the sitting room, plopping on one of the sofas. A moment later, Dexter left without sparing her a glance.

"Lady Reid," Colbert called.

She rose and went into his bedchamber. "I assume Prince Dexter went to get supplies?"

Colbert nodded. "He stitched me up the first time."

Not giving propriety a thought, Reid crawled onto the bed, settling beside him. Instead of saying that Dexter should have done a better job the first time, she asked, "Why don't you want a healer to do it?"

"Because no one can know I'm injured. I need you to promise you won't say a word to anyone."

"I promise." She couldn't help but wonder who'd cut him and why. Was it a training accident he'd been too embarrassed to tell anyone about? Or had there been some sort of altercation? She eyed him, trying to envision the different scenarios.

Dexter stomped into the bedchamber, pausing to glare at Reid before sitting on the chair. Scooting it closer, he opened a jar and scooped out a green gooey substance, gently spreading it over Colbert's wound. "That will prevent infection and numb the area." He put the lid back on the jar. "Try not to cry this time."

Reid studied Dexter's face. The right side of his mouth curved into a half smile. He must be joking then.

Finn sat next to the bed. After whining for a moment, he stood, preparing to jump on the mattress. Not wanting the dog to bounce on the bed as Dexter worked, Reid firmly told the dog to stay. Thankfully, Finn listened, curling up on the floor instead.

With that crisis averted, she returned her attention to Dexter, who deftly threaded the needle with large, steady hands.

"Look at me," she said to Colbert, wanting to distract him. "Why don't you tell me about yourself?"

"What do you want to know?" He hissed as Dexter started sewing his skin together.

Reid reached out, positioning Colbert's face so he focused on her instead of what his brother was doing. "Are you engaged?"

He grunted. "No, definitely not."

"Colbert is too busy reading books to be bothered with women," Dexter mumbled.

"When I saw the sofa in your office had been turned into a makeshift bed, I assumed you were addicted to the written word."

"The library is my favorite place," Colbert admitted. "That's why my office is there."

While Dexter finished sewing his brother up, Reid continued to ask meaningless questions about his dog, his schooling, and his favorite books. Beads of sweat pooled on his forehead, so she took the wet towel and dabbed his face, trying to cool him off. He reached out and clutched her hand, squeezing it.

"I'm done," Dexter announced. "Take your shirt off and get some rest."

Leaning closer, Reid started unbuttoning Colbert's shirt.

"What are you doing?" Dexter demanded.

"I'm helping him." Obviously, they didn't want his shirt to touch the wound and get stuck to it.

"Get out." Dexter pointed at the doorway. "Now."

"Are you always this rude?" she asked.

"Are you always this inappropriate?" he countered.

"This better not have anything to do with the fact that he's a man and I'm a woman." She climbed off the bed, putting her hands on her hips.

"That's exactly what it's about."

"I was raised as a boy. I've seen plenty of men in my lifetime. And it's not like I'm looking at your brother with lustful eyes. I'm simply trying to help him."

"You can't see my brother half naked."

"Why not?"

He ran his hands through his hair, muttering something unintelligible.

"You're insufferable," Reid retorted, leaning over to help Colbert remove his shirt. When she finished, she folded and set it on the end of the bed. To Colbert, she said, "If you need anything else, please let me know." She strode from the room, not acknowledging Dexter.

About halfway down the hallway, she heard Dexter jogging after her. Refusing to confront him, Reid continued as if she didn't know he was there.

He grabbed her arm, halting her. "Wait." When she faced him, he quickly released her. "I want your word you won't mention this to anyone."

She was half tempted to say something nasty. However, she'd already promised Colbert she wouldn't say anything. "I give you my word."

Instead of thanking her like a normal person, he simply nodded and went back into Colbert's room.

They weren't even married yet, and their communication already left something to be desired.

That evening at supper, Colbert was notably absent. Nara and Henrick sat at either end of the table while Reid and Dexter took their seats across from one another. A servant quickly removed the extra place setting. Once they finished serving the food, Henrick ordered all the servants out of the dining room.

"Where is your brother and why won't be he joining us?" Nara inquired.

"I asked him not to come," Dexter answered. "He happily agreed since he has a tremendous amount of work to do."

"Why don't you want him here?" Nara asked.

Dexter raised his eyebrows, giving his mother a *how could you even be asking that question* look. "Colbert doesn't need to be here while we discuss my personal life." He took a bite of his food, focusing on his plate.

Reid wondered if he spoke the truth or was only covering for his brother's absence.

"Lady Reid," Henrick said, capturing her attention.

"Please, call me Reid."

"Reid," he said, picking up his fork, "what has happened since the last time I saw you?"

After taking a sip of water, she explained how she'd returned to Ellington in order to speak with her father before facing the king. "I was only home for a few days when the princes arrived to escort me to the king's castle. Once there, I handed over the box. But when King Eldon opened it, the letters were gone."

Henrick paused mid-bite. "Gone?"

She nodded. "I think Ackley may have taken them."

"Ackley?" Dexter asked, his sharp gaze snapping to her. "You mean *Prince* Ackley?"

Reid mentally kicked herself for speaking so informally.

Henrick rubbed his forehead. "I need to think about this."

"The king sequestered me to my room," Reid continued. "Two weeks later, he summoned me to the throne room. There, he told me I was to marry Dexter. My father agreed to the king's request in exchange for a pardon and his deed. King Eldon then ordered me to spy on you and to find the missing letters."

"Which is interesting because your father had already sent me a letter inquiring about a union between you and my son long before the king did."

"Really?" Reid recalled seeing her father send out a rider the same night the princes had arrived to return her to the king's castle. Was that when her father sent a letter to Henrick about opening marriage negotiations?

"I offered my son in marriage to a daughter of any of Marsden's dukes to show I had no intention of going to war with northern Marsden. Your father accepted my proposal. Only, he didn't want you to marry Dexter and live in Ellington. He insisted you come to Axian where you would be safe and out of the king's clutches."

Dexter set his fork down. "Are you more than a spy for the king?"

Although she felt her face warm at his implication, Reid glared at him. "No, of course not. My virtue is still intact." Grabbing her goblet, she took a sip of water, trying to regain her composure. "Did no one else accept your offer?"

"Actually, several of the dukes agreed."

"Then why did you choose me?" What made her more enticing than the other ladies?

"Duke Ellington officially declared you his heir," Henrick explained.

"Me?" Reid asked, incredulous. Why hadn't her father chosen his eldest daughter?

"Nara and I spoke on the matter. We feel a union between you and Dexter is more advantageous."

The opportunity presented itself, so Reid took it. "Then I assume Dexter is your heir?"

The room went unnaturally quiet.

"The law is simple," Henrick stated. "The heir is the firstborn male."

"Yet, my father chose me, a woman and the youngest of his five children, to be his," Reid said. "No one knows Eldon is your son. Why allow him to inherit everything?" She raised her arms, the palms of her hands facing up to indicate not only the palace, but also the entire county. And it wasn't like Henrick was a stickler for the law. He allowed women to own land, hold jobs, and dress however they wanted.

"I often wonder the same thing," Nara said, her voice quiet.

"Eldon is my firstborn son," Henrick reiterated.

As he clutched his fork, Dexter's knuckles turned white. Reid suspected he'd already had this conversation with his father multiple times. And nothing he'd said had made a difference. That meant Henrick was stubborn. A trait shared by father and son. Reid needed to handle the situation carefully. "I understand Eldon is your firstborn son. I take that to mean when you die, the knowledge will be made public to the kingdom and...what? Eldon will inherit Axian? How does that work?" She didn't think a king could control a county. The dukes controlled the counties. The king oversaw the dukes.

"Did you know, Lady Reid," Nara said, "that Axian is where the king had always lived up until Hudson killed his father and took the throne?"

While Reid had her suspicions, she hadn't known it as fact. It made sense given the rich history of the city, buildings, and artwork.

"We don't have proof Hudson killed my father," Henrick said, rubbing his bearded chin.

"You were so determined to keep the peace, to honor your father's legacy, that you let Hudson declare himself the rightful heir." Nara folded her hands on her lap, watching her husband across the table. "Did you honestly think he would rule for a bit, then realize he wasn't cut out for the job? That he would suddenly understand you would be a better leader for our people?"

"There's more to it than that," Henrick stated.

"I don't fully understand what happened," Reid interjected. "Would you care to share it with me?"

Henrick twisted his goblet around, seemingly lost in thought. Finally, he looked at Reid. "My brother, Hudson, was born two minutes before me. He assumed he would rule. However, he cared more for women and hunting than he did for politics. I studied under my father, learning everything I could. Not because I wanted to rule, but because I enjoyed the studies. When we turned eighteen, Father declared me as his heir. Hudson went into a fit of rage, swearing to destroy the City of Radella and everything my father held dear. Around that time, I'd made an offer of marriage to Lady Leigh. Our parents were in the middle of contract negotiations when my father fell ill quite unexpectedly and died. I was shocked and heartbroken. After Father's death, my brother took control of the army. He declared he was going to marry Leigh instead. When my brother's actions toward me began to seem threatening, Leigh begged me to leave the city—to hide on her friend's estate. I complied, thinking it would give my brother time to calm down."

Reid had never heard any of this before. "But what of the dukes?"

"Hudson produced evidence, signed by my father, that proclaimed him as the rightful heir. While I believe he forged it, I have no proof. He claims Father changed his mind on his deathbed. There were supposedly two witnesses, both men loyal to my brother."

"What happened then?" Reid asked.

"Henrick came to my family's land," Nara said. "I was Leigh's best friend, and I promised to protect Henrick."

"Months later, when it was announced Leigh was with child, Hudson declared he was leaving the City of Radella. He traveled north of the Gast River to the City of Buckley, where he had a new castle built. One with a large wall. Since his wife was with child, the dukes supported him. Hudson said I could remain in Axian so long as I never crossed the river, so I agreed and came out of hiding. I returned to the palace where I've been living peacefully since."

"Why do you think Hudson left?" Reid asked. Why hadn't he stayed in Axian where the palace was far grander?

"I think he left because he couldn't handle the guilt," Nara said. "To live in the palace where he'd killed his father was too much for him. He ran from his childhood memories and what he'd done. In the City of Buckley, he started a new life, one separate from everything he knew in Axian."

"I agree," Henrick said. "The Gast River served as a line. He remained in the north, wanting nothing to do with me. I think if he had stayed here, he would have ended up killing me. However, the guilt of what he did to our father ate away at him, so he left, knowing he couldn't live with himself if he killed me, too. Not when we looked so much alike. It would have been like murdering himself."

"Why do you think King Eldon is determined to invade Axian?" Reid inquired. "Why not follow in his father's footsteps and remain in northern Marsden?"

Dexter, his eyes hard and fierce, answered. "Because Hudson wasn't Eldon's father—Henrick is. As long as Henrick is alive, Eldon is not the rightful king."

"You believe Eldon intends to kill his own father?"

"I do."

The room fell silent, no one contradicting him.

Finally, Henrick leaned forward and spoke. "I hope by joining the two of you in marriage, the king will leave Axian alone. If he doesn't, he will face Axian and Ellington's combined forces." He pointed at Reid's ring. "That's why your father gave you that. Not only to make sure the king doesn't hurt you, but also for you to have the power to call on the other dukes if necessary. Since I am a prince, I do not have that power."

"Duke Axian didn't produce a male child," Nara explained. "So Henrick took up the duke's duties. But he does not have the duke's ring."

Reid glanced down at the ring her father had given her. Henrick needed Reid to help prevent a war.

"I want to rally our people around this wedding," Nara said. "I want them to see Reid as a beautiful woman from northern Marsden who is here to help us. People need to believe your marriage will strengthen our counties."

And since Eldon had been the one to arrange it, he wouldn't see the union as a threat.

Nara had finished eating, so she shoved her plate away and crossed her legs, her attention solely on Reid. "I need to know if you will stand by my son's side. Your father sent you here for your own protection. However, I want my son protected as well. Where do you stand?"

Reid dared not glance at Dexter as she considered her answer. As much as she didn't want to admit it, this was an advantageous match. Aligning Axian and Ellington was a smart plan, one she fully supported. Although she didn't know Dexter that well, she didn't think he'd sit idly by just to preserve peace as Henrick had.

Considering their union objectively, Reid saw a new side to Dexter. Like Gordon, Dexter held a prominent position as a commander to the soldiers. Eldon had forced Gordon to marry a docile woman from a strong county loyal to the king in order to ensure the army remained devoted to him and to strengthen his own position. It was the king's way of making sure a powerful man like Gordon remained under his influence and control. Nara also wanted her son to marry a woman from a powerful county. However, she didn't want him attached to a docile and accommodating woman. Nara wanted her son to marry a woman who would fight the cause alongside him, someone who would challenge him, and someone who could help him lead Axian. Reid was here to fight on Axian's behalf.

Up until this point, Reid had viewed Nara as a powerful warrior. Now Reid understood that even a woman like Nara had her limitations. The princess needed Reid to help strengthen her son and protect Axian's future. The realization both humbled and honored Reid.

"I've been afraid marriage would make me weak. I didn't want to lose part of myself." Reid folded her hands, carefully considering her words. "I never realized the opposite could be true. That marriage could give me something."

Reid addressed Dexter. "I know we are not well acquainted, and you are hesitant to trust me. The feeling is mutual. However, I do trust my father, and he wants me here. I also respect both Prince Henrick and Princess Nara." After all, Henrick bore the mark of a Knight, and Nara embodied everything Reid admired.

Taking a deep breath to shore up her courage, she gazed directly at Dexter and said, "I do see the value of us marrying, and I am willing to give it a shot."

Dexter's penetrating eyes remained focused on Reid's, his face not giving away a hint of his thoughts or feelings. "My father and I have already spoken, and I agreed it's in Axian's best interest to align with Ellington." He rubbed the side of his face, along his strong jawline. "I also believe we can stop Eldon if we work together, which is why I severed my relationship with Gytha." He glanced at his mother as he said the last part.

Reid wondered how much of his decision to end things with Gytha had been based on his mother's tumultuous situation when she first married Henrick. She inclined her head. "I appreciate you ending things with your lover in order to give our marriage a try."

"I never said I was going to give it a try," he retorted.

Reid opened her mouth to argue, but he cut her off before she could utter a word.

"If we're going to do this," he said, his voice low and rumbling, "we both must fully commit. We don't try—we do." Fire and passion burned in his intense eyes.

Reid swallowed, not wanting to drown in the depth of his emotions. It felt as if his eyes pulled her toward him. Glancing away, she broke the connection, needing to make sure she maintained a clear head. No wonder he was such an effective commander. After one impassioned speech, she was willing to follow him anywhere.

"What do you say?" he asked, breaking her from her thoughts.

"I agree." Her voice came out slightly hoarse, causing her face to flush. She couldn't believe she found Dexter's fierce passion attractive.

"It's settled then," Nara said, saving Reid from having to say anything else. "We'll announce your engagement in two days. From this moment on, everyone must believe the two of you are in love. I want to give them romance and hope. Something they can believe in and rally behind."

"And I want the king to think Reid is here to do his bidding," Henrick said. "I don't want him to feel threatened. Then, hopefully, in time, the king will back off and leave Axian alone."

Nara and Dexter exchanged a brief look. It was obvious neither believed Eldon would leave Axian alone. And Reid was inclined to agree with them.

CHAPTER SIX

fter supper, Reid meandered around the palace, trying to get her bearings. Once she was confident where the main staircase, library, and great hall were located, she headed upstairs to see Colbert. His sitting room was dark, so she went into his bedchamber. A single lit candle graced his nightstand. Eyes closed, Colbert breathed evenly, his chest softly rising and falling, the sheets pulled all the way up to his neck.

She tiptoed over, gently touching the back of her hand to his forehead. His skin felt too warm. It could indicate the start of an infection or simply be from having too many covers on. The room had a slight chill since the fire in the hearth was low, barely producing any heat. Reid added a few more logs, stoking the flames back to life.

With her hands on her hips, she observed the prince. What had her sisters done when she'd fallen ill with a fever? They'd cooled her off with water. Reid grabbed the discarded bucket, then went to the bathing chamber to get fresh water. When she returned to his bedchamber, she sat on the chair next to his bed. Grabbing the towel, she dipped it in the bucket, wrung it out, and placed it on his forehead.

She needed to check his wound. Pulling the sheet down, she exposed his torso. A blood-soaked towel covered the injury. Slowly, she lifted it, thankful it didn't stick to his skin. The skin appeared slightly puffy and red. However, it didn't seem unnaturally swollen, nor was there any indication of infection. The stitches were small and evenly spaced. Dexter had done a surprisingly respectable job of sewing Colbert's skin together.

"Do you think I'll live?" Colbert asked, startling her.

She straightened, embarrassed he'd caught her with her face mere inches above his chest. "I do." After placing a clean towel over the wound, she pulled the sheet over him again, not wanting him to catch a chill. "Do you need anything before I leave?"

"Have you seen Finn?"

"No." He hadn't been in the room when she arrived.

The door opened. Dexter entered, Finn right behind him. The dog wagged his tail.

"There he is," Colbert said, a smile lighting up his face.

"I just took him out for a quick walk." Dexter stopped, apparently having just noticed her. "What are you doing here?" His gaze focused on Reid.

"I came by to check on your brother. Now that I know he's okay, I'll leave." She removed the wet towel, tossing it back in the bucket.

"Thank you," Colbert said.

She smiled kindly at him. "Any time." Reaching down, she scratched Finn's head before exiting the room. At the doorway, she glanced back. Dexter sat in the chair Reid had just vacated, clutching his brother's hand. It almost seemed as if he were apologizing. Again, she wondered how exactly Colbert had gotten hurt.

After putting on one of the dresses Nara had commissioned for her, Reid left the palace, eager to explore the city. Of course, it wasn't nearly as fun on her own as she'd thought it would be. A pang of loneliness filled her when she thought about Harlan preparing for his own wedding back home.

Reid wasn't sure if someone from the palace had followed her, and she didn't care. All she wanted was some fresh air, to peruse some of the shops, and to find the bookstore where she'd bought the map the last time she'd visited. Ackley had insinuated they would exchange correspondence through there. Not that she knew how it would work, but knowing Ackley, he already had a letter waiting for her.

After grabbing a bite to eat at a local bakery, she found the bookstore with ease. When she entered, she spotted the same worker as before. The woman stood on a ladder, searching along the top shelf.

Ackley had mentioned exchanging correspondences in a book. Meandering along the far aisle, Reid browsed the vast selection, hoping a title would stand out. Not finding anything of interest in the first aisle, she went down the second.

"The gentleman who was here earlier said I should recommend a book on knitting if a young lady with short brown hair came in," the woman said as she descended the ladder. "I think I have a few over here." Wiping her hands on her pants, she headed down the first aisle.

Knitting? Reid silently cursed Ackley. He was probably laughing somewhere at her expense. "Curious that a gentleman should recommend a book for me. He must know me well." And her hair wasn't that short. It had grown to just past her shoulders. Granted, it wasn't waist length like most women had, but it wasn't short like a man's.

The woman glanced over her shoulder at Reid, eyeing her from head to toe. "I'm not much of a knitter myself, but you do have the look of one." She squatted, then scanned the bottom two shelves. "Ah, yes, here we are. There are several books you may find of interest." She stood. "If you need any help, let me know."

"Thanks. I'll take a look."

The woman smiled before returning to climb her ladder once again.

Kneeling, Reid examined the books. Which one would Ackley have chosen? Probably the most boring one imaginable. She read the titles on the spines, trying to guess without having to flip through each book.

One's spine was so worn Reid had to pull it off the shelf to read the title. *The Origins of Knitting.* She groaned. Who would want to read such a boring book? Which was precisely why Ackley would pick this one. Settling on her bottom on the floor, Reid flipped through the ancient book. Nothing fell from between the pages. It didn't appear to have anything hidden inside. Maybe she'd chosen wrong. She closed the book, setting it on her lap. Although she hadn't known Ackley that long, she was certain he'd pick a book like this. Opening it again, she meticulously went through it, searching for even a scrap of paper hidden between the pages.

Toward the back, she found what she sought, deftly sliding the missive up her sleeve. After peering up and down the aisle to make sure no one was watching her, she slid the sketch of the ship entitled *Widow Maker* into the book. She'd scribbled details about Dexter's meeting with the ship's captain on the paper. Hopefully, the Knights could investigate further. She'd also noted that Eldon was Henrick's heir.

She gently closed the book, then re-shelved it.

An elderly gentleman entered the bookshop. "I'll be right with you, Walter," the shopkeeper said as she climbed down the ladder. "I have your order on my desk."

Reid used the distraction to exit the bookstore, eager to read the letter she'd acquired. However, she wouldn't dream of opening it until she was in her bedchamber with the door securely closed.

Since Dexter probably had someone watching her, she made sure to walk around in a relaxed manner as she took in the sights. Appearing eager or nervous would garner undo suspicion.

After making her way back to the palace, she went directly to the fourth floor. She had just reached for the door handle when someone called her name. Shock rolled through her as Dexter approached. "Yes?"

He stopped three feet away. "Do you have plans for this afternoon?"

"No, I do not." She eyed him warily, wondering what he was up to.

"Since you are free, I'd like to invite you to train with me over at the military compound. When we briefly fought in my parents' room, I recall you had some skill, though fairly basic. I think you would benefit from additional training."

Not sure if she should take offense to that or not, she decided she wouldn't—just to keep the peace. "After I change, I'll head over there."

He gave a curt nod and left.

Had Dexter decided to no longer ignore her since they agreed to have a real marriage? Reid watched him walk away, feeling an odd mixture of excitement and unease at the prospect of training with the army and getting to know this strange man who would soon be her husband.

Shaking her head, she went into her room, closing and locking the door behind her. After quickly checking each room to ensure no one else was there, she crawled onto her bed and slid the paper from her sleeve.

I hope you're doing well. I'd like to start off by apologizing. I know, I know, I'm not one to apologize. However, I feel this situation warrants one. I'm aware of your aversion to marriage. We are the same in that regard. Therefore, I'm apologizing for your upcoming wedding. You'd probably run away if you could. (You've considered it, haven't you?) The problem is you know this marriage has the potential to help our kingdom. And since you've sworn to protect Marsden, I hope you'll go through with it. Thank you for your sacrifice. I'm glad it's you and not me.

Even though the letter was unsigned, Ackley had clearly written it. Reid laughed. It wasn't like she was sacrificing anything on behalf of the kingdom or the Knights. She was a woman—as such, her father had the right to dictate who she married. Even if she weren't a Knight, her father would have still arranged this marriage. And, if circumstances had been different and she hadn't met the princes, she would have eventually married anyway.

She went over to the hearth, tossing the letter inside. There was just enough of a fire left to singe the paper, making it unreadable.

Now she had to find something suitable to train in. Searching through the armoire, she found pants and a tunic at the bottom of the last drawer. After quickly changing, she felt more like herself. The sleek pants made her legs look long, the slim shirt highlighting her curvy figure. Excitement coursed through her. She was going to train with soldiers!

After exiting the palace, she hurried across the lawn and past the lake until she came to the military compound. Not sure where to go, she ducked into the office building.

"I'm Lady Reid Ellington," she said, addressing the man behind the desk. "Prince, I mean Commander Dexter, is expecting me."

"Yes." The man stood. "I'm to give you a tour, then escort you to the training yard."

"Lady Reid," a familiar voice called. "I can't let this chap give you a tour." Markis patted the man's back.

"The commander gave me specific instructions."

"I understand," Markis said. "I truly do. But I'm free right now, and I can do it for you." He held out his arm. "Reid and I are old friends."

Reid eagerly took it, allowing Markis to usher her down the hallway.

They turned a corner, entering into a spacious room. "Is this an indoor training facility?" She'd never seen anything like it. Weapons lined the back wall. Several wooden boards were situated throughout at random intervals, probably serving as buildings or providing cover for various exercises.

"It is. It allows small groups to work on tactical drills." Markis led Reid from the room, then along another hallway. "This is my favorite place." He pushed the door open, allowing Reid to walk through first.

Curious, she entered the long, narrow room. It contained a dozen separated lanes, each with a round target on the far wall. Several bows and arrows were piled on a rectangular table by the entrance. "An indoor shooting range?"

"Isn't it fantastic?" Markis went over to the middle lane, picking up one of the smaller bows. He nocked an arrow, aimed, and shot. The arrow flew through the air, landing dead center with a satisfying *thud*. "Want to try?"

Was that even a question? Going to the adjacent lane, she chose a bow. After nocking the arrow, she lifted the bow and aimed it at the target. She tried to line the arrow up the way Markis had shown her. When she was confident she'd done so correctly, she released it. It soared toward the target, landing a foot below it. She burst out laughing. "I was so sure it would hit dead center, not miss the target completely."

He chuckled. "Try again."

She nocked another arrow.

"When I taught my sister to shoot, I always had to remind her to relax her stance and not be so rigid."

Reid took a few calming breaths, trying to make sure she was clear and focused.

Markis came up behind her. "Raise your left arm."

She did as he instructed.

73

He lowered his head closer to hers, looking along the length of her arrow. "You're aiming below the target."

"I am?"

He lifted her left arm slightly, then placed his hand on her right arm, adjusting it. Reid heard the door open behind her, but she didn't bother to see who entered. Her focus remained on the target.

"Good." Markis took a step back. "Now shoot."

Reid released the arrow. It cut across the room, landing with a *thunk* in the outer ring of the target. "Yes!" She beamed at Markis. "Thank you."

"Lady Reid," Gytha said. "What are you doing?"

"Shooting." Reid set the bow on the table, turning to address the woman.

"You're supposed to be getting a tour of the facility."

"I am," Reid said. "This is part of my tour."

"Commander Dexter wants you to join the novice training session. Come with me."

Novice? He thought Reid needed to train with the new recruits? Did he have so little faith in her? To test her, Ackley and Gordon had forced her to spar with someone far above her skill level. She still remembered the beast of a man she'd gone against. Yet now, Dexter wanted her placed with the beginners. Was there no happy-medium? On the bright side, she wouldn't look like a fool in a novice group.

"Thank you for the tour," she told Markis before she followed Gytha from the room.

Gytha led Reid to a different section of the building. When they came to a door, Gytha abruptly stopped, facing Reid. "What is going on with you and Markis?"

"He was giving me a shooting lesson." Reid's brows scrunched in confusion. "Why?"

"You are engaged."

"I know." It would officially be announced tomorrow.

"Then why are you spending time with another man?"

"Dexter wanted me to take a tour of the facility."

Gytha took a menacing step closer to Reid. "He did not instruct you to come here to flirt with one of his officers."

Reid snorted at the insinuation. "I wasn't flirting with Markis." She had no interest in flirting with him or anyone else for that matter.

"He was flirting with you."

"I can assure you he was not." Markis was just being kind.

Gytha shook her head. "Are you truly this clueless?"

"Markis is a friend." All Reid's friends were men. She was used to and comfortable with that fact.

"I will not sit idly by and watch you make a fool of Dexter," Gytha said, lowering her voice. "He deserves to be respected and loved."

The force of Gytha's words surprised Reid. She'd known Gytha and Dexter had a relationship that ended when Reid arrived in Axian. But, for some reason, she hadn't expected Gytha to still have feelings for Dexter, much less admit them to Reid. The fact the couple could no longer be together made guilt consume Reid.

"I'm sorry." The apology was inadequate, but she couldn't change anything. If she were in Gytha's position, she'd feel the same way. "Since I was raised as a man, I never had to worry about such things. I didn't think anything about it, nor did I realize it might seem improper. I promise it won't happen again."

Gytha narrowed her eyes as she studied Reid. After a long, uncomfortable minute, she nodded curtly. "This way." She opened the door, ushering Reid outside into one of the smaller training courtyards.

Short grass covered the ground and buildings surrounded the area on all four sides. There were around twenty-five people present, all about Reid's age. She scanned their faces—only a fourth were women.

Gytha whistled. "Line up."

Everyone immediately got into rows of five across and five deep. Reid moved to join them.

"You stay beside me," Gytha said, taking a spot in front of the trainees. "You will be my partner."

Reid did as instructed, clasping her hands behind her back.

"Today, we're going to practice what to do if someone tries to attack you from behind," Gytha announced. "Lady Reid, stand behind me and wrap an arm around my shoulders."

Reid did, already knowing what Gytha intended to do.

"If you find yourself in this position, lean forward," Gytha told the group. "Then use your attacker's momentum to flip them over your body. Like this." She demonstrated the move as she spoke.

Since Reid had been ready for it, she was able to land on her back without getting hurt.

"Now, it's your turn," Gytha said to the trainees. "Partner up with someone next to you, then take turns being the attacker and getting attacked."

Reid jumped to her feet.

"You know how to fight," Gytha stated.

"Yes."

Gytha shook her head, clearly nonplussed. "But you're a woman from northern Marsden."

"Who was raised as a man," Reid reminded her.

"I hadn't realized that included learning to fight."

"My father made sure I received extensive training." Although, he'd been sure to shield Reid from any sort of battlefield experience.

"Why are you with the novice group?"

"I assume Prince Dexter finds my skills lacking."

"What are your strengths?"

"I like to fight with twin swords rather than spar with my hands."

"Does the commander know this?"

"No." He hadn't bothered to ask. And when Reid had fought

him, the only weapon she'd had was a dagger—which she'd thrown at him.

"Just when I think I have you figured out, you surprise me."

Reid couldn't tell if she meant that as a good thing.

"There's a weapons class after this. How about you help me with these trainees, then you stay and join me for that class?" Gytha asked.

"I'd like that."

Gytha's smile was sly. "That's because you don't know what you're getting yourself into."

Reid assumed Gytha meant that as a joke, but she couldn't be sure. For the rest of the class, Reid went around to the trainees, giving pointers on their forms. It was fun to see other women learning and taking fighting seriously. It was something Reid had never experienced in northern Marsden. But maybe that would change one day. Maybe Reid could help make that change. Perhaps marrying the prince was a good thing. Not only would it put her in a position of power, but it would also provide her with the means to seek positive changes. And now that she was her father's heir, she would have even more opportunities to accomplish those goals.

When the class ended, everyone quickly dispersed. A minute later, a dozen men entered, Dexter bringing up the rear.

"Welcome," Gytha said, addressing everyone. "Today, we're going to focus on sword work. Grab a sword, and let's begin our advanced weaponry class."

Ah, hell. Reid had assumed this would just be a step up from the last class—not advanced weaponry. She eyed Gytha, who smiled smugly. Reid wanted to wring the warrior woman's neck.

CHAPTER SEVEN

Since a regular sword was simply too heavy for Reid to wield, she'd grown up using twin swords her father had commissioned especially for her. They were designed to be lighter so she could manage them effectively. But that had been against common foot soldiers in Ellington. The men in this training yard weren't ordinary soldiers.

Gytha instructed Reid to pick a sword.

"I'll just watch." There was no need to make a fool of herself. She knew her limits. It was obvious she was outmatched. From the corner of her eye, she spotted Markis. For some reason, it helped to know she had a friend here.

Gytha tossed a sword at Reid, who had no choice but to catch the thing. It was even heavier than she'd feared.

"Everyone, pair up," Dexter instructed.

"Need a partner?" Markis asked, suddenly at Reid's side.

"Yes." Relief filled her. She couldn't handle fighting a stranger right now. Not when she could barely lift her weapon.

"Do you even know how to use that?" Dubiously, he scratched the back of his head.

"Yes, although I'm used to a much lighter one."

"Hang on." He took her sword, then jogged over to a large bin. A minute later, he returned, carrying two wooden swords. "Let's use these instead, shall we?"

With a grateful smile, she took one of the wooden swords and stood opposite Markis. She tried to recall the training session she'd had with Ackley where he'd demonstrated how to modify what she knew in order to succeed against an unfamiliar opponent.

"Ready?" Markis asked.

Reid nodded, adjusting her grip on the hilt, trying to get a feel for the weight of the weapon.

He swung, and she easily parried the blow. She kept herself reined in, not wanting to go on the offensive until she had a better read on him.

"I'm not the best swordsman," he said. "My talent lies with the bow."

"While I have no doubt you are exceptional with the bow," she said while blocking a series of strikes, "you are one of twelve in an advanced weaponry class." Which meant he knew how to use a sword. Talking was probably a ploy to distract her. Her friend Knox often did that.

"Speaking of which, why are you here?" He circled around her.

She followed him, keeping her front facing his, so he couldn't attack her from behind. "Captain Gytha invited me. She made it sound like it was a good idea."

"That's what I feared." Lowering his sword, he glanced over to where Dexter and Gytha fought one another.

Fascinated, Reid watched as Dexter struck Gytha's side. In retaliation, she slammed the hilt of her sword against his shoulder. He twisted, ramming his elbow between her shoulder blades. When the blow knocked her to the ground, he put his foot on her back. Grunting, she punched the ground and conceded the match.

Reid swallowed. Dexter hadn't gone easy on Gytha. In fact, a trickle of blood ran down her face. Dexter reached down to help Gytha to her feet. They spoke quietly to one another. Reid was just about to turn away when Dexter gestured over at Reid and nodded. Wiping the blood from her cheek, Gytha started in Reid's direction.

Reid faced Markis, eyes wide, silently pleading for him to do something.

Raising his sword, he said, "Let's go another round."

She lifted her weapon, shoulders tense.

"Markis," Gytha snapped. "Go fight with Dexter."

"I'd like to finish my round with Lady Reid."

"It wasn't a request."

Markis nodded. "Yes, Captain." He gave Reid a worried glance before exchanging swords with Gytha.

At least Gytha now had a wooden sword instead of a metal one. Not that she couldn't do damage with a wooden one, but at least she wouldn't sever Reid's limbs.

"Let's see what you can do." With no more warning, Gytha raised her sword and viciously swung, aiming for Reid's side.

Reid barely had time to lift her sword to block the strike. The force was much stronger than she'd anticipated. Standing with her feet a little wider than usual to maintain balance, she warily eyed Gytha, waiting for the next attack.

The woman snarled, then came at Reid with a series of moves meant to back Reid into a corner while simultaneously wearing her down. Having no choice, Reid parried each blow as she took a step back, trying to think of a way to turn the situation around. Years of training kicked in. Her arms moved of their own accord, holding Gytha off. Within the first minute, Reid's arms ached—it had been far too long since she'd practiced. Regardless, she forced herself to remain strong and not to cower.

Growling in frustration, Gytha sped up her movements, her hits becoming more aggressive. She feinted to the left, then lunged, trying to hit Reid's left side. Reid managed to block the blow, her arms shaking from the impact. But then Gytha's foot slammed into Reid's shin, making her leg buckle. Before she could even think to defend herself, Gytha twisted, kicking Reid's exposed right side. Reid flew to the ground, her head slamming against the stone wall. Stars exploded across her vision, then dispersed into blackness that hovered around the edges of her consciousness.

Multiple blurry Gythas seemed to appear above Reid. "Maybe the novice class is better suited for you."

"Are you okay?" Markis asked, kneeling beside Reid. His fingers trailed over her head, examining it.

Reid couldn't answer. A ringing sound bombarded her ears, her vision swimming in a cloudy sea of images she couldn't quite make out. Everything hurt. She closed her eyes, trying not to vomit.

"What were you thinking?" Markis demanded.

"Watch how you address your superior," Gytha sneered.

"My superior? My superior would have *never* taken such a cheap shot." Reid felt arms slide under her body, vaguely aware when Markis picked her up.

She opened her eyes, blinking frantically. As everything started to come into focus, she noticed the soldiers no longer sparred. Instead, they stared at her. She couldn't even summon the energy to be mortified by the attention. Her body ached.

"I'm taking her to the infirmary," Markis said.

Dexter approached. "Don't move," he murmured. Then, addressing everyone, he raised his voice. "Back to work. Now."

The soldiers immediately complied.

Turning to Reid, he asked, "Are you okay?"

"Yes," she replied, her voice barely audible. "The force of the hit jarred me, but I'm okay."

"Can you stand?"

"Probably."

Markis tightened his hold on her. "You hit your head pretty hard."

"Set her on her feet," Dexter commanded.

Markis hesitated before slowly releasing her, setting her on her feet.

When Reid stumbled, Markis grabbed her shoulders, offering support.

"She'll be fine," Gytha said dismissively.

"What are you still doing here?" Dexter asked, his tone sharp. "I told everyone to get back to work."

Gytha's eyes widened and she opened her mouth to argue. Dexter merely raised his eyebrows, and she snapped her mouth closed. She grabbed Markis's arm, proceeding to drag him away. They both picked up their discarded swords, then began fighting.

Dexter's intense gaze pinned Reid in place. "Are you sure you're all right?" he asked again, his voice low and throaty.

Everything seemed to spin around her. "I'm fine." She reached up, touching her throbbing head.

He wiped his forehead with his arm. "Do you need me to fetch a healer?"

"No." She swayed, pinching her eyes shut against a wave of dizziness.

Dexter reached forward, encircling her waist with both his hands to steady her.

His touch froze her in place. She forced her eyes open, staring directly into his. As she focused on him, everything around her stopped moving. The tips of his fingers dug into her sides. "I'm fine," she insisted, more to herself than to him.

Cautiously, he released her. "You don't look like you're fine."

She could feel steady strength radiating from him. "I just need to lie down." Turning ever so slowly, she took cautious steps toward the exit, hoping she'd make it without falling and embarrassing herself further. She wanted to maintain what little dignity she had left—if she even had any.

After pushing the door open, she entered the building and made a left. Once she heard the door click shut behind her, she collapsed against the wall, willing herself not to vomit. Thankfully, the world no longer spun and the ringing in her ears had stopped. However, she felt nauseous and her head throbbed.

Not wanting anyone to see her hunched over in the hallway, she forced herself to stand straight as she made her way to the exit. Outside, she squinted against the bright light, trying to decide what to do. The city suddenly felt too busy, too noisy, too overpowering. Longing for the solitude of the country filled her.

Without a conscious decision, she started walking west, continuing straight until she'd exited the city. After half a mile, she spotted a field of lavender. She glanced over her shoulder, making sure no one followed her. Not spotting anyone, she trekked down one of the rows, being careful not to step on any of the plants. The fragrant scent permeated the air, smacking Reid with a wave of homesickness. She missed her father and her sisters. Her castle and her land. She missed her friends.

When she reached the crest of a valley that extended for miles, she paused and took in the sight. The wind brushed against her skin, and she basked in the smell, the feel, and the warmth of the outdoors.

A tear slid down her cheek. Reid folded to the ground, hugging her legs. She'd always considered herself strong and fierce. After all, she'd been raised as a man and took pride in not emotionally falling apart like other women. Yet, here she was, feeling like a wreck.

Resting her head on her knees, she stared at the valley. Field after field of agriculture extended for miles. Everything was so vibrant. She'd thought by coming here, she'd find her true home. Since men in Axian treated women as equals who could hold jobs, own land, and wear whatever they wanted, Reid thought she would finally have everything she desired. This was where she'd thought she belonged. So why did she feel so alone?

She rubbed her face, exhausted. Marrying Dexter was the right thing to do. She knew that. However, the thought of tying herself to another person, especially a man like the commander, terrified her. She'd never been romantically involved before. No one had ever even kissed her.

Today had been humiliating. Reid gingerly touched her head where she'd smacked it, assessing the lump that was already forming. Why did Gytha feel the need to challenge and belittle Reid? Dexter had willingly chosen to sever his relationship with the warrior woman. Reid hadn't known anything about it. If Gytha wanted to be mad at someone, it should be him. Gytha's eyes had been wild and furious as they'd fought. It had scared Reid, who hadn't been prepared for the woman's anger to flare.

Wiping the tears from her eyes, Reid decided there was nothing she could do to change the past. It was over. She could only focus on the future, though she was tired of others dictating her life. In Ackley's letter, he'd apologized for putting Reid in this situation. When he'd placed that queen chess piece in the box—presumably stealing the letters—he'd set a series of events into action. He had to be the mastermind behind everything. She wasn't sure if she admired his ability to think so far ahead, or if she truly hated the man. It could go either way. Love and hate—two powerful emotions—similar, yet so contradictory.

With her crying fit now over, Reid decided to stop feeling sorry for herself. She wouldn't let anyone take advantage of her again. However, what she could use right now was a friend—one she trusted. She rose, brushed herself off, and headed back to the palace. There was someone she wanted to see.

When Reid stepped into Colbert's bedchamber, she spotted him in a chair next to the window. "It's good to see you out of bed," she said by way of greeting.

The corners of his lips rose. "It's good to be out of bed." In loose pants and an untied robe that revealed most of his chest, he looked disheveled.

Reid imagined it would be considered improper for her to be alone with him in here, especially in his state of undress, but she didn't care. "Does your tattoo mean anything?"

He smiled. "Why do you ask?"

"I've never seen anything like it before."

Colbert rubbed the nape of his neck. "I spent a year traveling."

She sat on the chair next to him, waiting to see if he'd elaborate.

"The tattoo came from one of the kingdoms I visited. It means *Strength in mind and spirit.*"

Reid hadn't been sure the marks were even letters. The ink covered his entire collarbone and circled around the back of his neck.

"So, Lady Reid, what brings you to my humble abode?"

The first word that came to mind was *desperation.* Desperation for kindness, compassion, and companionship. She leaned back, about to answer. Instead, she winced.

"Are you okay?"

"I'm fine." She sat slightly forward, keeping the sore part of her head from touching the chair. Rubbing her temples, she asked, "How are you doing?"

"Don't change the subject," he said quietly. "We're talking about you. What happened?"

"It's nothing." She didn't need to cry to Colbert about Gytha besting her. Reid was a big girl who could take care of herself.

"You're dressed in training gear."

"I am."

"You appear to be in some sort of pain."

She rolled her eyes. "Fine. I hit my head."

His brows drew together. "Has a healer checked it to make sure you're okay?"

Chuckling, she said, "That's funny coming from you." She pointedly looked at his wound.

"I suppose you're right." He crossed his legs. "Will you at least tell me how it happened?"

"I'll tell you on one condition."

He waved his hand, indicating she should state her case.

"You won't say a word about it to anyone else."

"Why?"

Instead of responding, she stared at him, waiting for him to agree.

He tapped his hand on his thigh. "Fine. I promise not to say anything."

Satisfied, she proceeded to tell him about her incident with Gytha.

When she finished, he said, "That doesn't surprise me seeing as how she doesn't like to lose."

"Gytha is far more experienced with a sword than I am." Reid had been no match for the warrior woman.

Colbert grinned, seemingly amused. "Sometimes, Reid, your youthful age and naïveté shows."

She frowned, not liking the sound of that.

"I am referring to Dexter," he clarified. "Gytha always assumed she'd be his wife one day."

"Why didn't they marry?" Why had they carried on a relationship for so long without taking it to the next level?

"That's a good question. Clearly, she loves him and wants to get married. I know Dexter likes her, cares for her even. He's attracted to the fact she's a fierce fighter, a warrior like no other, and loyal. I'm not sure he's actually in love with her, though. He considers her a great friend to be sure, but beyond that, I don't know."

Colbert had no reason to lie. So why had he told Reid this? Was he trying to help her understand Dexter better? She supposed friends discussed this sort of thing. They also told each other the truth. "I've never been in love," she admitted. "And I'm scared to marry your brother. Especially since we're not even friends." She clasped her hands together, waiting for his reaction.

He nodded in understanding. "That doesn't surprise me, given your upbringing. Honestly, I'd feel the same way if I were you." He shifted in his seat, then winced and cradled his side.

"Are you all right?"

"Yes, I just twisted too quickly. I'm sure I'll be better in no time."

"How did you hurt yourself?" She tried to sound nonchalant instead of like she was fishing for information—even though she was.

"I was doing something I shouldn't have been. Which is why I don't want my parents or anyone else to know I'm injured. I feel bad enough—I don't need them hounding me."

"I can understand that." Reid chuckled. "Are you going to be able to attend the engagement party tomorrow?"

"Everyone expects me to be there."

"I don't want you to injure yourself any further."

"I'll be careful. Maybe I'll walk a little slower than normal and refrain from dancing, but I will be there."

She reached for his hand, squeezing it gently before releasing it. "I'm glad I will have at least one friend in attendance."

Reid tossed and turned, unable to sleep. Tomorrow, her engagement to Dexter would be formally announced to the people of Axian. Nara had pulled Reid aside after supper earlier to explain a small, private party would follow the event. The princess kindly reminded Reid that the newly engaged couple needed to dazzle everyone. Reid and Dexter were to be the champions everyone rallied behind. Quite frankly, Reid couldn't imagine Dexter being anything other than the commander of the army. The notion of him formally dressed, dancing and speaking cordially with other people, seemed like a foreign concept.

Reid flew upright in bed. Not only did she have to wear a lavishly fancy dress, but she would also have to dance. The last time she danced was with Gordon. When her face warmed, she immediately banished all thoughts of him—he was in her past.

Instead, she tried to picture what songs she'd have to dance to. Thankfully, her sisters had taught her all the important steps. Granted, Reid had always taken the man's part. But how hard could it be to switch over to the woman's? What would it be like to dance with Dexter? Would everyone watch them, expecting to see two people in love? And how would Dexter treat her? In the training area, when he'd grabbed her waist to keep her from falling, his hands had been strong and steady. The thought of being held in Dexter's arms as they danced sent a wave of anxiousness spiraling through Reid. She didn't understand why she was suddenly so nervous.

After slipping out of bed, she tiptoed over to the window, then lifted the curtain to glance outside. In the sky, a sliver of the moon shone. Most buildings in the city were dark, everyone tucked safe inside their own homes. Everything seemed so quiet and still. Except for the man who strode across the front lawn, his black cape billowing behind him. Reid squinted, trying to get a better look, but the hood concealed his face. His shoulders were wide, his gait long. It could be a soldier heading home after his shift, but Reid didn't think so.

When she'd scouted the palace, the sentries had been aware of her presence. She didn't think much happened around here that Dexter wasn't privy to. It was doubtful a guard would be crossing the lawn at this hour. Her gut told her it was Dexter. And that the sentries were aware of his movements. So where was he going this late and alone?

Ackley had given Reid an assignment—*discover where the prince goes at night.* Dexter's midnight stroll had to be what Ackley referred to.

She considered changing, then running after him. However, Dexter had too far of a head start. She'd never be able to catch up. Not only that, but he would also know if someone followed him. Even if he somehow didn't, the guards would spot her.

The Knights knew Dexter sometimes went somewhere at night, but they hadn't been successful in finding out where. And if a trained spy couldn't follow Dexter, Reid stood no chance. She'd have to get creative.

When Ackley tested Reid before making her a Knight, he'd sent her on a job no other Knight had been able to accomplish. She'd been successful because she'd used her ability to play the part of a man or a woman. Adapting to the circumstances, thinking quickly, and being able to talk her way out of any situation had allowed Reid to succeed.

She released the curtain, the fabric sliding shut. Once she'd climbed back into bed, she tried to figure out how to solve the mystery.

CHAPTER EIGHT

U pon entering the family's private dining room for breakfast, Reid found Dexter and Colbert seated at the table. "Should you be up and about?" Reid asked Colbert as she sat across from the brothers.

Colbert raised his eyebrows. "Not you, too."

"Excuse me?"

He chuckled. "I just got that very same lecture from Dex." When Colbert nudged his brother, Dexter only rolled his eyes and took a big bite of his oatmeal.

Reid plucked a slice of bread and placed it on her plate, then poured a cup of tea.

Dexter's leg jerked against the table, almost as if he'd been pinched. Colbert covered his mouth, muttering to his brother so softly Reid couldn't hear a word. Curious, she took a sip of her tea, wondering if she'd find out what was going on.

A moment later, Dexter cleared his throat. "How's your head?"

Reid blinked, studying him. Curling her fingers around the warm mug, she said, "I have a large lump, which is rather sore, but I'm fine. Thank you for your concern."

He inclined his head, then resumed eating without a word.

Colbert shook his head, clearly exasperated with Dexter for some reason.

Nara entered the room. "Lady Reid, I need a moment of your time."

Longingly, Reid stared at her untouched plate of food before rising. "Of course, Your Highness." She followed Nara to a quaint sitting room.

"We need to talk about tonight." Nara closed the door, then sat on a sofa, patting the spot next to her.

As Reid took a seat, her stomach growled. Instead of acknowledging her hunger, she waited for the princess to speak.

"I'm not familiar with how things are done in Ellington, but, in Axian, the county is divided into six regions," Nara began. "A family is in charge of overseeing each region. These families then report to Prince Henrick, who oversees the entirety of Axian."

Reid nodded to show her understanding. Ellington was run very similarly.

"As soon as Henrick signed the marriage contract for you and Dexter, he sent word to each family, asking them to send a representative to hear a special announcement."

"So what you're saying is the most important families from Axian will be in attendance tonight?"

"Yes." Nara smiled. "That is exactly what I'm trying to convey."

Reid fidgeted with the end of her sleeve. "I've only attended one formal function as a woman, and it was rather small." Even as a man, she hadn't been to many grand events. Her father tended to avoid lavish parties.

Nara patted Reid's thigh. "You'll be fine." She pursed her lips. "But there is something you need to know."

"What is it?"

Nara scrunched her forehead, clutching her hands together. "I'm not sure how to say this, but one of those families is *your*

91

family. Your mother's side. In other words, your grandparents are in charge of an Axian region."

Acute silence fell as Reid processed the information. Her father had recently informed Reid her mother was from Axian. For some reason, Reid had never considered the possibility her grandparents could still be alive. Since her father's parents were dead, she'd assumed her mother's were as well.

Abruptly, Reid leaned forward, putting her elbows on her knees and resting her head against her hands. She breathed heavily. "I'm going to meet my grandparents tonight?"

"No. Neither will be in attendance tonight. However, I expect them to be at the wedding."

Reid kept breathing through her mouth, striving for more air.

"Your grandfather sent his nephew's son as the family's representative. You'll meet your second cousin this evening."

"What if my grandparents hate me for killing their daughter?" Reid felt sick.

"You didn't kill your mother. She died in childbirth. It was not your fault." Nara rubbed Reid's back, the simple action soothing her.

"I wish I had known." Stupidity for not considering the possibility she had grandparents filled her.

"Since northern Marsden's relations are so strained with Axian, you wouldn't have had the opportunity to visit anyway, so knowing wouldn't have made a difference."

"My father should have told me."

"Speaking of your father, this arrived for you." Nara pulled a letter out of her pocket, holding it out to Reid. "You can open it in private later."

Reid took the letter, running her finger over her father's seal.

"Now that you understand we are hosting the most important and powerful families tonight, families whose support we need, I am going to ask a few things of you."

"Of course," Reid answered automatically, too overwhelmed

with the notion she had grandparents to focus. Clinging to the envelope from her father, she stared at Nara, hoping the princess would finish in a hurry so Reid could read her letter.

"It's imperative Axian remain strong. To do that, we need money, resources, and the support of the military. As of now, the only thing looming before us is an uncertain future."

Reid understood what Nara had implied. Even though Henrick hoped for peace, Nara planned to prepare for war—just in case.

"Tonight," Nara continued, "you will dress as the fine lady you are. People will expect you to be meek and docile. However, you will be the strong, confident woman I know you are. You will exhibit this through the words you use, the wisdom you convey, and the way your carry and present yourself."

"I can do that," Reid said, the lie rolling off her tongue. She had no idea if she could act and behave in such a way. However, if her doing so was what Nara needed, Reid would do everything she could not to let the princess down—even if it meant putting on a show. The letter still clutched in her hand, Reid rose to leave. Hesitantly, she asked, "What do you think the king is going to do to me?"

"Whatever do you mean?"

"King Eldon expects me to procure those letters between Henrick and Leigh. However, someone stole them."

"The only other person who has a key is Leigh," Nara stated.

Could Leigh have given Ackley the key? And if so, why? "The king will be furious with me when I don't produce the letters."

Nara stood, settling a hand on each of Reid's shoulders in a show of comfort. "You're going to be part of this family. We'll protect you." Her strong words rang true.

"Thank you."

"I have a few things to tend to before tonight." Nara released her. "People will be pleased when they see their future princess looks like one should. And when they find out you're also a warrior, they'll know what a real gem you are."

The word *gem* reminded Reid of something. "I think we need to investigate what's going on in the Bridger mines."

"Why do you say that?"

"I saw two groups of men who looked like miners from Bridger. Both tried to assassinate Ackley, Gordon, and Idina—but not the king." Then there was the fact at least one ship sailed from Bridger to Melenia to barter precious stones and gems.

"Have you shared this concern with anyone?"

"No."

"I'm glad you said something to me. I'll have my sons look into it."

Standing before the full-length mirror, Reid shook her head. "I can't." She'd never seen a dress like this in her life, much less wore one. "It's not appropriate."

"I beg to differ," Nara said, coming to stand beside her. "It's perfect."

Reid barely recognized herself. The midnight-blue dress left her shoulders bare, going straight across her bosom to fit snuggly along her torso. At her waist, the fabric loosened, flowing in soft, silky waves around her feet. A mixture of braids and soft curls, her hair had been gathered atop her head, then adorned with a circlet. When she moved, the tiny diamonds all over her dress transformed it into a night sky glittering with stars. Even Reid's makeup complemented her attire, the pale shimmery colors making her appear almost fairy-like.

"Don't you think it's a little too revealing? I've never seen anyone wear something like this before."

"It is revealing," Nara admitted.

"Shouldn't I wear something...like your dress?" The princess wore a deep green dress that covered her from neck to toe. Tan thread formed a pattern of intricate leaves on her tight sleeves and bodice. Although elegant, it managed to convey Nara's fierce side.

Nara rested a hand on Reid's shoulder. "You look like a woman, you look like a princess, and you look desirable. That, my dear, is what you must convey. We are announcing your engagement to my son. He is the most sought-after man in Axian. He is not only a prince, but also the commander of the army here. You must rise to the occasion and match him." She released Reid. "Let's go."

"No necklace?" Reid reached up, feeling her bare neck. She couldn't help but notice her cleavage.

"No jewelry." Nara opened the door, waiting for Reid to join her. "I think you look more appealing that way."

Taking a deep breath, Reid steeled her resolve and joined Nara. They went downstairs to a room off the great hall. Nara instructed Reid to wait there, wanting her to remain out of sight until the announcement.

As Reid sat there, she thought about her father's letter. He'd apologized for organizing everything behind her back, informing her he'd written to Henrick and arranged the marriage before the king had. Also, he'd said they needed this union—that everything would work out in the end. After he wished her luck, he'd ended with a promise to be there on her wedding day.

A soldier entered the room. "Lady Reid." He bowed. "I'm to escort you to where the announcement is being made."

"Isn't it happening in the great hall?" she asked as she followed him through the palace.

"The celebration will be in the great hall, but a platform has been erected on the lawn so the announcement can be made to the people of the city." They stopped at the front door.

How many people were out there? Did they expect Reid to speak? Why hadn't Nara mentioned this part to her earlier?

Someone knocked on the door.

"That's our cue," the soldier said. "Let's go." He opened the door, motioning for Reid to step outside.

The sky was dark, matching the color of Reid's dress. Evenly spaced throughout the front lawn and along the exterior of the palace were hundreds of torches, which provided soft illumination. The platform was about fifty feet away. All four members of the royal family stood atop it. They faced the crowd, their backs to Reid.

Hundreds of people milled around, eagerly waiting for the royal family to speak. Reid couldn't believe so many were in attendance. What if she tripped on her dress as she went up the platform stairs? She'd feel infinitely better if only she'd been allowed to wear her pants and boots. More like herself and not this stranger.

Stopping at the bottom of the platform, she waited for Prince Henrick to announce her. Not sure why she was sweating, she fanned herself, trying to cool off.

Prince Henrick thanked everyone for coming before saying, "We are so very pleased to announce our son, Prince Dexter Winston, is engaged."

The crowd exploded into applause.

"Without further ado, I'd like to introduce your future princess."

"Up you go," the soldier said to Reid.

She ascended the stairs, aware Henrick hadn't revealed her name. How would people react? Would they be upset their prince was engaged to a northerner? When she reached the top, she paused to take it all in. Henrick and Nara stood slightly to the left, both smiling at her with warm smiles lighting up their faces. Dexter and Colbert stood to the right, both facing forward. There was an empty spot between Henrick and Dexter, clearly meant for Reid. Taking a deep breath, she moved forward, ready to take her place at Dexter's side.

Colbert glanced back at her. He blinked, his expression almost awed, then nudged Dexter.

Dexter rolled his shoulders as he turned toward her. His eyes widened in shock. Reid stopped, sucking in her breath. Dexter wasn't in his commander uniform as she'd anticipated. Instead, he wore dark blue pants and a matching tunic with the Axian crest embroidered on the front. He'd combed his hair back, his face clean shaven. Under the moonlight with the torches glowing around them, he looked devastatingly handsome. Lifting an eyebrow, he extended his left hand.

Reid resumed walking. When she was close enough, she slid her hand into Dexter's. His fingers curled around hers. The simple act sent a shiver through Reid. Her heart pounded as she stood at his side in the middle of the platform with hundreds of people watching them.

Nara leaned toward Reid. "Don't forget to smile."

There were so many people staring at Reid. And she was holding hands with Dexter. Her future husband, who was striking in a way she hadn't allowed herself to acknowledge.

A few people shouted, asking for the bride's name.

Henrick cleared his throat. "Prince Dexter will be marrying the lovely Lady Reid Ellington one month from today."

The cheerfulness subsided, a ripple going through the crowd at the mention of her name. Many eyed Reid with wary expressions.

"We would hold the ceremony sooner," Nara added. "However, we want to give everyone traveling here from northern Marsden plenty of time to arrive."

"I'd also like to mention that Lady Reid is Duke Ellington's heir," Henrick added. "After the wedding, Prince Dexter will travel to Ellington with his bride. Once there, he will discuss the possibilities of opening trade, traveling freely between our counties, and joining our resources together."

Dexter's fingers tightened around Reid's. She didn't think Henrick was supposed to tell anyone she was Ellington's heir.

However, given the crowd's reaction, he'd probably thrown in that boon to appease everyone. Only, instead of excited cheers, people started whispering to one another. Reid heard her name cascade through the crowd like a rough wave as the new development and what it meant for Axian was discussed. She could practically feel the tension radiating from the crowd. The urge to take a step back and run from the platform inundated her.

"Thank you all for coming," Nara said. "Let the celebration begin!" Servants rushed forward, passing out food and drinks to those gathered. To Reid, Nara said, "Let's get you inside. Now."

Dexter released Reid's hand, wrapping his arm protectively around her shoulders as he quickly ushered her down the stairs. At the bottom, a handful of soldiers surrounded them, then escorted the royal family into the palace.

The minute the doors shut behind them, Dexter let go of Reid.

"After an hour, cease serving food and drinks," Nara said to the sentries standing guard. "Then have soldiers begin to disperse the crowd. Make sure it is done peacefully."

"Yes, Your Highness," one answered.

The royal family made their way to the small room just off the great hall.

"We'll wait in here until the guests we've invited are safely inside," Henrick explained. "I think we're expecting about two hundred to attend."

Two hundred? Reid thought the celebration was supposed to be a small, intimate gathering. "How many people were outside for the announcement?"

"Around five thousand," Nara answered.

Whenever Reid's father spoke to the commoners, they only had two or three hundred attend. The sheer size of the City of Radella always surprised her.

Dexter leaned against the wall, crossing his arms. "The king has spies here," he said. "We shouldn't have said anything about joining forces with Ellington."

"Besides the six we're already aware of," Colbert said, "I spotted two more tonight. That brings the total to eight."

"Not including Reid," Dexter added.

"Not including our dear Reid," Colbert confirmed, a sly smile on his lips.

"We can have the spies intercepted before they send word to King Eldon," Nara suggested.

"No," Henrick said. "Let them go. I want to see how things play out."

Dexter raised his eyebrows, about to speak, when a servant entered.

"Your Highness, the guests are all here. Shall I announce the royal family?"

Henrick cleared his throat. "First, just announce Prince Colbert, my wife, and me. Let's wait another fifteen or so minutes after that to introduce the newly engaged couple."

After a brief nod, the servant left.

Nara stood before Dexter, taking his hand in hers. "You and Reid need to start spending time together," she said. "You're too awkward around one another. No one will believe you're in love."

"Mother," he murmured.

"You're not making an effort to be friends."

Dexter glanced at Reid, not even bothering to deny it.

"The people in that room must believe in this union. So please, for the sake of Axian, at least pretend to care about her."

Reid abruptly stood, about to inform them how humiliating it was to be spoken about like she wasn't there.

"I was Reid once," Nara continued. "I know how it feels to be in an arranged marriage with someone who doesn't want any part of it. Don't do that to her—it's not fair." She squeezed her son's hand, let go, and left the room, Henrick and Colbert right behind her.

Dexter didn't move from his position against the wall. Reid had no idea what to say or do, so she started pacing. She hated feeling like a burden. Like she was unwanted. He didn't even like her. It grated on her nerves, making her want to scream.

"I'm sorry," Dexter said, his voice barely audible. "It was not my intention to be rude."

At that, she stopped and glared at him. "Are you sure about that? Since the moment I arrived in Axian, you have been anything but welcoming."

"Because the king sent you to spy." He shrugged.

Yes, well, there was that. Tired of being nervous, afraid, and curious about this man, she resumed pacing. "Didn't you say you wanted to make our marriage work?"

"I said I wanted our *union* to work."

Was there a difference? She cocked her head. Had he meant he wanted to be married to her for the betterment of Axian, but he didn't want to care about her? "What are you afraid of?"

He pushed off the wall, ignoring the question. "I'm sure it has been long enough."

Reid followed him down a short hallway. He stopped before a door and knocked, shifting his weight from foot to foot. She couldn't tell if it irritated him to wait or if it had to do with being in such a confined space with her. The door swung open, and their names were announced. People clapped and cheered as Reid and Dexter entered the great hall. Side by side, but not touching.

The room's transformation astounded Reid. Hundreds of candles hung from the ceiling, resembling stars in the night sky. She started to sense a theme. A long table covered with food was situated along the east wall while tables lined the perimeter of the room. The middle had been left open to form a dance area. At the front of the room, there was a raised dais. Colbert sat on one of the throne chairs while Nara and Henrick remained on the steps holding hands. A few musicians were set up in one corner, and they began to play a slow tune.

Reid knew she was expected to dance with Dexter. When they

stopped in the middle of the room, he raised his arm, silencing the musicians.

"We want to thank you all for coming to celebrate with us," Dexter said. "Please, feel free to eat, drink, and dance." He gave a curt nod before heading over to the food table.

Not sure what to do, Reid followed, forcing a smile. He picked up a plate, then started piling it with food. "I don't think you're supposed to be eating right now," she said under her breath.

He glanced up at her. "I'm hungry."

She was still too nervous to eat. "I think we should mingle first."

"That's because you're a woman from northern Marsden. No one cares about that sort of thing in Axian."

She rolled her eyes. "Don't be daft." It had nothing to do with being a woman or where she was from. This was supposed to be a show, and they had a part to play.

"Lady Reid," a woman said, capturing her attention. "It is so nice to meet you. I'm Clara Rothsborn."

Stifling her irritation with Dexter, Reid forced a pleasant expression as she turned toward the woman, not sure if Clara belonged to one of the ruling families. Not wanting to say something and offend the woman, especially if her name was one Reid should know, she replied with a generic statement. She'd thought Dexter would jump in the conversation to make the necessary introductions. Instead, he shoved a piece of bread in his mouth, completely ignoring her.

Reid noticed Colbert heading for the exit. Worried his wound had reopened, she excused herself and hurried across the room, catching him just before he reached the door. "You're leaving already?"

"I am."

"You didn't tear a stitch, did you?"

He shook his head. "It's healing nicely."

"Then why don't you stay?" Reid needed a friendly face—someone who treated her with kindness and was her friend.

"I don't think I should."

She nodded, even though she wasn't sure what he meant by that. "Your mother did a fabulous job organizing this event on such short notice. Even my dress matches the room. Everything looks beautiful."

"I agree," he said, his eyes never leaving hers.

"Would you like to dance?" she asked.

Closing his eyes, he took a deep breath. "Reid," he said, opening them and taking a step closer to her. "My brother is a lucky man. You should go over and ask him to dance. With him is where you need to be—where you ought to be." His brow creased.

"Are you okay? I can walk you to your room if you need help." She wouldn't mind escaping the party for a few minutes, especially since she didn't know anyone here. She'd never been around so many people, yet she felt so alone.

He smiled. "I can see you're as eager as I am to leave the party."

"I feel very out of place here," she admitted.

"If it's any consolation, you don't look out of place. You look like you belong here."

She glanced at Dexter. A woman hovered at his side, conversing with him. She had on a blue dress, though not nearly as dark as Reid's, that covered the woman's neck, shoulders, and arms, leaving only her face and hands bare. The bottom portion flared out a bit, appearing full but not detracting from the woman's height. Realization dawned. "Is that Gytha?"

"I think all the captains are here," Colbert said. "You should go talk to Dexter."

"He doesn't want me around."

"I know it seems that way, but that's not the case."

"He won't even have a conversation with me."

"He's just scared."

"Of what?"

"Go talk to him. Once you two realize how similar you are, I'm certain you'll become fast friends. And mark my words, you and Dexter will be a formidable pair—a force to be reckoned with."

The brothers seemed to be close, and Reid valued Colbert's opinion. "Do you think so?"

"I know so. Now, I must leave so history does not repeat itself. Goodnight." He winked before exiting the room.

She took a step after him, wanting to ask what he meant by that statement, when someone tapped on her shoulder.

"May I have the honor of a dance?" Markis asked as Reid shifted to face him. He had on his officer uniform.

"You clean up well." She almost didn't recognize him.

"So do you." He held out his hand, waiting for her to accept his offer.

"I'm not familiar with this dance." It was a fast tune, and the steps appeared rather complicated. For her first romp around the dance floor, she'd rather it be to something easy to follow.

"I'll guide you through it."

"I don't know." A man leading her in a dance wasn't something she was used to.

Leaning forward, Markis whispered, "Don't say I didn't try to save you." He straightened as another man approached.

"Lady Reid Ellington." The man bowed. "It is a pleasure to meet you. I am Lord Robert." He exuded an air of confidence mixed with a touch of arrogance.

Reid felt as if she should know who this man was, so she replied, "The pleasure is all mine."

"I can see why Prince Dexter is smitten with you. You are a lovely sight."

"Yes," Reid snapped, offended by his comment. "I am sure it has nothing to do with my intellect, my personality, or the fact I'm the heir to one of the largest counties in the kingdom."

He barked out a laugh. "So you are not like other northerners?

I'm glad to hear it. If our prince had chosen a meek and helpless thing, I would have opposed."

Who was he to think he could oppose an edict set by the king?

"May I have the honor of this dance?" he asked, extending his hand.

Markis discreetly tapped Reid on her back. From Lord Robert's impeccably tailored tunic, the crest of a castle and a sun, his elegantly styled hair, and his intelligent eyes, she could tell he was wealthy, powerful, and not to be trifled with. Her father had taught her to keep her enemies close—and this man was not her friend. Ignoring Markis's warning, she said, "You may." She slid her hand into Lord Robert's, trying not to flinch when his cold fingers curled around hers.

CHAPTER NINE

Lord Robert led Reid to the dance floor just as the song came to an end. The musicians immediately began playing a slow, almost haunting melody, which allowed the couples to take a break after the fast dance.

Reid faced Robert, taking his right hand while placing her left lightly on his shoulder. His free hand rested against her back. He took the lead, moving to the music. Read easily followed him, though it felt wrong. She despised giving this man any sort of control.

"Tell me, Lady Reid, have you met your esteemed grandparents yet?"

"No, I have not had that pleasure."

"What about your second cousin?" He asked, looking down his nose at her.

"I have not had the chance to meet him either."

His eyes widened in feigned surprise. "Why didn't your father maintain contact with your mother's family?"

"That is a question I cannot answer." Because she honestly didn't know. Duke Ellington very well could have maintained a relationship with them and never told her about it.

Lord Robert's hand pressed into her back, pushing her body against his. She stiffened, unable to relax. But she refused to show fear or cower before this man.

He lowered his head, his lips hovering near her ear. "You and Prince Dexter don't want to marry one another, do you?" She tried to put some distance between them, but he gripped her tighter. His fingers dug into her back, making her wince. "You're only forging this alliance to maintain peace. But not everyone desires peace."

"Lord Robert," Reid said, her words calm and smooth even though her insides boiled with rage. "You overstep your place." When she stopped dancing, they stood on the dance floor and stared at one another.

His smile was condescending. "Perhaps you are the one overstepping yours."

Her natural reaction was to punch him in the face. However, she couldn't behave in such a manner when surrounded by Axian's esteemed guests. She settled for sliding her hand over Robert's shoulder until her thumb hovered on a pressure point. When she opened her mouth to reply, she felt a subtle shift in the air.

Robert focused above Reid's head. "This is a dangerous game you're playing," he said, addressing the person behind her.

"Release my fiancée." Dexter's commanding voice sounded furious.

Robert's lips slyly curved. "I haven't yet finished my dance with her." His grip on Reid tightened.

She dug her thumb into his shoulder, right on his pressure point. He jerked in surprise, immediately releasing her. She took a step back, bumping into Dexter. "I'm sorry, Lord Robert, but I have finished my dance with you."

Dexter chuckled, draping his arm around her shoulders. "Thank you for celebrating with us," he said mockingly before turning to face Reid, effectively dismissing Robert.

Sneering, Robert stalked off.

Reid's heartbeat went into overtime as she peered into Dexter's warm eyes. Instead of speaking, he slid one hand to her waist while his other gently took hers, enveloping it. About to take a step, she remembered it wasn't her job to lead. It was his.

He took the step forward, and they started dancing to the slow music.

Reid felt delicate next to this tall, burly man. She wasn't used to the feeling, and it unnerved her. "Why are you staring at me like that?" she asked, flustered by his intense attention.

"I'm sorry Lord Robert was so forward with you," Dexter mumbled. "Are you okay?"

"I'm fine." She had to crane her neck to speak to him. "It was nothing I couldn't handle."

"Obviously." He raised an eyebrow. "It's hard to remember how you were raised when you look like this."

"I only feel exceptionally short when I'm next to you." When she glanced away, she spotted Gytha watching them, the warrior woman's face devoid of emotion.

"You look like…" Dexter began, recapturing Reid's attention. "Like a star yanked straight from the sky. You're stunning. I'd almost forgotten that appearances can be deceiving. But I'm sure that was my mother's plan all along. No one will suspect you're capable of so much more than looking pretty." He pulled her closer until their bodies touched.

Surprised by his admission and his nearness, she didn't know how to respond.

He glided his hand up her back, his fingers trailing over her bare skin making her shiver. A man had never behaved in such a way with her before.

"What are you doing?" she whispered. His seductive behavior seemed out of character.

He blinked, as if coming out of a daze. "Lord Robert questioned our union, didn't he?"

"He did."

"Everyone in this room must believe we're in love to give us a better chance of stemming off a war."

Of course he was only holding her close and touching her sensuously because they had an audience. Not because he wanted to. They barely knew each other.

While she understood Henrick would do whatever possible to maintain peace, she wasn't sure Dexter felt the same way. She tilted her head back to ask if he genuinely wanted to stop the war, but their eyes locked.

They stopped dancing. Dexter raised his hands, cupping the sides of Reid's face. He searched her eyes—for what, she didn't know. The heat from his palms sent a jolt of pleasure through her. No one had ever looked at her like this. It made her knees weak. Slowly, Dexter lowered his head and Reid's eyes fluttered shut. A moment later, Dexter's soft lips brushed against hers, making her want to melt into him.

People started cheering.

Reid's eyes flew open, realizing everyone saw the kiss. Had Dexter only done it for show? His hands slid to her shoulders, his eyes never straying from hers. A second later, he smiled, his former intensity gone.

She would have to be careful around this man. His allure and power weren't only in his ability to command an army and wield a sword. If she didn't guard her heart, she could get swept up in his act. And she had no desire to let that happen. Playing a part was fine so long as she didn't lose herself in the process. She had to maintain some sense of control.

"A toast to the newly engaged couple," someone called.

Everyone shouted in agreement.

Taking Reid's hand, Dexter pulled her onto the dais. As they faced their guests, silence descended.

"Lady Reid is an exceptional individual," Dexter said. "I have never met anyone like her. The way we met was rather unorthodox, and I didn't make the best first impression. However, she made a lasting impression with me. From that moment, I realized she was a woman I needed in my life."

"Is it true the king arranged this marriage?" Lord Robert asked. "That Lady Reid's father sold her to you to gain a title? That the king sent her here to be a spy?"

Dexter chuckled. "Lady Reid, would you like to address Lord Robert's concerns?" Letting go of her hand, he gave her the reins, allowing her to take control of the situation.

Reid glanced over at Nara. The princess nodded once, giving her support.

Focusing on Lord Robert as she spoke, Reid made sure her voice was loud enough so everyone present could hear. "You have raised some valid questions. But tell me, Lord Robert, why was my father in such a precarious situation where the king was able to blackmail him?"

There was a collective gasp when she said the word *blackmail*.

"Your father didn't have a legitimate heir," Lord Robert answered. "He sold you so he wouldn't lose his title and land."

Reid smiled, pretending he was a child who didn't know any better. "You are correct when you say my father had no legitimate heir." Then she addressed the crowd, trying to meet as many people's eyes as possible, willing them to believe her sincerity. "I was the fifth daughter born. My mother died while giving birth to me. My father never remarried, so he did not produce a son. As many of you know, the king has some pretty antiquated and unfair laws. One being that only a male can inherit. My father was forced to declare I was a boy in order to retain his land and title. Otherwise, all his holdings would have reverted to the king. It wasn't losing his land and title that concerned my father—it was giving the king more land and power."

The crowd hung on Reid's every word, and a rush of power filled her. "Many in northern Marsden are suffering under the king. Women are not allowed to work. They cannot leave the house unescorted. When I came to Axian, I reveled in your prosperity and treatment of individuals. Upon my return to Ellington, the disparity between our counties felt even greater. I told my father I wanted to bring positive changes to Marsden, and Axian was the prime example of how it can be."

She took Dexter's hand. "I told my father I wanted to live in Axian because it was a fair county where I'd met a man who challenges me, treats me as an equal, and who is my friend. My father was the one who worked in conjunction with Prince Henrick to secure a union between Prince Dexter and myself. The king's involvement came after."

"Are you speaking out against the king?" Robert asked.

"Lord Robert," Reid said, making her tone condescending. "I did not attend school in Axian. However, I'm certain your education can't be so lacking that you misunderstood me. What you are trying to do is manipulate and twist my words around to suit your own agenda. You need to think before you speak. You question my loyalty to Axian, yet I am simply assuring you that this wonderful county is now my home and my priority. When I inherit Ellington, Prince Dexter and I will decide together how we will oversee both counties. We love each other, and it is our plan to work together as equal partners."

Everyone burst into applause.

Henrick and Nara joined them on the dais, each holding a goblet. "And with that," Henrick said, "let's toast the couple."

The musicians started playing a lively tune as servants merged with the crowd to hand out drinks.

"Well done," Nara said, hugging Reid before kissing Dexter on the cheek. "However, I think it would be best if you two retire for the night. I don't want people bombarding you with questions right now."

Dexter still held Reid's hand, appearing in no hurry to let go. "Good idea." After bidding his parents goodnight, he led Reid off the dais and out of the great hall through a side door. Six soldiers surrounded them with orders to escort the couple to the fourth floor. Once there, Dexter dismissed the soldiers for the night, assuring them that neither he nor Reid would leave the fourth floor until morning.

"Why the added security?" Reid asked, eyeing the two sentries posted at the top of the staircase.

"It's an extra precaution since there are so many people here for the celebration." They headed down the corridor to the right. "There are always guards on duty. Usually, they're posted in discreet places. My mother hates feeling like she's being watched all the time."

Reid could understand that sentiment.

"Are you hungry?" Dexter asked.

"Famished." She'd never gotten a chance to eat at the party.

"Wait in here." He opened the door to the royal family's private sitting room. "I'll be right back."

The sconces on the walls had been lit and a fire blazed in the hearth, warming the intimate room. Reid went over to one of the windows, gazing out at the city.

"I can't figure you out," Gytha said, startling Reid.

She studied the warrior woman's reflection in the window. "I didn't hear you come in."

"You will never hear or see me coming. I'm too well-trained to make any noise."

While Reid felt vulnerable with her back to Gytha—especially with that potentially threatening statement hanging in the air—she refused to turn around and face her right now.

"I'm sorry about your head," Gytha said, surprising Reid. "I may have gotten a little carried away."

"A little?"

Gytha grinned. "Okay, a lot. I allowed my emotions to take control. It won't happen again."

"Thank you for apologizing." It meant a lot coming from someone like Gytha. Reid didn't think it was something the woman did often—if ever. Taking a deep breath, she turned to face her.

"I still love Dexter," Gytha admitted. "I didn't want him to end our relationship. I thought he could marry you in name only while still being with me. I don't care about titles or money. All I want is him."

Reid wasn't sure how to respond. However, she was thankful Dexter had ended his relationship with Gytha. He very well could have married Reid and taken Gytha as his mistress. And Reid wouldn't have been able to do anything about it.

"Listening to you tonight, I realized something." Gytha folded her arms. "You do not match me physically. I am stronger and better than you in any sort of combat situation." She stepped closer.

With the window at her back, Reid had nowhere to go.

"But you best me in other ways I can't possibly compete with. In ways that may be more important than physicality." She shook her head. "Dexter loves Axian, and he will do what's best for his county. I thought his marriage to you would be the end of Axian. But now, I realize it may be the best thing for it. Though it kills me to say it, you are not the idiot I thought you were."

That was a lot to take in. Reid now understood Nara's stance on Reid wearing dresses and embracing her feminism. There was no way Reid could compete with Gytha when it came to fighting, especially one on one. If she tried, she would fail. And that wasn't what Axian needed. They needed someone who could stand at Dexter's side—who could lead the people with him. They needed someone who was politically savvy. While Reid had never thought herself well versed in politics, she now realized how much her father had taught her by always having her present during contract negotiations, labor disputes, and criminal trials.

It was time to repair the rift between the two of them. Gytha was a formidable soldier, and Reid needed her support. "When I first met you, I was jealous. Not because of your relationship with

Dexter, but because you are everything I ever wanted to be. You're tall, beautiful, strong, capable, and the best female fighter I've seen. I would have loved to join the army and had the opportunities you do. When I see you, envy fills me."

"When I saw you next to Dexter on the platform outside, I knew you'd be my greatest competitor. You possess attributes I do not. You have a womanly figure, and you are beautiful in a way I will never be. But your looks aren't your greatest asset. Your intelligence is. I am by no means dumb, but I do not have the eloquent speech you do, I do not know how to forge alliances without a sword, nor do I have the patience to deal with people like Lord Robert."

"What are you saying? Are we calling a truce or is this the start of a war between us?" It could go either way.

"What if I say it's the start of a war? That I want Dexter and will do anything to get him?"

"I would say he is not a possession we can fight over. He is his own person who can make up his own mind. It is not our job to dictate who he loves or what he does."

"I agree." The warrior woman cocked her head, studying Reid. "Have you ever been in love?"

"No." With Gordon, Reid had felt the onset of something, but that was all.

"You do understand you and Dexter must produce an heir, right?"

Reid's face flamed. "We have not discussed that yet."

Gytha barked out a laugh, patting Reid's shoulder. "Don't worry. I could never share Dexter. I couldn't stand the idea of him making love to me and then going home to his wife to do his husbandly duty. The mere idea disgusts me."

"The truce is sounding like a better option," Reid mumbled, wondering how intimate Gytha and Dexter had been.

The smile fell from Gytha's face. "I saw Dexter's reaction when you stepped on the platform tonight. I also saw the way he touched you. The way he kissed you." Gytha's eyes became glassy. "He broke up with me to give you a chance. Please take it. Because if you don't, I will." With that, she turned and hurried from the room.

This night had been one surprise after another. Before Reid had a moment to consider what Gytha had said, Dexter entered, carrying a tray filled with food. He stood at the threshold, part terror, part curiosity written across his face.

"Come in," Reid said. "It seems we have a lot to talk about."

CHAPTER TEN

"I hope Gytha didn't threaten to kill you," Dexter said as he came into the sitting room, kicking the door shut behind him.

"How do you know I didn't threaten to kill her?" Reid countered.

A laugh escaped him. "You're not what I thought you'd be." He set the tray on the low table. "Help yourself."

Reid went over and picked up a plate, piling it with bread, cheese, and apples. She sat on the sofa, curling her legs under her.

"Gytha and I have a long history." Dexter grabbed a plate of food, taking a seat on the sofa across from Reid.

"I'm not particularly interested in your shared past." It wouldn't help Reid move forward. "But I am curious why you didn't marry her."

"She has asked me that several times over the years."

"And?" Reid wanted to know. Maybe it would help her understand this man before her.

He held up his hand, asking for a moment. Then he removed his tunic, tossing it on the floor. After pushing up the sleeves of his undershirt, he picked up his plate. "Sorry, I was hot." His wide shoulders pulled the fabric taut.

Even though he was fully covered, the thought of him so casually dressed felt intimate in the enclosed room. Reid plopped an apple slice in her mouth, needing to focus on something other than the muscles in Dexter's forearms. Honestly, what was wrong with her?

"I'd hoped to avoid marriage."

"So did I," Reid mumbled.

"What's your reasoning?" he asked around a mouthful of food.

"I don't want to be controlled. I don't want someone telling me what I can and cannot do." She took a bite of cheese. "And I don't want to be subservient to someone else."

"My reasons are pretty much the same."

"But you're a man," she pointed out. "You're not subservient to anyone." Especially as a commander and a prince.

"I guess I should qualify my answer then," he said. "I don't ever want to be in love. Love makes slaves of people, and I don't want to be controlled, manipulated, or emotionally attached to another person in that way."

Reid's eyes widened in shock. Why did he have such a negative view of love? She couldn't argue with him since she'd never been in love, but he sounded quite cynical. "You agreed to marry me even with the knowledge there would be no emotional attachment?"

"Yes."

Even though she expected that answer, it still stung. And she didn't know why since she didn't expect to have feelings for him either. "What about Gytha?" Because Gytha clearly loved Dexter.

He set his plate down, then propped his feet on the low table. "I admire her. She's an excellent fighter. We're friends. I enjoy spending time with her. But no, I am not, nor have I ever been, in love with her."

Then how did he know love would make him a slave? "Have

you been in love before?" Did something happen to make him this way?

"No. But I've experienced enough of the world. I've seen what love does to people. How it skews their reasoning and choices. What about you? Are you in love with someone?"

She shook her head.

"Given your upbringing, and what I've seen of you here, you seem a little naive when it comes to relationships."

"Just because I've never been in love doesn't mean I'm naive. It simply means I haven't met a man worthy of my love."

He smiled. "I like the fire inside you. I can see why my parents think you're a good fit for me."

Still trying to figure Dexter out, she set her plate down, clutching her hands together. "How do you see our marriage working?" The question was rather blunt, but she needed to know his answer since she had no idea what he was thinking.

"How do you see our marriage working?" he countered. "Why ask me first and give me the power to decide?"

"I asked how you see our marriage working, not how it *will* work. My question implied I'm curious to hear your thoughts. I am in no way giving you any power. And if I don't like your answer, I'll tell you. I'm not obliged to do whatever you say."

Rubbing the nape of his neck, he said, "I guess I envision us each doing our own thing."

"Yet, somehow working together to align our counties?" Did he not want companionship? Friendship? A partner?

"My father wants peace. My mother thinks there will be a war. All I can focus on right now is protecting Axian and my family."

"I can help you. Ellington will be your ally."

"Will your father provide soldiers if we need them?"

"I think so. Especially if I request them."

"And if my father says not to fight? If he wants to hand over Axian to King Eldon, then what?" His eyes shone bright and intense. As if her answer made all the difference.

"That's an intriguing question." But how to respond since she didn't know for certain? Should she—could she—stand by Dexter's side if he went against the king? Because if she supported Dexter, that meant fighting Gordon, Ackley, and Idina. Choosing her words carefully, she replied, "Do you know there is unrest in northern Marsden? Are you aware some of the dukes are questioning the king?"

"Are you implying we may be able to rally others to stand with us?"

Reid noted he chose his words carefully as well. He never said *rebel against the king* or *take over.* "I am. And if we can put enough pressure on the king, we may avoid a war while maintaining control over Axian."

"Are you siding with my father then?" he asked.

"No. I'm not saying we should be subservient or roll over like dogs to avoid a war. I'm saying we gain the necessary support to let the king know we're prepared to go to war if needed."

"And do you think Axian should remain a solitary county? Not trading with northern Marsden?"

"I don't know. I like Axian the way it is, and I don't want it to change or conform to the north's rules and ways of life. However, I think open trade is a promising idea. I'd like to be able to visit Ellington to see my family." And Axian was part of Marsden. "Unless..."

"Unless?" he asked.

"Unless Axian becomes its own kingdom." Would that solve their problems?

"The king would still see us as a threat."

Point taken. "I need to think more on the matter." She rubbed her eyes. "It has been a long day. I'm going to bed."

"Speaking of beds..."

Too shocked by the mention of beds to stand, she remained sitting. "Yes?" She had no idea where he was going with this.

"My mother is having a suite prepared for us. For after we

marry. I requested we each have our own room. She insisted on an adjoining room between them, which will have a large bed for us to share if we ever so decide."

"Oh." Reid had no idea what to say to that. This was the part of the marriage she refused to think about.

"Since we'll have separate rooms, we can maintain a platonic relationship."

"Our marriage will be in name only?" she asked.

"Yes."

Relief flooded her at the realization she wouldn't have to give her body to this man she barely knew. "What about an heir?" Since Dexter wasn't his father's heir, would Henrick insist they have a child?

Dexter ran his hands through his hair. "My father made it clear he expects me to have a child. He thinks it will be good for the people of Axian."

"Did he give you a timeframe?" Was it in their marriage contract?

He shook his head. "And who knows what'll happen in the next few years."

They had time to figure out their platonic, no-love marriage before they eventually had to produce a child. She rested her head on the armrest as she observed Dexter across from her, trying to envision what her life would be like ten years from now.

***

Reid awoke on the sofa, still wearing her dress. How long had she been asleep? When she sat up, she realized she wasn't alone. Prince Henrick stood with his back to her, gazing out the window. The sky was a dull gray, the sun just starting to rise. "I'm sorry," she said. "I didn't mean to fall asleep here."

Henrick turned to her. "It's fine."

Standing, she stretched before heading to the door.

"Lady Reid."

"Yes?"

With his right hand, he absently touched his left wrist where his Knight mark was hidden below his sleeve. "You've been summoned," he murmured. "A Knight is waiting in the stables to take you to our headquarters. There, you will meet the person in charge and spend a few days training."

Shock rolled through Reid. *Headquarters?* She hadn't known such a place existed. "Am I permitted to go?" Would there be enough time to make it there and back before the wedding?

"It's only two days on horseback from here. All you have to do is change and head to the stables."

"Aren't people going to wonder where I am?" And by people, she meant Dexter. He would notice her absence, and probably assume she was up to something nefarious.

"I will inform everyone you left with your second cousin to visit your grandparents for a few days. No one will suspect a thing."

Her grandparents. As excited as she was to go to the Knights' headquarters, she also wanted to meet her family. "Can I visit them as well?" Would there be enough time to do both?

"You can. However, it will have to be at a later date. Duty calls, so I suggest you get moving."

Reid rushed from the room. After putting on a pair of pants and a traveling shirt, she quickly packed a few essentials. Hoisting her bag on her shoulder, she exited her room. On the first floor, she tried to remember how to get to the stables. Not having any time to waste, she checked the library and saw light coming from the back rooms. After rushing to Colbert's office, she found him reading a book at his desk.

Finn jumped to his feet, throwing himself at Reid's legs and licking her hand.

"Don't you ever sleep?" she asked Colbert.

He glanced up from his book. "Occasionally." He smiled. "Where are you off to at this early hour?"

"The stables. Can you tell me where they are?"

He quickly gave her directions. "Are you going for a ride?"

"My second cousin is taking me to meet my grandparents."

"Right now?" He closed his book, setting it aside.

"He's already at the stables waiting for me." After giving Finn a kiss on his head, she exited the office.

"Reid," Colbert called after her.

"I'll see you when I get back!" She jogged to the stables.

A man in his late twenties already mounted on a horse asked, "Lady Reid?"

She nodded.

Pulling up his sleeve, he revealed his Knight mark. He looked at her, waiting.

Assuming he wanted verification, she yanked up her sleeve to show him her identical mark.

Seemingly satisfied, he said, "If anyone asks, I'm Victor, your second cousin." Dark brown hair topped his pleasant face. "The horse in the stall to your right is saddled and ready for you. Let's be off."

Reid led the horse from the stall, then attached her bag to the animal. She mounted, nudging her horse to follow Victor out of the stables.

"Sorry to make you wake so early," he said as they rode off the palace grounds and into the city. "I want to cover as much distance as possible today."

"It's no problem." It felt good to be back in a saddle again.

They exited the city and went southwest, pushing the horses hard. They only stopped once for a quick meal. When it became too dark to travel, Victor found a cave for them to sleep in. He woke Reid before the sun rose, and they set out, traveling hard and fast the entire day.

Just when Reid was about to ask if he planned to stop for the night, they came to a mountain, Victor steering his horse directly toward it. At the base, he started ascending in a back-and-forth pattern.

"It's almost dark," Reid said. "Are we to take shelter in another cave for the night?" She thought Henrick had said it was only a two days' journey from the palace.

"We only have a little bit farther to go."

The higher they went, the steeper it became. Afraid her horse would lose its footing and fall, she suggested they stop for the night.

Victor agreed, steering his horse behind a large boulder. Reid did the same. On the other side, a passageway cut directly between the mountain. Since it was too narrow to ride side by side, she followed close behind him. After a quarter mile, they exited to a flat area sunken in the middle of a mountain. The area had to be at least a mile in diameter. In the center, a castle had been built from stones. The place looked ancient.

Victor headed straight toward the castle.

"Is this it?" Were they at the Knights' headquarters? The deteriorating castle appeared abandoned.

He nodded.

An eerie sensation—like spiders crawling over her skin— unsettled her. "Victor," she whispered. "Are we being watched?" While she didn't see anyone, she could feel eyes tracking them. Were there unseen Knights following their movements?

He smiled over his shoulder at her.

Unease filled Reid, making her want to turn around and leave. However, she had no desire to descend the steep mountain since it was almost dark.

At the front of the castle, Victor dismounted, Reid doing the same. He went to the front door and opened it, waiting for her.

"Should I get my things?"

He waved her forward.

She glanced around, not seeing anyone but feeling like dozens of eyes were on her. Maybe she'd feel safer inside. She brushed past Victor to enter the castle. It was pitch black inside.

Victor placed his hand on her back, gently nudging her forward. "There is someone here who is dying to meet you."

The door slammed shut, startling her.

"I have Lady Reid Ellington," Victor said. "Just as you requested."

"You may pass."

Victor prodded Reid forward. "There's a curtain in front of you. Push it aside."

Reid did as instructed. Stepping past the curtain, she entered a brightly lit hallway. On her left, two open doors led to a sitting room.

Victor stepped around Reid and entered the room. There were two sofas and four chairs arranged around a low table. An enormous fireplace was situated along one wall, a desk and a bookshelf along another. A woman who had to be in her late forties stood near one of the chairs. She wore black pants and a black tunic, her brown hair in a single braid. Victor plopped on a sofa, then groaned in exhaustion.

"Please have a seat," the woman said.

Fatigued, Reid sat, taking note there weren't any windows in the room.

The woman smiled. "Lady Reid, I'd like to welcome you to the headquarters for the Knights of the Realm."

CHAPTER ELEVEN

Reid couldn't believe she was in the Knights of the Realm's headquarters. And that it was in Axian. Leaning forward, she rubbed her face. "What about you?" she asked the stranger who hadn't divulged her name.

"What about me?" Her voice was smooth and level, not revealing any emotion.

"Are you a Knight?"

Still standing, the woman gripped the back of the chair. "No. I am not officially a Knight."

"Who are you?"

"It's a long story."

"I have time."

"As do I." The woman's smile softened her face. "However, it's late. I'm tired, and you must be as well. We will discuss everything tomorrow." To Victor, she said, "Thank you for bringing her. You may leave." Then to Reid, she said, "I'll show you to your quarters."

Reid followed the woman from the room.

"Thank you for coming. I've been wanting to meet you."

Dozens of questions swirled in Reid's mind. However, she was too exhausted to voice any as they traveled along a seemingly endless corridor. When they came to a steep, spiral staircase, they climbed two flights, then traversed another long hallway, doors lining either side at evenly spaced intervals.

The woman stopped before the sixth door on the left. "You may sleep in here. In the morning, we'll talk."

Entering the room, Reid found a single lit candle, which revealed a narrow bed on one wall, a writing desk on another, and a tall dresser shoved in the corner. No window, no fireplace. She shivered. While the room was neat and clean, it felt cold and sterile. Reid spotted her bag at the end of the bed. She opened it, pulling her nightgown out. After changing, she climbed under the rough sheets.

The unnatural quiet gave the castle a haunted feeling. Who was the woman she'd spoken to? The exhaustion from traveling all day consumed her, and she quickly fell asleep.

Since there weren't any windows in the room, Reid had no idea if it was morning yet. Feeling rested, she stretched and climbed out of bed. When her feet hit the stone floor, she yelped at the frigid temperature.

After quickly dressing in pants and a tunic, she tied her hair back and exited the room. She headed downstairs where she found the woman from last night sitting at a desk writing.

"Good morning," Reid said, hoping not to startle her. "At least I think it's morning. I honestly don't know."

"It's after sunrise." The woman folded a piece of paper in half before sliding it in the top drawer. "Let's get something to eat while we talk."

"You still haven't told me your name."

"I'm Anna." She led the way to a rectangular dining room, where a table already loaded with food waited.

Reid sat, taking a plate and piling it with food. She'd barely had anything to eat over the past two days. "This is the Knights' headquarters?" From the little she'd seen, the facility seemed remote and secure.

"It is."

"But you're not a Knight?"

"No. I train the Knights. However, I've never taken the oath."

"Why not?"

"I'm married."

"So is Prince Henrick," Reid pointed out.

"He's no longer an active Knight, though he does help out when needed. For example, when we requested your presence, he made the arrangements to get you here." Her plate held only a piece of bread covered with raspberry jam.

Reid took a bite of her eggs. "Ackley told me there are twenty-five Knights?"

"You are the twenty-sixth active Knight. There are another twenty-five who are retired."

"What's going to happen once I marry Prince Dexter?" she asked, cutting into her fried tomato.

"You will no longer be a Knight."

That didn't seem fair. "Aren't the Knights trying to bring Axian's way of life into northern Marsden?"

"Why do you say that?"

Because people were treated fairly in Axian, which made Axian better than the other counties. Instead of saying that, she voiced another concern. "Don't you think Henrick is a more effective leader than Eldon?"

Pushing her plate forward, Anna folded her hands and rested them on the table. "What I think is irrelevant. The purpose of the Knights is to serve the kingdom. And right now, that means ensuring peace."

She sounded like Henrick. "Are you telling me the Knights support King Eldon?"

"No, I'm telling you the Knights support the people."

"The people in northern Marsden should have the same rights and liberties as those in Axian."

"That is your opinion—one I happen to agree with. However, we must look at the larger picture. Do you think those freedoms are worth the loss of thousands of lives? The destruction of farms, homes, people's livelihoods? Those are the questions we need to ask ourselves before we start talking about ousting a king."

Reid hadn't thought about it that way before. She took her last bite of eggs before shoving her plate away. "Since I'm to marry Prince Dexter in one month, I'm not going to be a Knight much longer."

"If you remained a Knight after you married, how would you feel about withholding information from your husband? How do you think your husband would feel about you not being honest with him? You'd have to lie, sneak around behind his back, and keep a part of yourself hidden. That's not a marriage."

No, it wasn't. But neither was what she was going to have with Dexter. "The prince and I will be married in name only."

Anna drummed her fingers on the table. "That may change as you become better acquainted. Regardless, the Knights' laws are absolute. A great many people have made sacrifices through the years to keep it so."

"Then why did you even bother to make me a Knight if I could only be one for a few months?"

"We need you to serve a specific role that no one else can."

"And what role is that?" Reid asked, not sure if she wanted to know. The room suddenly felt too hot, the walls too close, the air too thick.

"There are a series of plans in place right now. A lot of time and energy has gone into this. Dexter is becoming a liability. We need him controlled."

Reid snorted. She couldn't control that man. They weren't even friends.

Anna leaned forward, her eyes boring into Reid's. "You are going to get close to Prince Dexter. We know he's going somewhere a few nights a week, but no one has been able to find out what he's doing. I suspect he's leading a group of revolutionaries and he plans to incite a war. I believe he wants Axian to be its own kingdom, one separate from Marsden. Our resources are spread too thin to investigate further, so it is up to you. You will become Prince Dexter's shadow. Where he goes, you go."

"Isn't he on our side?" Weren't they fighting for the same thing?

"There are no sides. He has his own agenda. It might be the same as ours, or it might be in direct opposition. I don't know. What I need you to do is keep him on a leash, and report his movements to us."

Reid didn't miss the irony. She couldn't continue being a Knight once she married because that wasn't fair to her marriage. However, she could lie, spy, and report on her fiancé's actions now since they weren't wed yet.

Anna raised a single eyebrow, observing Reid. "You understand that if you fall in love, your loyalty to the Knights is compromised?"

A laugh escaped Reid's lips. "You don't need to worry about that." She couldn't imagine being in love with Dexter. Sure, she might admire his physique. And the way he wielded a sword. Even the curve of his lips when he bestowed one of his rare smiles. But love him? Absolutely not. Needing to change the subject, she asked, "What are the other Knights doing?"

"I'm not at liberty to discuss that with you. The less you know, the better."

Reid nodded, although she wasn't sure she liked the position she was in. She didn't want to blindly follow and trust. She may be going along with them for now, but that didn't mean she had to do what they said. She would do what she felt was right and what benefitted Ellington and Axian.

"Which brings me to why I brought you here."

Reid waved her hand, signaling for Anna to continue.

"I need to make sure you understand what's at stake."

"I do." War, death, destruction.

"I don't think you fully do." Anna came around the side of the table, perching on the edge of it beside Reid. "The speech you gave during your engagement party was out of line."

Shock rolled through Reid. One, how did Anna know about it since it just happened? And two, Reid thought her speech was what the people needed to hear to rally behind the engagement.

"You shouldn't give the people false hope," Anna said. "You can't make promises or expectations you can't deliver on."

"I disagree." How dare this woman tell Reid what she could or could not do? "You said that once I'm wed, I am no longer a Knight. That means I'm Duke Ellington's heir and a princess of Marsden. I will have the power to incite change. And I plan to use my position to do so." She stood so she was at eye level with Anna. "You can't marry me off for your convenience, then expect me to idly sit around for the rest of my life. I'll be in a unique position, and I plan to make the most of it."

Reid could have sworn the corners of Anna's lips rose ever so slightly, as if she fought a smile. Was the woman laughing at her? Did Anna think Reid young and naive?

Anna reached out, patting Reid's shoulder. "Even though you won't be an active Knight, I hope you'll work with us when we need you."

"We'll see." Reid folded her arms, taking a step back from Anna.

"Fair enough. The other reason you're here is because you lack some basic skills."

The woman was starting to get on Reid's nerves. "My father

taught me how to fight. I may not be the strongest person, but I can hold my own."

Anna stood. "I'm referring to a different skillset."

Reid's brow scrunched in confusion.

"You need to learn to spy, snoop, and stealthily gain information from someone."

"I can do those things." Otherwise, Ackley wouldn't have made her a Knight. They exited the dining room and headed down the hallway.

"Against an amateur, you can, but not against one of the king's Shields."

"Shields? What are those?" Reid had lived in the king's castle, yet she'd never heard the term before.

"Shields are the king's personal guards. Those closest to him. The king has a dozen men who bear the title."

"Are you certain?"

"Unfortunately. Prince Ackley informed us Prince Gordon personally trains the Shields. In fact, Prince Gordon even suggested the king should increase the Shields' numbers and duties."

Reid tripped on a loose rug in the hallway. "Gordon is a good man," she mumbled, feeling a headache coming on.

"Prince Gordon believes he is helping the king whom he's sworn fealty to. He also wants to make sure his brother's throne is secure. You of all people should understand Gordon's loyalty."

Reid had to bite her tongue to keep from uttering a snide comment. If she did, it would only add fuel to the fire, and she had no desire to stoke those rumors. While she may have found Gordon attractive and considered him a friend, that was all he could ever be. He was married.

They rounded a corner, stopping at a large door. Before Anna could open it, Reid asked, "Why wouldn't Ackley discourage Gordon from expanding the Shields? Especially since Gordon knows about the Knights?"

Anna's entire body went rigid. "What?"

"When I was at the castle, both Gordon and Idina knew Ackley was a Knight. They're aware of the organization."

Anna blinked, processing the information.

Feeling as if she'd made a huge blunder, Reid forged on. "Gordon and Idina even help Ackley. Idina gathers information, and Gordon allows a dozen Knights to function as a unit within his army." How did Anna not know any of this?

"And the three siblings manage to keep this from King Eldon?"

Reid thought so, but she couldn't be sure. The three brothers often spoke with one another behind closed doors. Neither Idina nor Reid were ever privy to these conversations. Based upon what Reid had seen at the castle, she believed Eldon knew nothing about the Knights. As to why Ackley would have told Idina and Gordon if he wasn't supposed to, she couldn't say. But one thing was certain—Ackley had a reason for everything he did.

"I'll think more about this later," Anna mumbled as she opened the door, revealing an expansive room lined with various weapons. "This is our training facility."

"It's quite big." It reminded Reid of where she'd worked with Ackley at the king's castle.

"We'll start here with a few simple exercises so I can ascertain your skill level."

Reid went to the sword-lined wall. Before she could choose one, Victor burst into the room, his shoulders heaving.

"We have a problem," he said, panting. "Prince Dexter was seen leaving the palace on horseback, accompanied by some of his men. He's tracking Lady Reid instead of going to her grandparents' house, and he's headed this way."

Dexter was coming after Reid? She couldn't fathom why he'd bother. He had plenty of other things to do besides follow her around.

"How far away is he?" Anna demanded.

"About ten miles."

"Are you sure he's tracking me?" Reid asked. Maybe Victor was mistaken.

Placing her hands on her hips, Anna started pacing the room. "Let's enact the contingency plan."

"I've already saddled two horses."

Anna stopped beside Reid, placing a hand on her arm. "Go get your bag and anything else you brought. You are to leave at once."

Instead of questioning Anna, Reid ran upstairs and collected her things. Then she headed to the front of the castle where Anna and Victor waited. After attaching her bag to the horse, Reid mounted. The only reason she could imagine Dexter chasing after her would be if something bad had happened. Fear gripped her. Was her father okay? Had one of her sisters fallen ill?

"I wish I had more time to work with you," Anna said. "You need proper training."

"What we need is to get moving," Victor reminded them.

Anna agreed. "It was nice to finally meet you, Reid."

"Likewise." Reid nudged her horse, following Victor to the narrow passageway. When she exited it, she was at the top of the steep mountain. Trying not to look down, she stayed behind Victor as he descended in a zigzag pattern.

When her horse's hooves slid, Reid's heart lurched into her stomach. She pulled on the reins, trying to help the horse regain its footing.

"Easy," Victor said, trying to soothe his own horse. "Slow and steady."

Reid's grip tightened. She had to force herself to relax so she wouldn't spook the horse. The animal had probably traveled this way dozens of times before. Reid had nothing to worry about. Her vision narrowed until the only thing that existed was the back of Victor's head and his horse's tail. Not once looking down the mountainside, she focused only on those images until they finally reached the bottom.

At the road, they headed south, pushing their horses hard.

"Where are we going?" Reid asked, wondering if they'd try to head Dexter off or return to the palace.

"Since we're supposed to be at your grandparents' house, we'll go there now. We'll just tell Prince Dexter we traveled at a leisurely pace."

If she hadn't been sitting on the horse, she probably would have fallen over. Jubilation at the prospect of meeting her grandparents filled her. Riding in silence, Reid tried to imagine what they would be like. Would she see her sisters in them? What about herself? She still couldn't get over the fact her mother was from Axian.

After several hours, Victor slowed his horse. "The estate is right over there," he said, pointing to the right.

As the tree-lined road curved, a square manor situated in a clearing appeared. "It's beautiful." A bright green lawn surrounded the estate.

At the front, they dismounted. Reid grabbed her bag before sprinting up the steps to the front door. She was about to knock when she heard hooves pounding behind her.

CHAPTER TWELVE

Reid swiveled around. Dexter rode up the narrow pathway, accompanied by a handful of soldiers. When he reached the steps, he dismounted, then handed his horse over to one of his men.

"What are you doing here?" Reid asked, trying to seem shocked by his arrival. She descended the stairs to confront him, not wanting an argument right in front of her grandparents' front door.

Instead of answering her question, he asked one of his own. "Are you only arriving now?" He eyed Victor suspiciously.

"We stopped along the way," Victor explained. "I pointed out a few landmarks to Lady Reid."

"Did you deviate from your course at all?" Dexter demanded.

Reid decided to let Victor handle this one.

"Yes. We left the road to find a safe place to sleep at night," Victor answered. "Why all the questions? Is something the matter?"

"I'm just surprised you're only arriving now, the same as me."

"What are you doing here?" Reid asked again.

Dexter rolled his shoulders. If Reid didn't know better, she'd swear he looked uncomfortable. "I came after you because I thought I should be here."

"I don't understand."

Dexter scratched the side of his neck. "Lord Victor, show my men to the stables and get them situated."

Taken aback, she blurted, "You know Lord Victor?"

"He's your second cousin."

Reid blinked. Her second cousin was a Knight? While she'd assumed her second cousin existed, she hadn't thought Victor was actually him. Disappointment filled her. She'd just spent a couple days with a new-to-her family member, yet she hadn't asked him a single personal question. He hadn't inquired about her life either. *What a waste.* Folding her arms, she waited for Victor to lead the soldiers and horses around the side of the property.

Dexter cleared his throat. "This is the first time you're meeting your grandparents, correct?"

Reid nodded.

"Well, as your fiancé, I figured I should accompany you. This is an important moment in your life. I want to be here for it...and for you."

Dumbfounded, Reid could only gape at him, not knowing what to say.

The door swung open, and a gray-haired woman with a round face appeared. "Welcome, Prince Dexter," she said.

"Duchess," he replied.

The woman's attention landed on Reid. Scanning Reid from head to toe, the older lady squinted. "Reid Ellington?" Shock laced her words.

"Yes." Was she Reid's grandmother?

A kind smile transformed the elderly woman's face. "Welcome, child. It's nice to finally meet one of our grandchildren." Still beaming, she waved Dexter and Reid inside.

The entryway was long and narrow, with several doors on either side and a staircase at the back. They entered the first door on the right. A single sofa and two chairs adorned the room.

"We have company," the duchess announced.

Seated at a desk under one of the windows was an older gentleman with thick gray hair. He somehow swung his entire chair around, then pushed it forward, all while still seated. With utter amazement, Reid realized there were two large wheels attached to the chair, which allowed him to move throughout the room.

He stopped before Reid, taking her hand in his. "After all these years, I can't believe you are truly here," he said, tears in his dark eyes. "Welcome."

"I'm sorry," Reid said, "but my father never even told me you were alive."

He squeezed her hand, then released it, waving her toward the sofa. She sat, facing her grandparents, with Dexter at her side, though he'd left a respectable space between them.

"I bet there's a lot your father never told you," the woman—Reid's *grandmother*—muttered.

"Lady Reid," Dexter said, his voice oddly formal. "I want to officially introduce you to Duke Gregor Axian and his lovely wife, Duchess Constance Axian."

While Dexter had referred to the woman as *duchess* earlier, the fact hadn't registered until now. Her grandparents were the duke and duchess of Axian? How had Reid not known this? Nara had said they were one of the ruling families, but she'd failed to mention their titles.

"You look a wee bit shocked," Gregor said, chuckling.

"We never had a male heir," Constance explained. "Our land reverted back to King Broc."

So many questions swirled through Reid's mind. She settled on one. "Why didn't my father tell me about you? For that matter, why didn't either of you ever try to contact my sisters or me?"

"I can't speak for your father," Constance said as she stood. "If you'll excuse me, I'll go and fetch some tea so you can warm up from your journey." She exited the room.

Gregor lifted his right leg with his hands, adjusting it to the side a bit more.

"Is there something wrong with your legs?" Reid asked. She'd only seen a wheelchair once before.

"I was injured many years ago," he replied. "Unfortunately, it has prevented me from doing many of my duties."

"I'm sorry to hear that." Her father had suffered a fall from his horse last season, which had allowed Reid to see first-hand the consequences of such an injury. Thankfully, due to her father's insistence she be trained as a man would, it had been a simple matter to take over his duties for a few weeks until he was able to ride again. If she hadn't been there—if he hadn't raised her as he had—she wasn't sure what he would have done.

"I heard your father named you as his heir," Gregor stated.

"He did." She held up the ring as if that were proof, wondering how the news had traveled so quickly.

"An interesting turn of events," he said, forehead creased in thought.

"I agree," Dexter said. "And I'm pleased Duke Ellington managed to do so given Marsden's strict laws."

Reid wholeheartedly concurred, especially seeing as how she'd spent most of her life trying to figure out a way around Marsden's laws.

Constance returned, carrying a tray that held four teacups. She set it on the side table, then handed each person a cup. "We hadn't anticipated our granddaughter or the prince coming to visit, so we don't have anything special prepared," she said as she resettled on the sofa. "Do you know how long you plan to visit?"

"Only a day or two," Reid replied.

"You're welcome to stay as long as you like," Gregor said. "But we understand if this must be a brief visit. From what we've heard, you plan to be wed in three and a half weeks."

Reid nodded, still not able to dwell on being physically married to Dexter.

"We'll be traveling to the palace for the wedding," Gregor announced.

"Speaking of weddings," Reid said, "how did my father and my mother come to be wed?"

"It was an arranged marriage," Gregor revealed. "Duke Ellington had just died, his title and land passing to Tatum, his son. Tatum wanted a strong alliance. I'd been friends with Duke Ellington, and I knew the sort of man Tatum was. I wrote to him, offering my condolences on the death of his father and mentioning the possibility of a match between him and my only daughter, Brianna. He agreed to the contract terms, and Brianna traveled to Ellington to wed him. At first, their relationship was rocky. Your mother is an extremely strong-willed woman. However, they quickly realized they had a lot in common and became friends. It didn't take them long to fall in love."

"Was," Constance stated, staring down at her tea. "She *was* a strong-willed woman."

"I'm…" Reid searched for the right words. "I'm sorry she died delivering me."

"It's not your fault," Constance whispered. "I should see about supper and your accommodations for the night." She set her tea down, then left the room once again.

Maybe Reid shouldn't have said anything about her mother. The subject was probably too painful for her grandmother to discuss.

Gregor cleared his throat. "There's a lake out back. If you want, you two can take a walk around it. Supper won't be ready for another hour or so."

"That's an excellent idea." Dexter stood. "Lady Reid?"

She joined him, allowing him to escort her through the front door of the manor. They walked around the side of the property, gravel crunching under their shoes.

Reid finally broke the silence. "Do you know how my grandfather injured his legs?"

"Duke Axian has been like that for as long as I can remember." As they traversed the narrow pathway leading to the lake, Dexter kept his hands clasped behind his back.

Trees towered on either side, leaves swaying in the wind.

"It's beautiful here," Reid commented. "Everything is so green and vibrant."

"Isn't it like this in Ellington?"

"No, it's not." When she took him to Ellington to visit, he would see for himself.

They came to the edge of the lake, the water calm and shimmering under the setting sun. To the left, a dock extended above the water. Reid headed that way, Dexter following. After pulling off her boots and socks, she settled on the end of the dock, rolled up her pants, and stuck her bare feet into the refreshing water.

Dexter sat next to her.

"You're not going to put your feet in the water?"

He scanned the area. "I'd prefer to keep my boots on."

"Is there something I should be aware of?" An unseen threat, maybe?

"No. If one of my men needs me, I like to be prepared."

She eyed him. "Don't want to be caught slacking on the job?"

He shrugged. "Technically, I'm not working. Still, it's hard to relax."

As much as she hated to admit it, she understood him. Wiggling her toes in the water, she asked, "Do you get the feeling that everything is about to change?"

He studied her for an uncomfortable minute before answering. "Ever since Eldon became king, I've had an ominous feeling. I can't say what it is exactly, but I fear something bad is coming."

"Every time I think I have a handle on things, something happens to throw me off." Like being taken to the Knights' headquarters and then meeting her grandparents. "I don't know why, but I think I'm supposed to be here. I think I can help save Axian."

"Colbert keeps telling me that you're on our side."

"I am," she answered without hesitation.

He scanned the area again. "How's the water?"

"Cold." It felt fantastic on her toes.

To her delight, he removed his boots and socks, then rolled his pants up. After he stuck his feet in the water next to hers, they sat in companionable silence, the setting sun casting them in a soft glow.

Reid stood in the middle of her mother's bedchamber. Constance had escorted Reid there, leaving her alone to freshen up for supper. Her grandmother had said no one had moved anything—except to clean—since the day Brianna left for Ellington. Reid trailed her hand over the dresser, the bed. She wanted to find something that revealed the type of person her mother had been.

Going over to the armoire, she opened it, expecting to find dresses. Instead, pants and tunics filled it. The thought of her mother wearing clothes similar to Reid's own made her smile. After closing the armoire, she went to the window to gaze at the beautiful view of the property. Shifting to face the room again, she noticed a target on the back of the door. Made from wood, it was riddled with dozens of arrow holes. Had Brianna known how to shoot?

Reid rushed over to the closet, then threw the door open. Four swords, a handful of daggers, two bows, and a quiver with a dozen arrows filled the space. She froze, feeling as if she'd stumbled upon a hidden treasure. Had Brianna been a soldier before she married Duke Ellington? Or did she just have a passion for weapons?

Reid closed the door and examined the room again, seeing it in a different light. If her mother had been a soldier, what would she think of her daughters? Would she be proud of or disappointed in the women they'd become? Reid's four older sisters always wore dresses, and none had even touched a weapon.

Brianna had left here at the age of eighteen to marry Duke Ellington. She'd had Reid at twenty-five. Reid supposed a lot could change during that time. Especially considering that during those seven years, Brianna had lived in Ellington, where there were restrictions on women's rights.

Although...Prince Henrick had gradually changed the laws here in Axian to allow women to wear pants, work, and join the army. Henrick had taken over Axian around the same time Brianna married, which meant she'd grown up under King Broc's rule.

The elements of her mother that Reid found intriguing—the clothes and weapons—had been hidden from plain sight. Which probably meant Brianna had been one person in the manor and another while out in society. Maybe Reid and her mother weren't so different after all.

During supper, Reid spent the entire time asking questions about her mother. Her grandparents indulged her, telling her everything they could about Brianna's life as a child—she'd always seemed to get into trouble; painting and drawing had been her favorite pastimes; and bread loaded with butter was her favorite food. They'd never mentioned anything about her mother knowing how to shoot a bow or wield a sword, though.

After Constance and Gregor retired for the night, Reid meandered to the sitting room where the fire slowly died in the hearth. Her mind buzzed with everything that had happened today.

Dexter sat on the sofa next to her, his legs propped on the low table. "I don't know how to break it to you, so I'm just going to say it. Your grandparents are lying to you about something."

"Why do you think that?"

"During supper, they kept glancing at one another. They seemed…uncomfortable."

Reid had noticed that, too. However, she'd assumed it was because her visit was unexpected. Or maybe because they were nervous with a prince in the house.

"Let's snoop," he said.

"I am not going to snoop in my grandparents' home." She folded her arms.

"Why not?"

"Because it's wrong."

"They're your family."

"Precisely."

He rolled his eyes. "Fine. But mark my words, they're hiding something."

Letting her head fall back against the sofa, she asked, "Where's the closest village?"

"About a mile west. Why?"

"I need to clear my head. Let's go." Besides wanting to see more of where her mother had grown up, Reid needed to get out of the manor so she could look at the situation objectively. And she wasn't tired enough to retire for the night.

Instead of arguing as she'd expected, Dexter stood and went to the door, putting on a cape.

Reid also grabbed a cape, wrapping it around her body. The chilly night air engulfed Reid as they exited the manor, making her shiver. They walked along the road, which led straight into the village. It was much larger than she'd expected, with several streets and stores. Since it was after supper, there weren't many people out and about, giving the place a sedate feel. Only a few lights shone from within the buildings.

When they reached the local pub, they went in. A handful of men sat at the bar, and about half the tables were full. Reid claimed an empty table in the back.

Dexter ordered two drinks, then sat across from her, pushing one of the mugs her way. "What do you want to talk about?" he asked.

Reid wrapped her hands around her mug. "Who says I want to talk?"

Dexter took a drink, not bothering to respond.

"Fine." She sighed. "Something's off." A feeling of being off kilter had inundated her since leaving the palace. "I can't say what it is exactly." She took a sip, not sure how to explain.

His right leg bounced under the table, proof he was restless, too. "I agree." He chugged the rest of his drink before he said, "I know you want to get to know your grandparents better, but I would prefer to leave tomorrow. They'll be at the palace for our wedding, so you can spend more time with them then. Is that okay with you?"

"Yes." Maybe she'd feel better once she returned to the safety of the palace.

"The way you were brought here, the feeling I'm getting, it adds up to something being wrong."

"What happened to Victor?" She hadn't seen him since they arrived earlier in the day.

"He went home."

Her cousin could have at least bid her goodbye.

Dexter abruptly stood, the legs of his chair scraping against the wood floor. "Let's play a game." He pointed at the dart board on the back wall.

Reid eyed it. "I should warn you—I don't like to lose."

Chuckling, Dexter responded, "Neither do I." He picked up ten darts, setting the five yellow ones on the table in front of her. "What do you say? Are you up for the challenge?"

"I'm not sure a game of darts is a challenge." She shrugged. "But you're on."

He stood ten feet back from the target, his toes on the white line. Fingering his first red dart, he raised it, aimed, and threw. It landed in the center ring, slightly to the right.

"That's too bad." Reid stood and picked up her first dart, sauntering over. Standing just behind the line, she lifted her dart and threw. It hit the center ring, slightly to the left. She cursed.

"That's too bad," he mocked.

"There's something wrong with these darts." Her dart should have struck dead center.

"I know. Otherwise, I would have one in the middle."

She stepped aside, allowing Dexter to take her place. He threw his dart. Again, it struck the center ring, a little too high this time. They went back and forth until they'd thrown all their darts. When they finished, they observed the board. All ten were in the middle circle, though not a single one was dead center.

Dexter strode forward to remove the darts from the board. "I'm calling it a tie."

"I agree. We have no choice but to play again. This time, we have to get a single dart in each ring."

"Good idea." He raised his hand, ordering two more drinks. "And they have to hit the top of each ring."

Reid picked up her darts. "Deal." This time, she went first, aiming for the outer line. Her dart landed right where she wanted it to.

Dexter's dart landed right next to hers.

The bartender slid two mugs on the table.

Reid took a sip of her drink before throwing her second dart. This game went the same way, ending in another tie.

"How is that even possible?" he mumbled, eyeing her.

She shrugged. While she was disappointed she hadn't won, she was thrilled she hadn't lost.

"There has to be another game around here we can play." He surveyed the pub. "I have an idea." He finished off his drink, then set his mug in the center of the table. "Do you have any money on you?"

She pulled a few coins out of her pocket, tossing them on the table.

"Excellent. You sit in that chair there. I'll sit directly across from you."

Reid did as he said.

"Hold a coin like this." He placed a single coin vertically on the table, holding the top with his pointer finger. "Then try to flick it into the mug like this." He hit the coin with his thumb and pointer finger. The coin went flying, smacking Reid's arm.

"Was that supposed to happen?" she asked.

"It should have gone in the mug." When he tried again, the coin hit the outside of the mug.

Reid positioned a coin, then flicked it right into the mug on her first try. Throwing her hands in the air, she screamed, "Yes!"

Dexter narrowed his eyes. "That was a lucky shot."

"We'll see." She lined up another coin. When she hit it, it sailed into the mug. She smirked.

Dexter tried again. His coin pelted Reid on her forehead. When she squeaked in surprise, he burst out laughing.

"Did you do that on purpose?"

He couldn't stop laughing.

Irked, she grabbed another coin, aimed for Dexter's face, and flicked it. It smacked his right cheek.

"Hey now," he said, still chuckling.

Reid did it again, hitting his left cheek.

He sat up straighter. "You did that on purpose."

She lined up another, hitting his forehead.

Dexter scrambled for a coin, snapping it at Reid. She ducked, easily avoiding it. Perturbed, he tried again. She dodged it.

"The coins aren't cooperating," he muttered, trying again. He missed. Now it was Reid's turn to laugh. "You really don't like to lose."

"Not if I can help it. And I'm not against playing dirty when it's called for."

CHAPTER THIRTEEN

Reid peeled her eyelids open, moaning at the bright light shining in through the bedroom window. Rolling onto her side, away from the window, she cradled her pounding head. The ale they'd consumed last night must have been particularly strong. When she shoved the covers off, she realized she still wore yesterday's clothes.

Brain feeling muddled, she slid her feet over the edge and stepped on something hard, yet warm.

Cursing, she jumped back on the bed, peering down.

Dexter lay face down on the floor, without a pillow or blanket, unmoving.

"Dexter," she whispered, trying to rouse him. Nothing. She reached down, shaking his shoulder. "Wake up."

Turning his head to the side, he mumbled incoherently.

"You need to get out of my bedchamber before someone sees you."

His eyes flew open. "Why am I in here?"

"I have no idea. Just get out."

He rolled onto his back, and Reid's eyes widened. There were welts on his face from where she'd struck him with the coins.

"What is it?" he asked, blinking against the morning light. Cringing, she bit her lip. "Nothing."

"You're a terrible liar." He sat up and rubbed his eyes. "If it's okay with you, I'd like to head out after breakfast."

"I'm fine with that." There would be plenty of time for Reid to get to know her grandparents after the wedding.

"I need to inform my men of our plans. There's only four, so we'll have to be vigilant on our way back." He stood and stretched before leaving the room.

Since Reid was in Brianna's room, she slid out of bed and went over to the closet. Wanting something of her mother's, she picked two daggers at random, tucking them into her pants. When she went to close the door, something caught her attention. A leather armored vest hung from a peg on the wall. Before she could change her mind, she snatched it off.

It was hard and thick, entirely too big to fit in Reid's traveling bag. The only other option was to wear it. She slid her arms in the holes, hoisting the vest on, then cinching it together. It fit like a glove. Examining herself in the mirror, Reid couldn't help but think she looked like Nara.

Not wanting Dexter or anyone else to question why she had on armor, she pulled her tunic over it. After grabbing her bag, she headed downstairs. She found her grandparents eating breakfast in the dining room.

"I see you have your bag with you," Gregor said. "Does that mean you're leaving?"

Taking a seat across from her grandmother, Reid answered, "I am. Prince Dexter and I must return to the palace. There is much to be done to prepare for the wedding."

"We will make every effort to be there," Constance assured her.

It surprised Reid that neither insisted she stay for another day. It was almost as if they didn't mind her leaving—which didn't make any sense. Unless, as Dexter pointed out, they had something to hide. But why would her grandparents withhold information from her? Didn't they trust her?

"I want you both to know how sorry I am that I didn't know you were alive until recently. Now that I'm living in Axian, I hope we can see one another frequently."

"Your grandmother and I would like that," Gregor answered. "You're welcome here any time."

Reid was about to say something when she caught sight of a painting on the wall behind her grandfather. Family portraits covered the entire space. However, one in particular stood out. It was a painting of a girl who looked to be about fourteen. "Is that my mother?"

Constance's face went stark white.

"It is," Gregor replied. "Now if you're ready to leave, we'll walk you out."

Reid absently nodded as she stood. Instead of following her grandparents from the room, she went over to examine the portrait. The girl—her mother—looked vaguely familiar with her thick brown hair flowing around her shoulders. Her eyes stared directly at Reid, as if she knew a secret. Her mother wasn't smiling, but the corners of her lips tilted slightly up, hinting at mischief. Searching the girl's features, Reid tried to find similarities.

"Are you coming?" Gregor asked from the doorway.

"She's beautiful." If Reid had the time, she would spend all day staring at this portrait. Her father didn't have a single one. Tears filled her eyes. "My oldest sister looks just like her." She tilted her head to the side. "And so does Kamden." They had the same nose.

"Lady Reid?" Dexter said. "My men are ready to go."

Forcing herself away from the painting, she exited the room. Were there additional portraits of her mother in the manor? Would her grandparents give her one?

"Are you okay?" Dexter whispered.

She nodded.

He put his hand on the small of her back, escorting her out. In the entryway, Reid hugged her grandparents, bidding them farewell.

Outside, Dexter's men waited, already mounted. Reid went over to her horse, attaching her bag. After climbing onto the saddle, she adjusted the reins. Her grandparents were framed in the doorway, and Reid studied them.

"I'm surprised you're traveling with so few men," Gregor said, addressing Dexter.

"It'll allow us to travel faster. There's no need to worry—I'll protect your granddaughter."

Gregor smiled. "I have no doubt you are more than capable of caring for Lady Reid. But please make sure to take care of yourself as well. Axian needs you."

"I have four of my most skilled men with me," he assured Gregor. "We'll be fine."

With that, Dexter nudged his horse and they set out. Dexter and Reid rode side by side, two men in front, and two men behind.

"Your most skilled men?" Reid said. "I would have thought that included Markis and Gytha."

"I lied to your grandfather," he admitted. "I left in such a hurry I didn't have time to find Markis and Gytha. Instead, I grabbed the first four soldiers I encountered and ordered them to come with me."

She chuckled. "Then I'm surprised those two didn't come after you."

He smiled ruefully. "Even though you haven't been in Axian long, you seem to know and understand a great deal."

"I saw their loyalty to you the moment I stepped off the boat."

"Speaking of that day," Dexter said, "I want to apologize for the way I treated you."

Why was Dexter being nice to her now? Did he finally trust her or was he only trying to gain information? She needed to proceed with caution. "When King Eldon informed me I'd be marrying you, I was furious. Given the fact I'd snuck into your home and tried stealing from you, I hadn't expected a warm reception." She spoke softly so the soldiers escorting them wouldn't overhear.

"I'll admit, when you first arrived, I feared you were here to assassinate my father."

Yet, he'd still ended things with Gytha. Interesting. "You know that's absurd, don't you?" Reid was many things, but an assassin was not one of them.

"Is it absurd?" He eyed her. "King Eldon sent you here to acquire an object for him. That speaks volumes about what he thinks of you and what you're capable of."

Because Eldon didn't employ women. "But stealing is very different from murder." She'd only ever killed someone once— when they'd been ambushed by assassins in the forest. And even then, she'd only done so to stay alive. Rubbing her forehead, she banished all thoughts of that night and what she'd done. It was too hard to think about.

"After watching you," Dexter said, adjusting his reins, "I could tell you weren't interested in my father. When you formed a friendship with my brother, I thought maybe you'd been sent to assassinate him. But that didn't seem logical. You had nothing to do with me, so I figured you weren't out to kill me."

"Why do I have to be killing someone?"

"Once I realized you weren't an assassin, then next logical reason was you were a spy."

"I've already admitted to that. The king wants me to spy on your family. I assumed that was obvious."

They rode in silence for a few minutes. "I feel like there is something I'm missing," he admitted.

Well, there was the part about her being a Knight tasked with discovering where Dexter went at night. How was she supposed to gain this man's trust when he was so distrustful? And did she have the right to go behind his back? After all, she would only be a Knight for a couple of more weeks, whereas she'd be married to Dexter for the rest of her life.

"So, Lady Reid," he said, her name rolling off his tongue like water, "where did you go on your way to your grandparents' house?"

She pursed her lips, trying to decide what to say. "Why do you think I went somewhere?"

"Because you should have arrived the day before me, not at the same time."

Good point. "I'm not familiar with these roads. I'm not sure which way Victor took me."

"Ah, yes. Victor."

She cringed at the way he said the man's name.

"Why would you leave the palace with a man you don't even know?" he asked.

Well, she wouldn't have. The only reason she'd gone with Victor was the confirmation of his Knight mark. Ackley had told her to trust any Knight she encountered. Instead of saying that, she replied, "Your father told me that my second cousin was in the stables, waiting to escort me to my grandparents' house. I trust your father." Because Henrick was a Knight.

"I plan to speak with my father about that." Dexter looked sidelong at her. "Mark my words, Lady Reid, if you're hiding something, I will discover what it is."

Leaning toward him, she lowered her voice. "Mark my words, Prince Dexter, I'll discover whatever it is *you're* hiding."

If she hadn't been staring right at his face, watching for a reaction, she would have missed the slight twitch in his lips, a sure sign he was also hiding something. Straightening, she focused on the road, shocked she was finally getting somewhere with Dexter. He was starting to make sense to her, and she was no longer scared of him.

The group of six continued riding until the sun began to set.

Then Dexter gave the order to pull off the road. They set up camp in a spot nestled between two huge oak trees.

Dexter approached Reid. "I'd like a moment of your time. In private."

She followed him about thirty feet away from his men.

"We can't keep secrets from one another," he said. "We have an opportunity to work together to achieve something."

"I agree." Her father's army was mighty. With the backing of Ellington and Axian, she could implement positive changes. But none of that would happen if she was constantly butting heads with Dexter. They had to start working together.

"Tell me what you're hiding."

"You tell me what you're hiding," she countered.

He ran his hands through his hair. "This is what I mean. We have to stop bickering."

Reid hesitated. Ackley had told his siblings about being a Knight. She could probably tell Dexter. At least he knew how to keep a secret. "I agree. But one of us has to go first, and we are both too stubborn."

"Of all the women my parents could pick from, they chose you!" He stalked back to camp, shaking his head and mumbling the entire time.

"Trust me," she called, "the feeling is mutual."

———

The next day, neither Reid nor Dexter spoke as they made their way east toward the palace. Reid yawned, exhausted from not having slept well. Not only was the leather armor vest uncomfortable to sleep in, but so was the particularly rocky ground Dexter had chosen to make camp on for the night.

"There's something blocking the road up ahead," a soldier in front said. "Looks like a wagon."

"The two of you in back, go see what it is," Dexter ordered.

They immediately veered off, then headed toward the wagon.

"Looks like the wheel came off," Reid said, halting her horse. "Strange it's angled across the road, not pushed to the side instead."

"Agreed," Dexter mumbled, scanning the trees on either side of the road. "Let's backtrack and go around just to be safe."

Reid nudged her horse to turn it around just as a whistle rang through the air. A dozen men burst from the back of the wagon, bows and arrows in hand. The two soldiers who went to investigate withdrew their swords. The men raised their loaded bows, arrows striking the soldiers before Reid could even blink.

"Ride low," Dexter commanded as he positioned his body alongside his horse's neck.

Reid did the same, urging her horse faster to keep up. The two remaining soldiers rode close behind them. A *hiss* cut through the air, followed by two sickening *thuds*. One of the soldiers cried out. Glancing over her shoulder, she saw arrows protruding from both soldiers' backs. One fell from his horse while the other slumped forward, barely hanging on. More arrows sailed through the air, aimed at Reid and Dexter.

Terror filled her. They wouldn't be out of range for another twenty seconds—more than enough time for another round of arrows to find them. Something hit her back, the force almost knocking her from the saddle. She clung to her horse, realizing an arrow must have struck her. Her mother's armor had saved her life.

Dexter wasn't quite as lucky. An arrow protruded from his left arm. He broke the arrow off, tossing it on the ground. Blood soaked his sleeve.

They rounded the bend, finally out of striking range. Dexter halted, dismounted, and hit his horse's rump. The animal took off, not needing any more encouragement. Reid slid from her saddle. The second her feet hit the ground, Dexter swatted her horse's rump. It quickly followed the other horse.

Dexter ran up the slope on the left, into the cover of the trees. Reid chased him, almost losing her footing on the slick, leaf-covered ground.

"There," someone shouted.

Reid glanced back. Two riders approached. The right one pointed at Dexter. The left one raised his bow and aimed.

Without thinking, Reid sprinted to the prince. She threw herself at him, covering as much of his torso as possible. An arrow struck her upper back, the impact making it hard to breathe. Between her weight and the force of the arrow that hit her, Dexter fell forward, Reid landing on top of him.

"I got her," the man crowed. "She'll be dead in no time."

Dexter twisted around, his eyes wide with panic. "You're hit?"

"I'm fine. I have armor on." Her voice came out squeaky.

He reached behind her, pulling the arrow free from her armor, then he examined the tip to make sure there wasn't any blood. "We need to go before they come after us."

She slid off him, and they crawled the remaining three feet to the top of the rise. Once they were certain they were out of sight from their pursuers, they scrambled to their feet and ran, dodging between the trees.

After a mile, Dexter stopped. They'd reached a section of the forest covered with thick ivy. "Let's hide here until we're sure we're not being followed." The blood from his wound had soaked through his sleeve all the way down to his wrist.

Reid scanned the area for a good hiding place. The ivy reached her knees, trailing over rocks and up tree trunks. She approached one of the larger boulders and stretched out on her side, nestling below the ivy. The likelihood of a horse trampling her this close to the boulder was slim. She settled in, assuming she would be in this position for some time.

A moment later, rustling sounded to her right, about five feet away. "Are you okay?" she whispered.

"Yes. I ripped a section of my tunic off, then tied it around my arm to stop the bleeding. Once we're safe, I'll need to remove the arrowhead."

The mere thought soured Reid's stomach. She breathed in and out through her nose, trying to remain still and not make a sound. Her back began to throb where the arrows had struck her. Bone-deep bruises would no doubt blossom by tomorrow.

Birds chirped overhead. The wind rustled the leaves. The sun slowly moved across the sky, casting eerie shadows through the trees. Hours passed.

"I think it's safe," Dexter finally said.

"They're probably looking for our bodies." She carefully sat up, scanning the area for threats. Not seeing anyone, she stood and stretched.

"We need to return to the City of Radella by a different route." Dexter sat, leaning against the boulder.

"I figured."

"And we'll have to walk."

"How far is it?"

"Thirty miles."

That wasn't too bad. "We can't go anywhere until we remove that arrowhead."

He examined his arm. "It's up high in the muscle. No major damage."

Reid knelt at his side. "Take your shirt off so I can see what I'm dealing with."

He raised his eyebrows. "I'm perfectly capable of removing the arrow."

"Really? I thought you were right handed."

"I am."

"And you can use your left hand to remove an arrow from your right arm?"

"Sure."

She rolled her eyes. "Come on. Let's find some water to rinse the blood off."

"Okay." Dexter stood. "But we need to travel south, then to the east. I don't want to deviate from that and end up lost."

Reid agreed, and they set out. They trekked through the forest, neither talking in case the assassins were nearby.

"Is that the sound of water?" Reid whispered.

"It is. I have a vague idea of where we are."

After a quarter of a mile, they came to a ten-foot-wide river, the water moving rapidly over rocks. "It doesn't look very deep," she said.

"It's pretty shallow here. In other sections, you can't even see the bottom."

It was deep enough to clean Dexter's wound. "Go ahead and remove your shirt," Reid said as she squatted on the riverbank, thinking about what she needed to do. She hated this sort of thing. Back home, whenever her father or one of her sisters fell ill, Kamden always tended to them. Never Reid. "If you can't, I'll just rip your sleeve off."

Not only did she not have the necessary tools to start a fire, but also starting one when they didn't know the location of the assassins was probably a bad idea. In that case, heating the tip of her dagger and placing it on Dexter's wound to cauterize it wasn't an option.

Pulling out a dagger, she stuck it in the water to clean it.

Dexter removed his shirt, then tossed it on the ground.

Throughout Reid's life, she'd seen plenty of men naked. When she'd sparred, most of her opponents had been shirtless. Even when she traveled with Ellington's soldiers, she'd seen hundreds of men strip. They'd always assumed *she* was a *he,* so it never mattered. But this was different. Dexter knew she was a woman. Somehow, seeing his bare chest felt intimate. And Reid didn't like intimate.

"What's wrong?" he asked, sitting on the ground beside her.

"I'm just thinking about what needs to be done." His shoulders were broad, his skin tan, and, holy kingdoms, the well-defined muscles of his stomach appeared as if etched from stone. She swallowed, mentally chiding herself. Now was not the time to drool. She needed to focus.

Imbedded parallel to his arm instead of inward, the arrow couldn't be very deep. Using the tip of her dagger, she gently placed it at the edge of the arrowhead. "I'm going to try to push the arrow out."

"I've never had a woman tend to me like this."

"I'm sure Gytha has stitched you up once or twice." Reid couldn't believe she'd mentioned the warrior woman. As if she were jealous. Which she wasn't.

He chuckled. "Oh, she has. She's just not...how should I put it? As kind as you are?"

Reid felt her face heat at the compliment. At least she thought it was a compliment. Maybe it wasn't. Taking a deep breath, she carefully pressed the dagger into his skin, then sideways, pushing the arrow out. It fell to the ground, blood spurting out of the wound. She grabbed Dexter's shirt, dunking the bloodless sleeve in the water before cleaning the area around the wound. The blood kept oozing out, so she tore off a piece of fabric and pressed it against his arm.

"Hold this here," she murmured. He did as instructed. Reid ripped off another piece of fabric, wrapping that piece around his arm to hold the fabric in place. "Hopefully, the bleeding will stop."

"Reid."

She peered into his eyes, wishing she hadn't. A million questions and emotions swirled inside them.

"Why did you throw yourself in front of that arrow for me?" His low, rumbly voice made her shiver.

"I had to save you." If she hadn't, he'd be dead now.

"Why?"

She shrugged. "Because it was the right thing to do." This close, his eyes were mesmerizingly beautiful. She couldn't look away.

"And now? Why are you helping me?"

"I don't know."

"You could have let me fend for myself."

She rolled her eyes. "Oh, please. You couldn't have removed the arrow without me." Then, to ease the building tension, she picked up his shirt and rinsed the bloody sleeve in the water. When she finished, she handed it to him.

"Your turn."

"What do you mean?" She wasn't injured.

"Let me see your back. I want to make sure the tip didn't cut you."

"I'm fine." It was the truth. She was sore, but fine. "We need to get moving." She offered him a hand up.

Dexter grabbed her hand, using it to rise. "Did you get a look at their faces?"

"I did."

"And did you recognize them?"

"Yes."

CHAPTER FOURTEEN

T he men who'd tried to kill Reid and Dexter had looked like the miners from Bridger. They had the same build, hair, and accent. As they trekked through the forest, Reid told Dexter about her previous encounters with the men, starting with the assassination attempt when she was with Ackley and Gordon and they'd been ambushed in the middle of the night. She thought it strange two dozen men had been sent to kill two princes, yet they'd failed. Which led her to believe that maybe they weren't trained assassins. She explained how she spied on the men staying at the inn in the City of Buckley, telling Dexter how she found the journal indicating they planned to kill Ackley, Gordon, and Idina. Then, she finished with how she'd seen men resembling the assassins working in the mines in Bridger.

At first, she'd assumed Eldon must be working with Duke Bridger, employing the miners as assassins. However, some things didn't add up. The men had a distinctive look, accent, and skin color. In all her studies about Marsden, she'd never learned about any county having such differences. "Do you think the men could be from another kingdom?" Reid asked.

"Colbert has been gathering information," Dexter replied. "We believe Eldon may be forging an alliance with a kingdom to the east of here, across the ocean."

"Melenia?" she asked, remembering Dexter's conversation with the sailor.

"Yes." They continued in silence for several minutes. The river to their right made a soothing sound as water rolled over rocks. "I must admit, I'm surprised they tried to kill you, too. I assumed the king would want you alive."

"I know Eldon's secret—that he is not the legitimate king. And since my father gave me his ring, the king can't harm me. That's why he is using assassins from outside Marsden. No one can know about his involvement." If she could prove the king sent those men, Reid could rally the dukes to overthrow him. However, did she want to do that? Henrick had no intention of accepting the throne, so who would Marsden's leader be? If Eldon died, Gordon would ascend to the throne. She had a hard time imagining the commander ruling Marsden.

"What are you thinking about?" Dexter asked.

Beads of sweat coated his forehead even though it wasn't hot out. His wound didn't appear to be bleeding anymore. Regardless, Reid would have to watch for signs of an infection.

"I'm considering who should be king."

"So am I."

"What are you thinking?" Reid asked.

"I'm tired of my father bending over backward for Eldon. I get he's his son. But it's not fair to my mother, Colbert, or even to me. We've stood by his side and supported him all these years."

"What do you want your father to do?"

"I don't know," he admitted. "But I do know I don't want my father to allow Eldon to invade and take over Axian."

"What about your father giving Axian to Eldon?"

Dexter regarded her coolly. "How would you feel if your father handed Ellington over to the king?"

"I wouldn't stand for it." Granted, she didn't know what—if

anything—she could do to stop him, but she wouldn't sit idly by and allow the king to destroy everything her father had worked so hard for.

"Even though Eldon is the king?" He climbed over a fallen tree.

"But he's not." Reid clambered up behind him, scraping her hands as she did so.

"He was crowned king."

"That's my point—Eldon can't succeed King Hudson since he's not Hudson's son. The throne should belong to Prince Gordon or it should revert to Prince Henrick." She slid off the tree, resuming her place behind Dexter.

"My father has no desire to sit on the throne. Since he's declared Eldon as his heir, Eldon ends up the king regardless."

Reid noticed Dexter hadn't acknowledged the possibility of Gordon ascending to the throne. "What if your father chose someone else as his heir? Typically, it's the eldest son, but there is nothing in the law that prevents your father from declaring you or Colbert." Granted, that didn't solve anything at the moment since Henrick didn't want to be king.

Reid's boots sank into the muddy ground, squishing as she walked. Dexter's pace slowed.

"If we want to reveal Eldon is not Hudson's son, those letters would be proof, correct?" Dexter asked.

"Yes."

"And you believe Prince Ackley has those letters?"

"I do."

"Whose side do you think Prince Ackley is on?"

A good question. Originally, she'd believed Ackley was solely dedicated to the Knights. Now, she wasn't so sure. He'd told Gordon and Idina about the Knights, which he wasn't supposed to do. He'd also stolen the letters with Leigh's help. While Reid had thought Ackley loved and supported his brother Eldon, she couldn't be certain. Especially considering the fact Eldon was trying to kill his siblings and Ackley seemed to be working in direct opposition to him.

"I don't know," she answered. Ackley kept his secrets closely guarded.

Dexter swayed.

"Are you okay?" Reid lunged forward, wrapping her arm around his waist to steady him.

"I'm beginning to fear the arrow was tipped with poison."

"You lost a lot of blood when I removed the arrow," she said. "Maybe you're just weak from blood loss?"

"I don't think so." He leaned against a tree, breathing heavily. "Colbert was in an altercation and stabbed. He became ill within a few short hours. Suspecting the knife had been tipped with poison, I put charcoal on the wound to neutralize it. He started to feel better within minutes."

Reid wanted to ask more about that altercation, but now was not the time. "If there's poison in your system, we need to do something about it." It had been hours since he'd been shot. What if it was already too late? Putting her hands on her hips, she started pacing.

"Now's your chance to do away with me," he said. He'd obviously meant it as a joke, but his voice came out weak.

It would be so much easier if Harlan were here. He could whip up something to take care of the poison in no time. Dexter said charcoal had worked for Colbert, but she didn't have anything like that readily available. The palace was too far away. What other options were there? "Are there any homes nearby?"

"One mile east, on the other side of the river. I think."

"Let's go." She wrapped her arm around his waist, hoisting him upright. "I need you to push yourself for twenty minutes, then you can rest."

He nodded.

Since the river looked shallow here, Reid and Dexter crossed it. Some of the rocks on the bottom came loose, almost causing Reid to lose her footing. However, she managed to remain upright, still supporting Dexter. His face paled with every passing minute, sweat dripping down his cheeks.

Once safely on dry land again, Reid pulled Dexter along, maintaining a fast pace since he didn't look like he could last much longer. If he passed out, she wouldn't be able to carry him.

They trekked along, Reid taking more of his weight with each passing minute, until they came to a single-story wood home with smoke rising from the chimney.

"Hello," Reid called out. "I need help!"

A man came around the side of the house, an axe in hand. He wiped his sweaty forehead with his arm. "What can I do for you?"

"This is Prince Dexter," she said, her voice fast and urgent. "He's injured and needs immediate attention."

The man tossed his axe on the ground, rushing over to help. Dexter wrapped his good arm around the man's shoulders, allowing the stranger to help him inside. Reid hovered right behind them.

Inside, a woman kneaded bread dough on a small table. "What happened?" She wiped her hands off and rushed over, helping Dexter sit on the bed.

"We were ambushed by assassins," Reid explained. "Prince Dexter was shot with a poisoned arrow."

"I have something we use for wounds like this," the woman said. "But I'm not sure if it'll help against poison."

"Get whatever you have and bring it here." Reid removed Dexter's shirt, then helped him lie back, propping his head on a pillow.

The woman began to rummage around the kitchen area.

"Get charcoal," Dexter ordered the man. "Now."

He dashed over to a basket in the corner, pulling out a handful of black rocks. "What do you want me to do with them?"

Dexter clutched Reid's hand. "I need to ingest some, and I need you to put some on my wound. Leave it on for an hour, then remove it. Once the wound is clean, apply the stuff the woman has, then stitch me up."

Reid nodded, acknowledging the directions he gave in case he passed out or was too weak to talk. Her stomach twisted at the thought.

"Look at me," Dexter commanded.

She gazed into his eyes.

"You're pale."

"I'm fine," she insisted.

"Can I trust you to do this?"

"I can do it." She turned to address the man. "Grind the charcoal up. I want two batches. One in water so the prince can drink it, and the other in a bowl so I can put it on his arm."

The man got to work.

"What are your names?" Reid asked.

"I'm Rick, and that's Ava."

"Thank you for helping us."

"We'd do anything to aid our prince," Rick said.

Reid removed the fabric tied around Dexter's arm. When Rick handed her a bowl with tiny pieces of charcoal in it, she sprinkled some onto Dexter's open wound. He pursed his lips, but he didn't make a sound. Then Rick handed Reid a cup of water mixed with finely ground charcoal.

She carefully placed the cup on Dexter's lips, slowly pouring it into his mouth. After he swallowed a few gulps, she withdrew the cup, hoping it was enough.

"Ava," Dexter called out. "I need a favor."

"Of course, Your Highness." She curtsied.

"Check my fiancée's back."

"I'm fine," Reid assured him. Her voice came out weaker than she'd intended, shocked by Dexter's use of the word *fiancée*. He probably only said it so these people would know she wasn't a soldier.

"She was also struck by an arrow," Dexter explained.

"However, she was fortunate enough to have armor on. I want to be sure the poisoned tip didn't penetrate the armor and scratch her back."

"Yes, Your Highness."

"I'll leave so you can have some privacy," Rick said, exiting the house.

"Lady Reid." Ava gestured toward the corner of the room.

Seeing no way around this embarrassment, Reid went over and removed her tunic. After untying the vest, she took it off, carefully setting it on the table. Withdrawing both daggers, she set them beside her armor. Facing the corner again, she pulled her shirt over her head, exposing her bare back to Ava.

"Is there a puncture wound?" Dexter asked.

"There are two small marks," Ava answered. "While I don't see any blood, both spots are pretty swollen."

"I want you to put charcoal on them just to be safe," he ordered. "And I want Lady Reid to drink some of the charcoal, too."

Reid didn't think either was necessary. However, Dexter needed to rest so he could fight off the poison. He wouldn't do that until Reid was cared for. It was easier to comply than fight.

"Would you prefer to sit on a chair or lie on the bed?" Ava inquired.

"She'll lie down," Dexter said. "That way she can leave the charcoal on for a full hour."

"But I don't have a shirt on," Reid said. "I can't lie next to you." Her breathing sped up.

"Reid, don't be so difficult. We're going to be married in a few weeks."

Heat scorched her body, and there was nothing she could do to hide her utter embarrassment. It was awkward enough having a woman she didn't know tend to her. However, it was doubly awkward having Dexter in the same room, let alone the same bed.

He tilted his head, facing her, and managed a weak smile. "Don't tell me you're shy."

Mortification set in. The longer she waited, the worse it would get. "Look the other way and close your eyes."

Thankfully, he complied. Clutching her shirt against her chest, she scurried over to the bed and plopped on her stomach, making sure the sheet fully covered her breasts. Since the bed was so tiny, her arm inadvertently brushed Dexter's.

Ava approached. There wasn't enough room for her to sit on the bed, so she stood next to Reid to apply the charcoal to the two spots on her back. "When my husband returns, I'll have him grind up some more so you can drink it."

"Take some out to him and have him do it now," Dexter said. "I don't want to wait in case there is poison in Lady Reid's system."

Ava did as he said, slipping outside.

"I'm fine," Reid insisted. "I don't feel off."

"I'd rather not wait to find out." His voice sounded stronger than before, giving Reid hope the charcoal was already working to neutralize the poison.

"You know," she said, repeating the words he'd said earlier, "now's your chance to do away with me."

He tilted his head toward her. "If I wanted to get rid of you, I would have done so by now."

She blinked, trying to decide if he was joking. Probably not. She doubted he did anything he didn't want to. He'd agreed to their marriage for a reason. "Sorry you're stuck with me." Her sister, Kamden, would have been better suited as a princess who portrayed the image Nara desired. "I'm moody and not the doting-wife type."

He chuckled, his focus on the ceiling. "I'm fairly certain I'm not the doting-husband type either."

While neither wanted this marriage, at least they both cared for and sought what was best for their people. United in that, they

JENNIFER ANNE DAVIS

could learn to be friends, couldn't they? And since neither was seeking love, they wouldn't have to worry about losing their hearts.

Ava entered carrying a mug. She handed it to Reid, who begrudgingly drank the nasty contents.

"I hate to ask this of you," Dexter said, "but I need you to put the fire out. If anyone is searching for us, I don't want them to see the smoke and come here."

"Of course," Ava replied. "I'll get my husband to toss dirt on it."

Once she left, Reid said, "I think Eldon is trying to kill all contenders for the throne since he knows he's not the true king."

"That makes sense."

"He won't stop until he succeeds."

He patted her hand. "Then we'll just have to stop him before he does."

"How do you suggest we do that?"

"I'll figure it out later. Right now, I'm going to close my eyes and rest."

Reid supposed she should do the same.

Reid woke up to find Dexter staring at her. Before she could say anything, Ava patted Reid's shoulder.

"It's time to remove the charcoal and apply the healing salve."

"Okay." And Reid needed to use the privy. If there was one.

Ava used a soft cloth to wipe off the charcoal. Then she applied a cool salve to Reid's back. "All finished."

"Thank you." Reid twisted away from Dexter and sat up, clutching her shirt to her chest. She quickly put it on. Ava handed Reid her tunic, so she slid that on as well.

"Now that you're dressed, I'll go get my husband," Ava said. "Then we can prepare something for you to eat."

When she exited, Dexter said, "We'll stay here tonight. But I want to leave first thing tomorrow morning. We need to get home in case there's been an attack on the palace."

Reid understood his concern, though she didn't think the assassins would be able to get anywhere near the palace.

Rick and Ava entered. They started rummaging around the kitchen area, pulling out plates, bread, and carrots.

"Without a fire to cook, the meal is going to be meager," Rick said. "I'm sorry we don't have something suitable for a prince."

"Anything will be fine," Dexter replied. "I'm grateful for your help, and I don't care what we eat. Your hospitality and kindness are more than we could have hoped for."

"Is there a privy?" Reid asked, tucking her two daggers into her pants.

"Yes. It's around back," Ava replied.

"Rick, can you please escort Lady Reid?" Dexter said.

Reid glared at Dexter, unused to him acting concerned or overbearing.

"Sorry." Dexter raised his hands. "But the assassins are out there somewhere. The last thing I want is for them to kidnap you to use against our families."

"Fine." She followed Rick out of the house. Walking around the side of the place, she breathed in the pungent smell of pine and damp dirt. The sun had recently set, casting the area in a dull, murky gray.

Rick sat on a tree stump thirty or so feet from a small shack that served as the privy. After relieving herself, Reid exited the shack, not seeing Rick anywhere. She froze, observing her surroundings. No birds sang, no forest animals scurried nearby. Something was wrong.

Withdrawing her daggers, she analyzed the situation. If someone were out there, not only was the front door too far away and exposed, but it was also probably being watched. The two windows on the side of the house were closer. If she made it

169

through one into the house, she'd have the cover she needed. However, she'd be trapped in there with no way out. If the assassins called in reinforcements, then Reid and Dexter wouldn't stand a chance. To survive, she needed to draw the assassins out and eliminate them.

Since no one had shot at her, they must not be aware of her presence at the back of the house. Most likely, they were watching the front door. Moving slowly, she made her way around to the rear of the small shack. A twig snapped about ten feet in front of her. She raised a dagger, about to throw it, when Rick stepped out from behind a tree, one finger on his lips and an axe in hand. She relaxed, and he joined her.

They leaned against the shack. Rick held up three fingers. Reid understood it meant there were three assassins.

Tilting his head toward her, Rick whispered, "Front of the house. One up in the tree on the right, one behind the largest boulder, and one squatting behind the tree on the left."

"I'll take care of the man behind the boulder."

He dipped his chin. "And I'll take care of the other two."

Rick motioned for Reid to follow him, then led the way deeper into the forest. After fifty feet, they split up—Reid going to the right, Rick to the left. As she swung around, making her way to the front of the house, she focused on where she stepped so she wouldn't make any noise. Their plan would only work if they took the assassins by surprise.

Creeping through the forest, Reid couldn't believe she was about to take on a group of assassins. If her theory was correct, they weren't anything more than hired mercenaries. Had these men been trained assassins—like Ackley—Reid would already be dead.

At the front of the house, she hid behind a tree and scanned the area, searching for the three men. The one in the tree was easy to spot since he was on one of the lower branches, which exposed most of his body. He had his bow aimed at the front door.

With a dagger in each hand, she peeked around the other side of the tree. The man behind the boulder focused on the front door, his back to her. If she ran straight at him, she could strike him from behind. The hit would have to be hard and well-placed in order to do any damage. And she'd have to be quick before the man in the tree shot her. Taking a deep breath, she prepared to attack.

Rick's axe flew through the air, startling Reid. After a sickening *crunch*, a man tumbled onto his side, an axe protruding from his head. Vomit rose in her mouth. She hadn't even seen the third assassin hidden behind the tree about twenty feet away. Rick burst through the area, heading straight for the fallen man.

He must be running for his weapon—which meant he was exposed to the man in the tree. Whirling, Reid aimed her dagger at the archer, who already had his bow trained on Rick. Reid threw her weapon, the dagger striking the assassin's arm. His head swung to the side, easily spotting her from his elevated position. A cruel smile twisted his lips.

Rick put his booted foot on the fallen man, his hands wrapping around the handle of his axe as he yanked it out of the guy's head. The assassin behind the boulder had withdrawn his sword, and he stalked toward Rick.

Reid squinted at the archer in the tree. She only had one dagger left, so she couldn't afford to throw it at him. There were several smaller rocks on the ground. Keeping her eyes on the archer, she squatted and picked up one the size of her hand.

The archer pointed an arrow directly at her. She hid behind the tree so he couldn't strike. Her heart beat frantically as she readjusted the rock in her hand. Peering around the trunk, she breathed a sigh of relief the archer hadn't moved from his spot.

Rick and the third assassin circled one another, neither sparing her a thought.

Sucking in a breath, she chucked the rock at the archer's head as hard as she could, striking him in the temple. He fell from the tree, landing on his back, his bow snapping in two. Reid ran at him, dagger in hand, prepared to make the killing blow.

The archer sprang to his feet, facing Reid. She skidded to a halt. His fingers curled as he came at her, swinging his fist toward her face. She ducked, twisted, and rammed her dagger into his exposed stomach. Grunting, he punched her in the side. She stumbled to the ground, gasping in pain. He reached down, picked her up, and threw her. She sailed through the air, landing five feet away flat on her back. Pain exploded through her body, stars floating across her vision. Reid couldn't breathe.

Out of the corner of her eye, she saw Rick hack off his assailant's arm. Unable to watch, she choked back a gag and focused on the archer stalking toward her. He withdrew her dagger from his arm, then stood above her, glaring as she lay on the ground, unable to move or defend herself.

A hissing sound reached her ears. The archer crumbled to the ground, an axe protruding from his back.

Rick knelt next to her. "Are you okay?"

Tears slid down her face. Everything hurt. "Are they dead?" she wheezed.

"Yes. All three are dead."

"Good." She stared up into his face. "Thank you. I'm glad you know how to fight. I wouldn't have survived on my own." Breathing was painful, and she feared she'd broken something.

His grin was fierce. "I've chopped a lot of wood over the years. Never realized how handy my axe was until now." He reached down to help her sit up.

She hissed, pain piercing her side.

"It's okay," he said. "I've got you." He picked her up, then carried her toward the house.

CHAPTER FIFTEEN

The door flew open. "Is she all right?" Dexter demanded.

"She's fine," Rick said. "I think she may have a broken rib." He stepped into the house, carefully setting Reid on the bed.

"You can come out," Dexter called to Ava.

Ava stepped out from the closet, a kitchen knife in hand. Rick rushed to her side, enveloping her in a hug.

"Reid," Dexter said, sitting beside her on the bed. "Look at me."

She did as he asked, tears streaming down her face.

"How many fingers am I holding up?"

"Two," she answered.

"Does it hurt to breathe?"

"It's getting better."

He lifted the hem of her shirt, examining her stomach. "I'm going to touch your ribs. Let me know where it hurts." His fingertips trailed over her right side, then her left.

She hissed. "Right there. In the middle." Where the archer had punched her before tossing her like a rag doll. Her back and arms felt scraped raw, but that was nothing compared to the stabbing sensation in her torso.

"It's already turning purple." He lowered her shirt. "You probably have a broken rib. First, I need to clean up the mess outside. When I come back, I'll wrap your torso to help with the pain."

"What about your shoulder?" she asked.

"I had Ava sew it when you left to use the privy. I know how much you hate that sort of thing."

Reid hadn't realized he'd noticed her reaction when he'd sewn Colbert up. "Please be careful. You don't want to split it open."

He nodded, then instructed Ava to stay with Reid while he and Rick went outside to dispose of the bodies before they attracted attention—whether animal or human.

"If you'll allow me," Ava said to Reid, "I'd like to clean you up while the men are out."

Reid gratefully agreed, not wanting Dexter to tend to her ribs. His touch on her skin was too intimate.

Ava made a paste to help reduce the swelling, then applied it over the already-forming bruise on Reid's ribs. When she finished, Ava wrapped a strip of fabric around Reid's torso to help stabilize her ribs. Sitting up and being bandaged brought tears to Reid's eyes.

"There now," Ava said when she finished. "Let's put a clean shirt on you. This one has some blood." Setting Reid's shirt aside, Ava then retrieved one of her own and helped Reid put it on.

"I'm so sorry we've barged into your life like this," Reid said, sniffling.

"It's fine. A little excitement now and then is good. Of course, this is enough to last us for years." She smiled. "Should I start a fire?"

"No. There could be more assassins out there."

"I'll get some blankets then. The temperature will drop drastically now that the sun has set." After shutting the curtains, she lit a candle. She put one quilt on the bed and one on the floor. "I never managed to cook supper."

"Just some bread will be fine." Reid wasn't hungry, but she needed to eat to keep her strength up.

Silently, they ate two slices of bread each. Sometime later, the men returned with wet hair. They'd probably washed off in the nearby river after getting rid of the bodies. After the men ate and it was time for bed, Ava and Rick insisted on sleeping on the floor. No amount of protesting on Reid's part could change their minds. She made a mental note to send this kind couple something special once she returned to the palace, so they would understand how thankful Reid was for their hospitality.

Dexter took the first watch. In the middle of the night, he crawled in bed and Rick stepped out to take the second watch.

Freezing, Reid snuggled next to Dexter, trying to stay warm in the frigid house.

The following day, Dexter was eager to start their journey home. Since Rick didn't have any horses, Dexter and Reid had to walk. Although it would take them longer on foot, Reid was secretly glad she didn't have to ride in her condition.

With the possibility of more assassins showing up, Rick and Ava decided to leave the comfort of their home and travel south, no plans to return for weeks. Once safely back at the palace, Dexter intended to send soldiers to patrol the area to ensure no further harm came to the couple.

Armed with daggers, knives, and bread, Dexter and Reid set out, heading southeast.

"Are you sure you can walk?" Dexter asked for the tenth time in less than thirty minutes.

"If I said no, what would you do? Carry me?"

"Hmmm," he murmured. "Possibly."

She glared at him over her shoulder, making him chuckle. He'd insisted on remaining behind her in case she stumbled or slowed.

"Head more to the left," he said.

"How do you know where we are?" Everything looked the same to Reid. With the trees towering around them, it was hard to keep track of the sun's position.

"I've studied Axian's land and terrain all my life. Aren't you intimately familiar with your county?"

"The land around my castle, yes. But not all of Ellington."

"I suspect that's because your father was hiding you. If you'd been a normal male heir, you would have traveled throughout Ellington. You'd have ended up knowing most towns and lakes."

Every step sent a sharp pain shooting through Reid's torso. Each breath made her cringe. How could one little broken bone hurt so badly? She focused all her concentration into putting one foot in front of the other.

When it became too dark to safely travel, they stopped. Since neither had a traveling bag, they'd taken one blanket from Ava, who'd filled it with bread. Dexter untied the blanket, then handed Reid half a loaf. After eating, they nuzzled next to one another, trying to stay warm. Instead of spreading the blanket on the ground, they used it to cover their bodies.

"We shouldn't be in this position," Reid mumbled as she tried to get comfortable. The leaf-coated ground was damp, a trail of ants not far away. Closing her eyes, she tried not to think about what else could be crawling around nearby.

"I know," he said, his whispered voice tickling Reid's ear. "I should have had more guards with me. I apologize for our predicament."

"I meant we shouldn't be next to one another like this." The back of her body pressed against the front of his, every inch of her touching him. Although, it was easier being this close to him when she didn't have to look at his face. For some reason, when she noticed him watching her, it made her breathing speed up, her stomach clench, and her face warm. His gaze was too piercing, he saw too much, and he noticed everything.

"Since we're already in a compromising position, this shouldn't matter." He wrapped his arm over her hip, resting his hand against her stomach.

She froze, unsure what to think or do. He was touching her—not in any sort of a romantic way, of course—and he was purposefully doing it. And...she liked it.

"Are you okay?" His voice vibrated through her body.

Why did he have this effect on her? No one had ever made her feel this way before. On a few occasions, she'd felt the start of something with Gordon. But nothing like this. This—this scared her because she was starting to like the man curled around her. "I'm just cold," she said, shivering.

After tucking her head under his chin, he tightened his arm around her body. Her heart pounded so loudly she feared he could hear it.

"Better?" he asked.

"Yes." Her voice came out hoarse.

"How's your rib doing?"

"It's sore but manageable."

"Good. I want to look at it tomorrow." He trailed his fingers up her torso, skimming lightly over her ribs. "If it gets any worse, please tell me." His fingers hovered just below her left breast before he swept them down her torso, stopping at her waist.

Reid wanted to press against his warm body, but she forced herself to remain still. She didn't want to embarrass herself by acting like a love-struck idiot. Not that she *was* love-struck by any means. They were simply acquaintances who were getting married. Well, maybe they were more than mere acquaintances. She supposed they were friends now. Probably friends. Becoming friends at least.

"Reid," he murmured, sending a chill down her spine.

"Yes?"

After a pause that lasted a little too long, he whispered, "Never mind. Go to sleep."

Sleep was a long time coming.

———

Reid peeled her eyes opened. At the sight before her, she jerked her head back, smacking into Dexter's chin. He cursed.

"What are you doing?" Gytha demanded. She squatted in front of Reid, inches from her face. A dozen soldiers stood fanned out behind her.

"We *were* sleeping," Dexter mumbled.

Gytha's eyes narrowed. "We killed six assassins. According to the one we questioned, there are still six unaccounted for. And you were sleeping?"

It was too early for this. Yawning, Reid rubbed her eyes.

"Three," Dexter said.

"What?" Gytha asked, her brow wrinkling.

"Reid killed three, so only three are unaccounted for."

"Lady Reid killed three men by herself?" Gytha asked, her voice betraying her doubt.

"Yes. Now, take the soldiers at least thirty feet away and wait there for us. I need a moment alone with Reid."

Face blank, Gytha stood and gave the order.

Once they were gone, Dexter asked, "How are you feeling?"

"Better." Reid rolled onto her back, grimacing from the pain. Not only did her ribs hurt, but so did her side from sleeping on the hard ground.

Dexter chuckled. "I hate to break it to you, but you drool. There's a line of dirt stuck to your face from the corner of your lip to your ear."

"And I hate to break it to you, but I don't care." Using her sleeve, she wiped her face off. She probably had dirt and leaves stuck in her hair as well. "And just so you know, you snore."

"I do not."

"Except you do." She smiled at him.

After rising, he brushed the dirt from his body. He grabbed the blanket, folded it, and set it aside. "I've broken a rib before. It's no fun." He squatted next to Reid, then helped her to a sitting position.

Being sure to move slowly, she got to her knees before attempting to stand. Everything hurt worse than it did yesterday.

"I was going to help you up."

Shrugging, she replied, "I didn't need your help."

He placed his large hands on her shoulders, forcing her to meet his eyes. "I know you don't need my help, but you can't fault a guy for trying."

No, she supposed she couldn't.

He released her. "My soldiers will escort us back to the palace now."

As she followed him, she thought about what Gytha had said—they'd killed six of the twelve assassins. Had Gytha's group encountered them while searching for the prince? Or had the assassins managed to infiltrate the palace? If something had happened to a member of the royal family, Gytha would have mentioned it. Reid had to assume everyone was all right.

"We thought you'd each have a horse," Gytha said as Reid and Dexter approached.

Reid didn't want to ride a horse right now. The animal's movement would be too jarring.

Dexter ordered a smaller soldier to dismount and double with someone else. After, he told Gytha to ride that horse while he commandeered hers. He brought the animal to a stop in front of Reid.

Skeptically, she eyed the huge beast, knowing she couldn't climb on it in her condition. Dexter must have realized the same because he slid his hands onto Reid's hips, hoisting her up. After she settled in the saddle, he mounted behind her.

"What are you doing?" she asked, thankful she had pants on and could sit normally.

"You're small, and we're short a horse."

Well, yes, she knew that. But it didn't mean he had to ride with her.

"Would you be more comfortable with Gytha?"

Quickly, she shook her head.

"That's what I thought." Reaching around her, he grabbed the reins. "By sitting so close to you, I'll know if the horse jars you too much. If it does, we'll stop for a break."

His thoughtfulness surprised her. Instead of thanking him, she mumbled, "I'm perfectly capable of steering the horse."

"I know. But this way, I can make sure you don't topple off."

She sighed. His soldiers would think she was an incompetent fool who couldn't care for herself.

"Listen up," Dexter said, addressing everyone. "My fiancée, Lady Reid, is injured. She has at least one broken rib. In addition, my shoulder is recovering from an arrow wound. We'll be riding slow."

With that, Gytha gave the order to set out. The rocking movement only hurt Reid's ribs slightly.

"You can lean against me," Dexter said. "I won't bite."

He may not bite, but she was afraid she would enjoy the comfort and warmth of him too much. She tried to remain slightly forward, away from him. However, it was no use. Giving up, she relaxed against him.

"Gytha," Reid said, capturing the woman's attention.

Gytha rode directly in front of them. Shifting her horse to the side, she waited for them to catch up until they rode side by side. "Yes, Lady Reid?"

"How did you know Prince Dexter had been attacked by assassins and was in need of assistance?"

"Princess Nara sent us after the prince. She said he'd left the palace with only four soldiers, which was simply inadequate. We stumbled upon the wagon. One of our soldiers was still alive. He told us what happened and which direction you'd gone."

"Did you send him to the palace for medical treatment?" Dexter asked.

"Yes. I don't know if he'll make it," Gytha said. "But I had two soldiers escort him back."

They exited the forest and turned east, traveling on a dirt road.

"We've been searching for two days," Gytha said.

"I'm sure I'll get a long lecture when I get home," Dexter muttered.

"As you should." Gytha nudged her horse. The animal sped up, returning to its previous place in front.

"When we stop, I'll need to check your wrapping," Dexter said.

"Gytha can help me with that." Reid had no intention of removing her shirt in front of Dexter.

He chuckled. "I can tell it's no use trying to convince you that I'm better than Gytha at treating injuries. I know I am, and I'm fairly certain you do, too. In that case, you must be serious and your mind unchangeable if you want Gytha's help."

Reid rammed her elbow into his stomach, which only made him laugh. Gytha glared at them over her shoulder.

"I guess we need to be quiet in case there are assassins lurking nearby," he whispered in Reid's ear.

Why was Dexter acting as if he and Reid were good friends? Was it because of what they'd just been through? No, she was certain his kindness had started before then. She couldn't pinpoint when exactly, but it had been before this trip.

When they stopped to set up camp, Dexter led Gytha a few feet away, then spoke quietly with her. The soldiers began to unroll their bedrolls and prepare a meal. One female soldier offered her bedroll for Reid's use, then unpacked it for her.

Dexter approached with Gytha. "She is going to take you far enough away so no one can see you. Then, she'll unwrap your bindings to check your rib and back." He left no room for argument.

Reid followed Gytha into the cover of the trees. "When you're done helping me, I want you to have someone look at Prince Dexter's shoulder to make sure infection hasn't set in."

"Yes, Lady Reid."

Reid had never heard the woman agree so readily. Or take an order from Reid for that matter.

Once they'd gone far enough, Reid removed her shirt and wrap.

Gytha examined her. "It looks like two cracked ribs. How did this happen?"

"An assassin punched me, then tossed me on the ground."

"Commander Dexter informed me that you saved his life by throwing your body in front of an arrow."

Clearly, the woman was fishing for information. Reid wanted to make sure she conveyed her loyalty. "Yes. I couldn't let anything happen to him. He is too valuable to Axian."

"Let me see your back," Gytha said, her voice soft and without its usual harshness. "It's swollen, but it looks fine." She rewrapped the fabric tightly around Reid. "I know this is uncomfortable, but it will help."

When they returned to camp, Reid felt off-kilter over this nicer version of Gytha.

Late the following night, they reached the palace. All Reid wanted was a hot bath and a soft bed. A soldier had ridden ahead to let Prince Henrick know Prince Dexter and Lady Reid were about to arrive and both needed medical attention. When Dexter steered his horse into the stables, a dozen people Reid didn't recognize waited for them.

Dexter ignored them as he dismounted. Reaching up, he

placed his firm hands on Reid's waist, lifting her off the horse and setting her on solid ground. "Besides being seen by a healer, you don't have to talk to anyone tonight," he murmured. "They can all wait until tomorrow." He took her hand, leading her toward the exit.

Nara, Henrick, and Colbert entered the stables. When Nara threw her arms around her son for a hug, Reid wiggled her hand free.

"I want Lady Reid seen by a healer," Dexter said. "She has at least one broken or cracked rib."

Nara released Dexter, then scanned Reid from head to toe. "Then I won't hug you. Come, I'll help you to your room and see you're taken care of." Nara hooked her arm with Reid's, leading her out of the stables and into the main portion of the palace.

"Can you please make sure someone looks at Dexter's shoulder?" Reid asked. She hadn't seen any sign of infection. However, until a healer examined it, she would continue to worry.

Nara ordered one of the soldiers they passed to fetch a healer for the prince. "The soldier who arrived before you only said there were injuries sustained. He didn't say what happened."

"We were ambushed by assassins. Twice. Dexter was shot in his arm by an arrow. I was punched and thrown." A short, succinct version of what happened. Dexter could fill Nara in on the details later.

Entering her suite, Reid found the candles already lit. Joce had a hot bath waiting, too. Nara helped remove Reid's leather armor, clothes, and the wrap around her torso. Then, both women assisted Reid into the bath. Reid would have protested if she had the strength. But the hot water seeped into her muscles, relaxing her. After washing, she got out of the bath and dressed.

Nara asked Joce to fetch the healer. When the lady's maid was gone, Nara helped Reid get into bed.

"You don't need to stay with me. I can manage on my own." Now that Reid was in bed, her eyelids became heavy. She was certain Nara had better things to do than tend to her—like making sure Dexter was okay.

Nara laughed. "I'm happy you're home. Helping you gives me something to do while allowing me to express my gratitude."

The word *home* still applied to Reid's castle in Ellington—not this grand palace in Axian. Tears filled Reid's eyes, but she blinked them away. She could miss her father and sisters when she was alone. Now, she needed to remain strong and in control.

Nara reached out, pushing stray tendrils of hair away from Reid's face and gently stroking her cheeks. "I always wanted a daughter."

Instead of responding, Reid closed her eyes and willed her tears away. She would not cry.

The healer entered. "I've been summoned by multiple people to check on Lady Reid." She sat on the bed beside Reid, flashing a kind smile. "I hear you may have broken ribs?"

Reid nodded, lifting her nightshirt so the woman could examine her.

"It feels like one cracked rib to me," the healer replied. "I'll put a salve on it for swelling and wrap your torso. That's all that can be done."

While she worked, Nara stood at the window, staring out into the night.

"There," the healer said as she finished, pulling Reid's shirt back down. "If the pain becomes too uncomfortable, send for me. I'll bring some medicine."

Nara showed the healer from the room, then moved around the perimeter of the bedchamber, snuffing out the candles. When she finished, she pulled the blankets over Reid, adjusting them.

Having grown up without a mother, Reid had never had someone fuss over her like this. The only reason she had tears in her eyes—*again*—was due to her injury and exhaustion. Nothing else.

Nara perched on the edge of the bed. "I want to thank you."

"It's not a big deal," Reid mumbled. "Anyone would have done the same." She closed her eyes, sleep threatening to take over. "And my mother's leather armor saved me, so it all worked out."

"The armor saved you?" Nara asked.

"Yes, from the arrow I took in the back for Dexter."

"You didn't tell me about that."

"Then what are you thanking me for?" Confused, Reid opened her eyes to survey the princess.

Nara squeezed Reid's shoulder. "I was thanking you for bringing my son some joy."

That seemed like an odd thing to say considering what Reid and Dexter had just been through.

"Dexter closes himself off to other people. He doesn't have many in his inner circle. Even those closest to him, he keeps at a distance. Tonight, when I saw how protective he was of you, when I saw him holding your hand, I knew you'd finally broken through his barriers."

"I don't know about that. We've just been through a trying experience is all."

Smiling, Nara stood. "You don't give yourself enough credit. The first time I met you, I knew the two of you would be good together."

"Please tell me you didn't send the assassins after us in order to bring us closer together."

Nara barked out a laugh. "Although that's an intriguing idea, I would never do that. Now if you'll excuse me, I need to go check on my son. We'll talk more in the morning." She paused in the doorway. "I'm glad you're home safe and sound, Lady Reid. Right where you belong."

The following morning, Reid woke up to find Nara in her bedchamber, a tray filled with food in hand. "Oh good, you're awake. I brought breakfast." Nara placed the tray next to Reid, then sat beside her. "I need you to meet with the seamstress today so she can finish making your wedding dress." She bit the tip of her thumb while eyeing Reid.

"What is it?" Reid asked, pushing to a sitting position.

"I sent messengers to personally invite guests to the wedding. Some of the responses we expected. For instance, your father, your sisters, your grandparents, and all the dukes."

"Really? I'm surprised the dukes would want to travel so far." Reid took a bite of oatmeal. Would Harlan attend the wedding? Maybe he'd come with his new bride. What about Knox? Reid couldn't envision Knox there.

"I assume the dukes want to see Axian for themselves," Nara said.

Which made sense since trade and travel had stopped between Axian and northern Marsden for the last two decades. Reid took a sip of her tea, the hot liquid sliding down her throat and warming her.

"Which brings me to those we did not expect to attend the wedding."

Setting her teacup on the tray, she waited for Nara to continue, an ominous feeling starting to rise.

"The king is coming."

"That's unfortunate." Reid had hoped to never see the man again.

"I agree." Nara stood and went to the window, pushing the curtains aside to let in the bright morning sunlight. "Which means we have a lot to do to prepare for his arrival."

"I'll get dressed so I can help."

"No, my dear. You need to rest today. Otherwise, my son will have a fit."

Reid wasn't sure she could remain in bed all day long. Besides, staying busy would keep her mind off the fact Eldon was coming.

"Up for visitors?" Colbert asked from the doorway.

"Come in." Reid smiled, glad to see him.

"I'll leave you two to chat," Nara said. "I need to attend a meeting on security."

"Why does it seem like one of us is always injured?" Colbert said as he came into the room, folding his arms.

"Maybe it's a sign for us to be more careful."

He grinned. "Well, there's someone who's dying to see you if you're up for visitors."

When she nodded, he whistled. Finn bounded into the room, Colbert yelling at him not to jump on the bed and hurt Aunt Reid. She laughed, loving the nickname he'd bestowed upon her.

"How are things around here?" she asked, petting Finn's head. He licked her hand.

"Since we found out the king is coming, Mother and Father have been in endless meetings."

It looked like he wanted to say more, but he refrained from doing so.

"Is something the matter?"

Arms still crossed, he studied her before saying, "No, Lady Reid, there's nothing the matter. But I need to go. I have a meeting of my own I must attend." Finn ran after him, wagging his tail.

CHAPTER SIXTEEN

Reid spent the day lounging in bed. The only time she got up was when the seamstress came to take her measurements. After the sun set and darkness blanketed the city, Reid became antsy, no longer able to handle her confinement. Sliding out of bed, she went over to the window, gazing out at the city. Colbert's words kept replaying in her mind. Who was he meeting with? What exactly did Colbert do in the library all day?

On a whim, she decided to snoop. After dressing in pants and a tunic, she pulled her hair back and grabbed a dagger. Not that she needed a weapon in the palace. However, she felt better having one in case another assassin showed up.

She eased out her door, then crept along the dark hallway. At the top of the staircase, she encountered two soldiers.

"Can we escort you somewhere, Lady Reid?" the one on the right whispered.

"No. I'm just going to get something to eat." Thankfully, they didn't insist on accompanying her. She slowly made her way down the steps, her ribs not nearly as painful as yesterday.

On the first floor, she headed to the library. With none of the hallway candles lit, odd shadows filled the corridors. Someone had propped the library doors open. Pressing against the wall, Reid listened but didn't hear anything, so she peered around the corner. Two figures headed right toward her. She hid behind the door, hoping neither had spotted her. Were they sentries on patrol? Or could it be Dexter and Colbert?

The pair exited the library and turned left, walking away from Reid's hiding place. She poked her head around the door, watching them retreat. Based upon their heights and body shapes, she believed it was Dexter and Colbert. At the end of the hallway, they made a left. Reid hurried after them, unable to run because her torso hurt too badly. At the corner, she peeked around the edge, watching as they exited the palace.

Taking a deep breath, she considered her options. Follow them or go back to bed?

She smacked her head against the wall. The Knights had tasked her with discovering where Dexter went at night. This was her chance. So why was she hesitating? Well, for one, her ribs hurt. Two, the last time she'd tried spying, it hadn't worked out so well. She could just ask Dexter about his nightly escapades, but he probably wouldn't tell her what he was doing. And did it matter whether she got the information the Knights requested? Was she truly loyal to them above all else? Especially when she was only going to continue being a Knight for a short time? Most importantly—to her, at least—did it matter to Reid if Dexter was the leader to a group of revolutionaries seeking to make Axian its own kingdom?

Cursing, she exited the palace and hurried across the lawn in the same direction the brothers had gone. Looking at the situation objectively, if she'd been on her way to the kitchen for food and saw Dexter leave the palace in the middle of the night, she would have followed him out of curiosity. So, in actuality, she was doing this for herself and not the Knights.

When she reached the first set of buildings, she peered down the main street, searching for the brothers. Only a handful of people were out at this late hour. The streetlamps were dim, the city fairly dark. A few windows in the surrounding buildings were illuminated. In order for this to work, she needed to make sure she behaved normally, not like a spy snooping around. She straightened, rolling her shoulders back and trying not to wince.

Strolling around the corner, she acted like she had somewhere to be. Even though she didn't see Dexter or Colbert anywhere, she refused to stop or deviate from her current course. She walked with purpose while scanning the doorways and side streets. A thought suddenly occurred to her—how would she get back in the palace if the doors were locked? Would she be forced to knock? The entry and exit points had to be monitored. Last time she'd been here with Harlan and tried her hand at spying, she'd assumed security to be lax because she hadn't seen any sentries. How wrong she'd been. The same was probably true tonight. Someone had to see her leave. Would they report her absence to Dexter? This had been a terrible idea. She should have thought this through before she'd left the palace. Why had Ackley ever made her a Knight? She suspected it was simply because she could act like a man when needed since she was the worst spy ever.

Leaning against the nearest building, she closed her eyes. She should be in bed, not traipsing around the city on a stupid endeavor. Returning to the palace and pretending this night never happened was her best bet. She'd just tell the Knights she'd failed.

"Care to explain what you're doing here?" Dexter asked, his voice low and calm.

Reid's eyes flew open, her heart pounding. Both Dexter and Colbert stood in front of her.

"Are you following us?" Colbert asked, folding his arms across his chest.

Glancing between the two brothers, Reid felt as if she'd violated their trust. "I'm sorry," she whispered. "I know I shouldn't be here. I was just about to return to the palace."

"We were actually wondering how long it would take you to follow us," Colbert said.

"The first day you arrived at the palace, we made a bet," Dexter explained. "You lasted longer than either of us thought."

They didn't sound furious, nor had they attempted to drag her back to the palace. "Is it safe for you two to be out here like this? Especially seeing as someone tried to assassinate you not too long ago?"

"Are you concerned about our well-being?" Colbert asked, his eyes alight with mischief.

"Of course I am. Are you at least armed?"

"Are you?" Dexter chuckled. "Don't answer that—I'm sure you are." He took a step closer, invading her personal space. "You're not the first person who has tried, and failed, to follow us. Let's go."

"That's the wrong way." He was headed away from the palace, not toward it.

"Aren't you curious?" Dexter asked.

About what the brothers were up to? "Yes, but you don't have to tell me. I don't want to impose on whatever it is you are doing."

"You're not imposing," Colbert assured her. "I've been wanting to tell you. It's your fiancé who's been on the fence. Seems he's finally decided to trust you."

Trust. That was a big, important, and loaded word. Suddenly, Reid wasn't sure she wanted to be included. Whatever they were up to, the Knights wanted to know about it for a reason. "Wait." If she didn't discover their secret, she'd never have to worry about violating their trust.

"What is it?" Dexter asked.

"I'll go back to the palace. You don't need to include me."

"Are you sure?" Dexter asked.

"I'm sure."

He eyed her. "Sometimes I can't figure you out."

"The feeling is mutual."

"All right. Follow me." Dexter led the way into a narrow alley.

Reid thought he was returning her to the palace in a roundabout way. However, he stopped before the door to a tall, narrow building. He unlocked it, then ushered her and Colbert inside.

A long hallway stretched out before them. Dexter opened a door on the right, and they descended a steep staircase. At the bottom, a single torch revealed a plain, empty room that had to be underground. There was a door on the wall opposite the stairs.

"Is there anything you'd like to tell me?" Dexter asked.

Colbert leaned against the wall, not saying a word as he watched Reid.

She pinched the bridge of her nose, trying to decide what to do. If, as Anna suspected, Dexter was leading a group of revolutionaries, who were in direct opposition to what the Knights were trying to accomplish, it would force Reid into a precarious position.

"Now's the time to reveal any secrets you may have." Dexter waited for her to speak, his body tense but face relaxed.

It was obvious he knew she was keeping something from him. Given his well-trained soldiers, he probably had a network of spies to rival Ackley's. "I barely know you." Maybe the change she'd sensed in him lately was an act. Maybe he was only trying to gain her trust so she'd tell him everything she knew—about the Knights, about Ackley, about the king.

"We're on the same side," he insisted. "I'd like for us to start working together."

Were they working toward the same goals, though? Could she —should she—trust Dexter? Her gut instincts insisted he was trustworthy. With the Knights, she'd been told to trust them. However, she always questioned if trusting them was the right thing. Sometimes, it didn't feel natural to blindly accept their word. With Dexter, those hesitations were gone. "There's one thing I haven't told you."

"What is it?"

"I'm sworn to secrecy." Although, Ackley had told Gordon and Idina.

"What if you showed me?" he asked, taking a step closer.

He knew—she was sure of it. He'd looked at her wrist once before, as if searching for the Knight's mark. Maybe his father had told him about the secret organization. Or he could have figured it out. Thinking back, she'd been in bed next to him without her shirt on. Maybe he'd spied her mark then? Or Gytha could have noticed it when Reid removed her tunic to let the warrior woman inspect her injuries. Reid smacked her forehead. She'd forgotten Nara and Joce had helped her bathe. So many people had the opportunity to see the tattoo on Reid's arm.

Reid needed to tell Dexter. Keeping it from him would only complicate their budding friendship. Besides, the other part of her assignment was to gain his trust. Revealing her tattoo would certainly do that. She pushed her sleeve up, then twisted her arm to expose the rose with a dagger tattooed on the underside near her elbow. His eyes widened slightly, as if he'd suspected but hadn't honestly believed it until now. Lowering her sleeve, she waited for his verdict, eyes trained on him.

"Thank you for trusting me. Now, I'm going to trust you."

Colbert pushed off the door, then opened it to reveal another dark hallway. When he stepped inside, Reid followed. Dexter grabbed a torch, then joined them.

Every door that closed behind them had the distinct sound of a bolt sliding into place. No wonder the Knights hadn't discovered where Dexter was going. This was the only way in—having Reid gain his trust so he'd bring her along. A wave of dizziness washed over her. Feeling faint, she leaned against the wall. "Wait."

"Are your ribs bothering you?" Dexter asked.

She shook her head. "Something's wrong."

"What do you mean?"

Pieces started to fall into place. "I feel like I've been put here for a reason."

"Explain," Colbert said.

"I don't have any evidence. It's just a feeling that someone wanted me to get close to Dexter, to gain his trust, in order for him to bring me here. And I don't know the reason."

"Why do you think that?" Dexter asked.

"Comments people have made, things I've seen, places I've been. It's like a game of chess, and I'm a pawn. Someone has been moving me into position. Now, it's their time to strike." And she didn't know if she wanted to be used that way. What if she didn't agree with the outcome? She didn't like having her choices taken away from her.

Dexter chuckled. "And by strike, do you mean take down the king? Checkmate?"

"Exactly."

"If that's the case, is that a bad thing?"

They were on dangerous ground. She didn't think he referred to a game of chess any longer. "I don't know. But if I go through that door, everything will change."

"You're right," Colbert said. "Everything will change. But it's your choice. You can come with us or you can return to the palace. Just know we wouldn't have invited you along tonight if we didn't believe this is something you'd embrace."

Reid noticed his use of the word *invited*. Had everything been a setup? Was she simply a pawn to everyone?

Dexter placed his hand on her shoulder. "Are you in or are you out?"

She focused on his vibrant eyes, trying to understand this man she'd been so careful to shield herself from. Only, over the past week, she'd gotten to know him better. But had it been the real Dexter or a façade he wanted her to believe?

He raised his eyebrows. "What's your hesitation?"

"That I'm a disposable pawn." That Dexter didn't care for her at all and was only using her.

He squeezed her shoulder. "You're my fiancée." His voice was strong, assured. "We're getting married. I'd like to have a partner. Someone with the same goals as me. I'm asking you to work with me. We can accomplish more together."

She teetered on indecision. Whatever was behind that door would change everything between her and the Knights. It had the potential to alter Reid's entire future. However, if she'd learned one thing through the years, it was to always trust her instincts. Everything about Dexter and Colbert felt right.

"Okay, I'm in."

Dexter's shoulders relaxed ever so slightly as he shot her a grin. "I was hoping you'd say that."

"Let's go." Colbert opened the door.

Reid stepped through the doorway into a dimly lit room filled with what had to be over fifty men and women of all ages. Most sat on chairs arranged in rows facing the front, while a few stood at the back.

"He's here," someone announced. "Now we can begin."

Dexter strode to the front as if he'd done this a hundred times before. Colbert inclined his head for Reid to follow, leading her to the back. She leaned against the wall, observing those in attendance. Most everyone wore regular, generic merchant clothing. Reid straightened, taking a second look. The man in front of her had calluses on his hands. They could be from wielding an axe, plough, or a sword. The woman next to him had her sleeves rolled up to reveal strong, muscled arms. These were no ordinary merchants. A band of revolutionaries perhaps?

"Thank you all for coming," Dexter said. "We're still monitoring the ports. I believe the king is working with Melenia— a kingdom to the east of Marsden. It's about a two-week journey by ship."

"Do you know what he's planning?" someone asked.

"I do not. However, we believe small groups of men, maybe soldiers, have been arriving over the past month or two."

"Are they here in Axian?" a woman called.

"My sources report they are mostly in Bridger. However, we will continue to monitor the situation." His commanding voice was assured, easily capturing and maintaining everyone's attention. "The main reason for the meeting tonight is to discuss something of the utmost importance. An opportunity has presented itself, and I think it's time to act."

"So soon?" another woman said.

"This opportunity is too good to pass up," Dexter answered. "We may not get another chance. But it requires us to act quickly."

"What's the opportunity?" a man in the front row asked.

"We just received word that King Eldon will be in attendance for my wedding. He'll be staying in the palace. We won't get a better chance to assassinate him."

Reid jolted, almost smacking her head against the wall in her shock. Assassinate the king? That was what these people were here to discuss? She gaped at Colbert. Was he on board with this plot?

Colbert actually winked at her.

She'd thought about the possibility of Dexter's group wanting to split from the kingdom of Marsden to become their own kingdom. However, she hadn't considered they'd actually assassinate the king to take over.

"I'm thinking we can arrange for him to take a tour of the city," Dexter said. "An accident could happen during it."

Reid raised her hand, and Dexter pointed at her. "If you decide on this path, I suggest where, when, and how it happens is very carefully chosen," she said. "It needs to be clear that Prince Dexter, Prince Colbert, and Prince Henrick are in no way aware of or involved in the king's demise. Otherwise, Marsden will face a nasty civil war—which is what we are trying to avoid, correct?"

"Correct. Let's brainstorm some ideas."

Everyone started talking at once.

Slumping against the wall, Reid considered the ramifications of assassinating the king. "Colbert, your father doesn't want to be king."

"No, he doesn't. But we don't always get what we want."

Leaning closer to Colbert, she whispered, "Why don't we bring the king's legitimacy into question? Wouldn't that be easier than killing him?"

"We don't have proof."

"It doesn't matter," she replied. "We just have to plant a seed of doubt. And you never know—those letters may show up." If Ackley had them as Reid suspected, he might have a plan to use them when the right time presented itself. The other option was to ask Leigh to tell the truth about Eldon's father. However, that would cause two problems. One, Leigh had lied about who his father was in the first place, so why would anyone believe she was telling the truth now? And two, it forced Leigh to choose between her children. Telling the truth would strip Eldon of the crown, therefore making Gordon eligible for the throne.

Reid raised her hand again. When the room quieted, she said, "I think we should send letters to the dukes informing them Eldon is not Hudson's legal heir."

The room erupted in chaos.

"If we decide to go that route," Dexter said, reclaiming everyone's attention, "we need to do it now. *Before* everyone arrives for the wedding. The issue with that route is it allows for the possibility of two rulers—Prince Henrick versus Prince Gordon."

"The dukes would interpret the law, ultimately deciding who is crowned king," Reid added.

"We don't know what the outcome would be," Dexter said.

"What of the assassination?" someone asked.

"Maybe we should wait?" Reid suggested.

"We can't," Dexter replied. "This opportunity is too perfect. We won't get another chance like this."

"Once Eldon is dead," Reid said, "how do we know Prince Gordon won't ascend to the throne? After all, Prince Gordon is King Eldon's heir."

"She has a point," someone shouted.

"If the king accidentally dies while he's here, and all the dukes are present, then maybe we can contest the throne then?" someone said.

"What if the dukes decide to crown Prince Henrick, but he steps aside again?" someone else said. "The crown will go to Prince Gordon. Maybe we need to talk with Prince Henrick to see where he stands on the matter?"

In other words, these people wanted confirmation Prince Henrick would cooperate. Unfortunately, Reid didn't think he would.

"In order for the assassination plan to work," Reid said, unable to believe she was discussing murdering someone so casually, "we'll need to reveal that King Eldon is not Hudson's legal heir. I propose we write letters to the dukes and the other prominent families, throwing Eldon's birth into question. That way, once the king is eliminated, Prince Gordon won't automatically be crowned. If Prince Henrick refuses to accept the throne, I don't know what to do. The only suggestion I have is to hope we can convince him it's in the kingdom's best interest."

"Or maybe the family's," Colbert said. "Especially if Prince Dexter and Lady Reid announce they are expecting. That would solidify the throne."

At that exact moment, Reid happened to be looking right at Dexter and he at her. She felt her face go up in flames. If she were to get pregnant, as Colbert so eloquently suggested, she would need to be intimate with Dexter. That was something they'd touched upon earlier, when he'd said they were going to have separate rooms. She thought she'd have plenty of time to deal with that issue. Later. Much, much later.

"You two will need to get busy!" one of the men shouted boisterously. Hoots, laughter, and whistles rang throughout the room.

Mortification filled Reid. Not only was she not there to be sacrificed as a brood mare for *the cause,* but she also wasn't even certain she was ready to be intimate with Dexter. He probably felt the same way.

"I want everyone to think of plausible ways to take out the king while making his death appear accidental," Dexter said, expertly changing the course of the conversation back to the appropriate topic—if assassination could even be considered an appropriate topic. "Remember, it must look like an accident. We'll meet back here in one week to solidify plans."

Everyone exited the room, conversing in small clusters. When only Dexter, Colbert, and Reid were left, she plopped on one of the chairs, wincing from the movement. Reid was at a complete loss for words. If she opened her mouth, she was afraid only a plethora of questions would come out. Did they realize how insane they were for planning to assassinate the king? Were they aware that if the king found out, everyone involved would be killed? What did they plan to do about the fact Henrick didn't even want the throne? Couldn't they see there were other, less extreme ways to accomplish what they wanted without resorting to treason and murder? Oh, and did they genuinely understand she in no way wanted, was ready for, or could even imagine having a baby right now?

Colbert sat next to Reid. "You seem stressed."

"Wonder why," she mumbled.

"What are you thinking?" Dexter asked, straddling the chair in front of Reid so he could face her.

"That you're both crazy." Reid understood why they wanted to eliminate Eldon—she just didn't think it was the best course of action to take. She needed time to process the idea. She'd assumed she and Dexter would begin to implement the changes they wished to make over the years to come. She hadn't realized he'd planned to do something so extreme right now.

"We need to head back," Colbert said. "This is the tricky part."

"Sure...that's exactly what I was thinking," she muttered sarcastically. She rose, pain sparking in her ribs. "Getting back to the palace unnoticed is *definitely* the hard part. Not assassinating the king, not taking over Marsden, not any of those other seemingly impossible tasks, but simply returning home." She rolled her eyes.

"Come," Dexter said, ignoring her sarcasm. "We'll talk more about this when you're not so tired and the shock has had time to wear off." He took Reid's hand, leading her through the side door.

Reid glanced at their joined hands. It suddenly hit her like a ton of bricks—she was in over her head in all possible ways. Because she was fairly sure that she shouldn't feel a mix of comfort, strength, and desire every time she touched the man who was going to be her husband. How had she gone from being scared and intimidated by him to seeking his friendship? To maybe even wanting more?

CHAPTER SEVENTEEN

Dressed in a nightgown, Reid stared out her window, mulling over last night and what may or may not happen in the near future. If life were a game of chess, she needed to plot her next move carefully. No longer having the luxury of lying around in bed again all day—even if she did still need to heal—she went over to her armoire. There was too much to be done.

Pulling out an elegant green dress, she tossed it on the bed and considered the role she needed to play. Nara didn't want Reid to be a warrior—the princess wanted her to be a refined lady from the north. But that didn't mean Reid couldn't fight for what she believed in and wanted.

Joce entered the room to help Reid dress. Once Reid was presentable, she exited the bedchamber and headed to the royal family's private sitting room down the hall.

Nara and Henrick sat beside each other on the sofa, deep in conversation.

"Good morning," Reid said, loud enough to be certain they heard.

Henrick waved her forward, so Reid entered and sat across

from them. There was a detailed map of the palace on the low table between the sofas.

"What do you need me to do?" she asked.

Nara crossed her legs, leaning back against the sofa. "Dexter is at the military compound with his soldiers. He's assigning them various positions. Some will act as prominent merchants and landholders from throughout the county. Others will be on security detail. All visitors will be interspersed throughout the palace so we can maintain control at all times."

"Excellent." Reid examined the map, noting strategic locations where sentries would be placed in the palace. Some would be highly visible, while others would be hidden.

"Colbert is in the library going over your marriage contract," Henrick said. "He's making sure everything is in order. When your father arrives, he will look it over and sign it."

"What sort of stipulations do you have in place?" Reid had never thought to ask before now.

"On my end, I want it clear what happens when your father dies and you take over Ellington. What is Dexter's role going to be?"

An opportunity presented itself, so Reid decided to take it. "I'm certain my father isn't aware that Dexter is not your legal heir. This changes things, does it not? After all, once you pass, Dexter will have nothing. I'm not sure it's advantageous for me to marry Dexter."

"That's not necessarily true," Henrick said.

Nara pursed her lips, and Reid suspected the princess was pleased with this line of questioning.

"Eldon is Dexter and Colbert's half brother. Once I die, I'm sure they'll find a way to work together."

"You obviously don't know your son that well," Reid scoffed. "Eldon seeks power. Once he discovers he's your heir, he will take over Axian. He won't care about either of your sons. If anything, he'll see them as a threat and have them eliminated. Oh, wait, he already tried to do that with the assassination attempt—the one Dexter and I managed to survive."

"There's no proof Eldon sent the assassins."

Reid didn't feel like arguing with Henrick. If he refused to see reason, truth, and what was right in front of him, it was his loss.

"As long as Eldon doesn't see us as a threat, we'll be fine," Henrick added. "Once he realizes we want to remain here peaceably, he'll understand. He's my son, not Hudson's. Eldon is good."

Reid didn't want to tell Henrick how very wrong he was. "Regardless, once my father learns Dexter is not your heir, I'm not sure he'll go forward with the wedding contract." Deciding she'd said enough, she stood and exited the room, her hands shaking.

As she headed down the hallway, she heard someone approaching from behind. She turned to see Princess Nara actually sprinting toward her.

"Lady Reid," Nara said as she approached. "I want to talk to you privately." She pulled Reid into the closest room, which happened to be filled with portraits.

Before Nara had a chance to say anything, Reid said, "I'm sorry. I didn't mean to be so forward with you and your husband."

Nara wrapped Reid in a hug, surprising her. "No, my dear. I'm happy you said something." She held Reid at arm's length. "Everything you said is true. My husband only wants to see the good in people—especially those he loves. It's hard for him to look at the situation objectively."

"My father may already know Dexter is not Henrick's heir." And he may not care. His sole concern had been getting Reid to safety and maintaining his land and title.

"Everything happened so quickly that I don't remember the particulars. Colbert would be the one to see about that." Nara gave Reid another hug before they left the room.

Reid headed straight to the library. She found Colbert in his office with Finn curled on top of his feet. "My father will never sign the marriage contract once he learns Dexter isn't your father's heir."

"That's what I'm planning on." Colbert set his quill down, then leaned back in his chair.

"How'd you get him to sign the preliminary one?" she asked, perching on the chair across from him.

He pushed a piece of paper toward her. "When your father sent us his draft," he tapped the paper, "he mentioned you being his heir, but he left out anything regarding Dexter. My father agreed and returned it, stating we would finalize the details later." He pushed a second piece of paper toward her. "The king sent us this one."

Picking up both contracts, Reid quickly examined each. It was clear both assumed Dexter to be the heir, though neither specifically said so.

"I've amended the contract between our fathers, stating the particulars. For example, what happens when your father dies and you return to Ellington? I took the liberty of mentioning that since Dexter has no obligations in Axian, he is free to move to Ellington with you."

"When my father reads this, he's going to be furious."

"I would assume so." Colbert grinned. "I'm counting on it to force my father into changing his heir."

"Funny you should mention that...because I just had a conversation with Prince Henrick about this very thing."

"I knew there was a reason I liked you," Colbert said with a wink.

She shifted in the chair, wanting to discuss something with him, but not sure how to go about it.

"Reid, what is it?" he asked, leaning forward, his elbows resting on the desk.

"So, I thought of something..."

"Oh no, no more thinking," he teased.

She playfully kicked him under the desk, being careful not to hit the dog. "It's about the other night," she whispered, not wanting anyone to overhear their conversation. "If everything goes as planned and your father changes his heir and we're successful in that other endeavor..." She didn't want to say anything about assassinating the king in the palace. "That would mean Dexter would..." Again, she didn't want to say anything about Dexter ascending to the throne in case someone lurked nearby.

"Ah, you're finally figuring things out. Yes, that means Dexter would be the king."

Was that something Dexter even wanted? She certainly had no desire to be the queen. Maybe they should just leave Eldon alone.

"Reid," Colbert said, reaching across the desk and taking her hand. "If we do nothing now, we only prolong the inevitable. At some point, someone has to deal with this. Our fathers didn't, so now here we are. We still face the same issues. Let's take care of this once and for all."

"I don't want to rule." Just the idea of being responsible for thousands of people made her head spin.

"No one who *deserves* to rule ever *wants* to. That's how I know you'll do a phenomenal job." He squeezed her hand once before releasing it.

"I'm not sure about any of this." Sighing, she rubbed her aching forehead. Why did everything have to be so complicated? Why were there no clear answers? No matter how she looked at it, what was right and what was wrong always blurred depending on the variables. "I'm going to see if Dexter needs my help." Maybe he had a task she could perform in order to keep her mind occupied.

"You two seem closer than before." It was a statement, but also a question.

She shrugged, not wanting to have an in-depth conversation about her feelings. Talking about the subject meant she had to think about it—which she didn't want to do.

"You two could be great together. I hope you give my brother a chance."

"We'll see." She left his office before he could ask her anything else.

Out in the main portion of the library, she spotted Gytha striding toward her. "Lady Reid." Gytha bowed her head. "Prince Dexter sent me to fetch you."

"Is he at the compound?"

"No. He's here in the palace, working on security." Gytha led Reid to one of the interior courtyards. "Wait here. I have another errand to take care of."

Reid hadn't been in this particular courtyard before. A tall water fountain graced the middle of the space with several hedge-lined walkways leading up to it. A handful of tall trees were spread throughout the area, benches near each one.

At the water fountain, Dexter talked to a group of two dozen soldiers, pointing at the interior palace balconies as he spoke. The soldiers nodded. When Dexter saw Reid, he excused himself and joined her.

He leaned in and kissed Reid's cheek, surprising her. Instead of moving away, he whispered in her ear, "The king has left his castle and is on his way here. He is expected to arrive in two weeks." He took a step back.

Two weeks wasn't a lot of time to organize a failsafe assassination. Unease filled her. "I have a bad feeling about this."

"No one in the palace will be involved. I'll make sure of it."

"What if something goes wrong?"

He took her hand and pulled her along one of the walkways, away from his soldiers. "We'll have several plans in place in case one fails."

"I think it's too soon." Something of this magnitude should take months to plan and execute.

"I agree." Dexter squeezed her hand. "But he is coming here to

Axian. We must strike while we can. We'll never get this opportunity again."

"Have you considered he's planning something similar?" The king's assassins may have failed the first time, but would they fail a second?

"I'm sure he is." Dexter stopped near a tree. "Eldon is probably coming here with the intention of taking over. He is going to use the excuse that Axian plans to invade northern Marsden. He will be the savior to his people by heading off a war before it begins."

"And since he's the king, everyone believes what he says." Reid sat on the bench, pulling Dexter down with her.

He reached out, fingering the fabric of her dress. "Don't get me wrong...you look pretty in this dress, but it doesn't suit you. I like it when you wear pants."

"Prince Dexter," one of his soldiers called. "An urgent message just arrived for you."

"I need to go take care of this," Dexter told Reid. "Why don't you rest? I'd like you healed as much as possible before the king arrives. Just in case."

Reid hoped she wouldn't have to defend herself any time soon. However, she wanted to be able to deftly wield a weapon before the king stepped foot in the palace. Even though she didn't want to lie down, she knew her body needed the rest.

Winding her way through the palace, she caught a glimpse of the front lawn with the city in the backdrop. Should she take a detour to the bookstore to send a note to the Knights? She'd completed her tasks—she knew where Dexter went at night and she'd gained his trust. However, the thought of revealing Dexter's secrets didn't sit well with her.

Entering her suite, she headed straight to her bedchamber, eager to remove her dress for something more comfortable. She smiled when she recalled Dexter saying he preferred her in pants. That meant he saw her for who she was.

On her way to the closet, movement caught her attention. She froze. Someone was in her room, and it wasn't Joce. Slowly, she turned to face her intruder.

The man casually sat on Reid's chair, his booted feet resting on her dresser. He slapped the book he'd been reading closed. "Morning, princess."

"Ackley! What are you doing here?" He was the last person she expected to see.

He tossed the book on the dresser. "I've been sent ahead of the king to prepare for his arrival." When he stood, his gaze roamed over her from head to toe. "The real question, Lady Reid, is what are you doing here?"

"You would know since you're the one who sent me here." He didn't even flinch, confirming her suspicion that he had a hand in this.

"I must say," he gestured to her and the room, "it appears you've taken to your new position with astonishing ease."

"I'm gifted that way." She folded her arms, waiting for him to get to the point of his visit. Had he discovered Dexter's plot to assassinate the king? Was he here checking up on her?

"I'm disappointed in you, Reid. I expected a warmer welcome. I'm beginning to think you're not happy to see me." His shrewd gaze zeroed in on her.

"I'm tired is all."

His face instantly softened. "Are you okay?"

She nodded.

He stepped forward, wrapping his arms around her. "I'm sorry," he whispered. "There wasn't any other way. I never meant to do this to you."

"I know." And it wasn't just Ackley. Her father had done this to her, too.

"Idina said Dexter is a good man. I would never have sent you here otherwise."

"He is." So why were there tears in her eyes? Wanting to change the subject, she asked about Idina and Gordon.

"They're both doing well." He held her at arm's length. "Listen, Reid. We need to talk. Idina discovered something. There's—"

"What's going on?" Dexter asked, startling Reid.

She glanced over her shoulder to see him in the doorway. He watched her, face unreadable.

Ackley's hands tightened on her arms.

"Come in." She waved Dexter over. Ackley released her, a mask of haughty indifference sliding over his face. "I'd like to introduce you to Prince Ackley. Ackley, this is Prince Dexter, my fiancé."

The cousins stared at one another.

Finally, Dexter spoke. "How'd you get in here?"

"Does it matter?"

Reid knew Dexter took security seriously. The last thing she needed or wanted was the two of them fighting. Placing her hand on Dexter's arm, she said, "Is everything all right?" She assumed he was here because of the message he'd received.

He focused on her. "Yes. I wanted to see if you needed anything. I thought you'd be in bed resting by now."

"Why would she be in bed?" Ackley demanded.

"The king sent a group of assassins after us." Dexter glared, fists clenching. "Reid fought one. Came out of it with a cracked rib."

"Ah, yes. Sorry excuse for assassins if you ask me." Ackley plopped on the chair, kicking his feet up on Reid's dresser.

"They're not from Marsden, are they?" Reid asked as she sat on her bed, curling her legs under her.

"And that is what I need to discuss with you." He laced his hands behind his head. "Idina has discovered a few things." He kept glancing at Dexter, who stood at the end of the bed.

"You can speak freely in front of him," she said.

Ackley raised his eyebrows. "Can I?"

"I've been investigating men from Bridger going to Melenia to

209

trade," Dexter said. "It seems that every time a ship returns, it contains more men than it set sail with."

Ackley nodded. "Turns out they're soldiers. Idina uncovered correspondence between Eldon and the king from Melenia."

"Soldiers?" Reid asked. Her ears began ringing, her stomach twisting. This was so much worse than anything she could have imagined. "Does Gordon know?"

"He knows."

Reid's heart sank. "He's going to support his brother and king no matter what, isn't he?"

Ackley shrugged. "I can't be sure. Eldon is keeping us apart— so we have little opportunity to converse."

Reid fidgeted with the end of a string on her dress. "Where are these Melenia soldiers?"

"Some are in Bridger. Idina said something about them mining for precious gems as part of their payment. Others have been dropped off somewhere along the Axian coastline."

Dexter started pacing. "How many soldiers are accompanying the king here?"

"Eldon has ordered half of Gordon's men to stay behind in the city. The other half are coming with him to Axian."

"That's not nearly enough for an invasion," Dexter commented.

"No," Ackley said, "it's not. Which leads me to believe Eldon will be using the Melenia soldiers."

Dexter rubbed his face. "I need to send word to the men I have watching the ports and inns." When he reached the doorway, he turned to Ackley. "Let's go."

"I want to talk to Reid."

"*Lady* Reid needs to rest. And we should make your presence known. Come, I'll introduce you to my parents."

Ackley stood and stretched. "I suppose that's wise. That way, my brother can keep track of me. He has enough men here spying for him." He came over to Reid, giving her a hug.

"What's that for?" she asked, unused to physical affection—especially from Ackley.

Chuckling, he whispered in her ear, "I just wanted to see Dexter's reaction. Now that I have, I must ask, what's your relationship with him?"

"It's complicated."

"Aren't they always?" He winked and strode across the room, joining Dexter.

———

At supper that night, Ackley sat in the place of honor, to the right of Prince Henrick. Nara sat across from her husband, Reid next to Dexter, and Colbert next to Ackley.

"If we'd known you'd be arriving early," Nara said, "our cook would have been able to prepare a nicer meal."

Reid eyed the lamb, potatoes, and carrots. The meal was nicer than anything else she'd eaten here.

"Oh, I suppose my brother intended for me to catch you off guard." He took a sip of his wine.

Henrick dismissed the servants, telling them to shut the doors as they left the dining room. "We need to speak frankly with one another. What does King Eldon intend to do?"

Ackley swirled the wine in his goblet, considering Henrick. "I'm sure you already know the answer—he intends to take over Axian. He has everyone convinced you're going to invade the north. He'll take control of Axian, claiming it's to prevent a nasty war and to maintain peace."

"Once King Eldon is here, I'll talk to him. I'm sure we can come to mutually agreeable terms," Henrick said.

Ackley reared back in disbelief. "Why do you believe that misguided notion?"

"Because Eldon is my son."

Ackley snorted. "And he's my half brother, yet that didn't stop him from trying to assassinate me. It didn't stop him from sending his mercenaries after Dexter, his other half brother." He took a sip, then set his goblet down. "He will strip you of everything you love and hold dear."

"Are we speaking of Hudson or Eldon?" Nara asked.

"Exactly," Henrick replied. "Eldon is my son, not Hudson's."

"That may be, but Hudson raised him," Ackley pointed out.

"What's your plan, Ackley?" Reid asked. "Because I know you have one."

The corners of his lips curled into a slight smile, his eyes sparkling with mischief. "I always have a plan." Casually, he leaned back in his chair. "I'm just not sure I want to share my plan with any of you."

Reid moaned. "We don't have time for this. Let's work together to stop Eldon."

Ackley stared, seeming to consider her.

"Will you stop appraising my fiancée like she's a piece of meat?" Dexter snapped.

Ackley's eyebrows rose. "Me?"

"Yes, you. I don't like the way you're looking at her. She's not yours."

Ackley's face went sly, his lips curling in a devilish grin. "She isn't? Are you sure about that?"

Reid felt like her entire body erupted in fire as mortification set in. She wanted to crawl under the table and melt away.

Colbert chuckled. "I haven't had this much entertainment in ages."

Reid eyed Dexter. He'd balled his hands into fists, and he hadn't yet touched his food.

"Ackley," Reid said, belatedly realizing she should have used his title. "Prince Henrick is a former Knight, I'm a Knight, and you're a Knight. We all want the same thing. Let's work together to accomplish it. Please, just tell us what you have planned."

He glared at her, then took another sip of his wine, stalling.

"I've been told to stand down. The Knights are going to allow Eldon to take over Axian. After all, he'll have it one day anyway." Bitterness seeped through each word.

"And what's to happen with my family?" Nara asked, setting her fork down.

Ackley shrugged. "The Knights said if Henrick won't take the throne, then he is not their concern. Their focus is on protecting the vast majority of the people in this kingdom. You," Ackley tipped his goblet toward Henrick, "clearly don't give a rat's tail what happens to the people who live and work here."

"I do care," Henrick insisted. "That's why I'm standing down. Sometimes it takes more courage to not say anything than it does to pick up a sword and fight."

"What you call courage, I call giving up." Ackley stood. "I'm done. Lady Reid, I need a moment of your time. Now."

Reid followed him from the room, feeling everyone's eyes on her. She'd been set to argue that Ackley was a prince and outranked them, but then she realized they were all on equal footing. By leaving with Ackley so readily, she'd inadvertently implied that her loyalty was to him. She groaned.

Out in the hallway, Ackley turned left, entering a sitting room Reid had never been in before. He closed the door. "We need to talk."

"I gathered that."

He plopped on the sofa, rubbing the nape of his neck, his expression vacant.

"Ackley?" Reid asked, sitting next to him and rubbing his back. "What's the matter?" She'd never seen him like this before. He usually kept his emotions hidden away.

Shoulders hunching forward, he shook his head. "Everything is a mess."

"Talk to me." Ackley always had a plan. And a backup plan. And a backup plan for the backup plan. Nothing rattled him.

He peered up at her, his look freezing her in place. "I

suspected, but I didn't truly think it possible." His eyes glazed over with a sadness that pierced right into Reid's heart, gutting her.

She took hold of his hand. "What's the matter?" she asked, not really wanting to know.

"Eldon killed my father. I'm certain of it." He squeezed her hand, seeming to need to anchor himself to something. Anything.

Reid held on tightly. "Why would he do that?" she asked, trying to make sense of what he'd revealed.

"To be king."

What kind of person killed someone just to inherit the throne? Reid pinched the bridge of her nose with her free hand. It felt like a thousand rocks had landed in her stomach. "The assassins in the forest and the castle?"

"Eldon hired them to kill Gordon, Idina, and myself."

"I'm so sorry." Because she didn't know what else to say. She'd suspected Eldon was trying to eliminate all contenders for the throne. To have it verified was another matter entirely. "You're his half brother. You have the same mother." Did Leigh know?

"When Idina figured it out, she told our mother. Mother believed it impossible, so she confronted Eldon. Gordon, Idina, and I were present. He denied everything. And then my mother divulged the truth of his birth to my siblings. She told them about the letters, which she revealed she had in her possession. Eldon demanded she hand them over. She refused, saying if all he said were true, then he should trust her with them. He was so furious he wrapped his hands around her neck and squeezed. Gordon stopped him."

"Is your mother okay?"

Ackley nodded, rubbing his face. "Idina is taking care of her."

"They're not still at the castle, are they?" If they were, there was nothing and no one to stop Eldon from trying to kill Leigh again.

"No. I sent Idina and Mother somewhere safe."

Relief filled Reid. "Good." As to where they would be safe from the king, Reid wasn't sure.

"Eldon knows the letters aren't here in the palace." He squeezed her hand again. "Which means he has no further use for you either."

Thankfully, Reid wore her father's ring. With it, the king couldn't hurt her. If he did, she could call on the dukes to rise against him. "I'm aware Eldon is on his way here for the wedding. Is he going to seize the palace when he arrives?" Or would he come back and do it at a later time? Was this visit just for the purpose of seeing what he planned to conquer and solidifying how? She couldn't imagine an army coming into this beautiful city and destroying it.

"As far as Idina and I have been able to piece together, that's his plan."

Reid figured as much. "What can we do to stop him?"

He released her hand and leaned forward, resting his elbows on his legs while his hands covered his face. "The Knights ordered me to stand down."

Reid rubbed his back again, wondering who called the shots for the Knights. Anna? "I didn't ask what the Knights are going to do. I asked what *we're* going to do."

He chuckled, the sound humorless. "You're not going to do anything."

"What are you planning?" she asked, cold fear slithering down her spine.

"I'm planning to avenge my father's death."

CHAPTER EIGHTEEN

A ckley's words rang in the air. He planned to assassinate the king without the support of the Knights. "I think you need to talk to Dexter," she whispered. Since Dexter also planned to kill the king, they should work together to coordinate the assassination. The chance of success would be much higher.

"Why?"

She didn't want to violate Dexter's trust, but she would be helping Dexter by telling Ackley this vital information. "You're both planning the same thing."

"It's not his place."

"Of course it is," she said, curling her legs under her. "Eldon plans to invade Axian. Dexter has a right and a duty to protect his people and his land."

"Eldon is *my* brother."

"He's just as much Dexter's brother as he is yours."

"Eldon killed my father."

Doing something purely out of revenge was never the right reason to kill. However, she couldn't tell him that when he was vastly more experienced in the art of murder than she was.

"Having grown up with Eldon, knowing him so intimately, could you actually kill him? What's that going to do to your mother?"

"Reid," Ackley whispered, reaching out and clutching her hand again. "There's so much I need to tell you."

"Right now, we need to focus on the future and come up with a plan."

The door clicked shut. Reid glanced over her shoulder. Dexter and Colbert had entered the room.

"Explain what you mean by *focus on the future*," Dexter almost snarled as he prowled closer, his eyes zeroing in on Reid and Ackley's joined hands.

Ackley chuckled softly. "Easy there, cousin." His face instantly transformed from sulking to aloof indifference.

Reid removed her hand from Ackley's. "We're talking about working together instead of independently since we all have the same goal—to eliminate the king." She looked pointedly at Dexter. "If we pool our resources, we may be able to pull this off."

Dexter blinked, his shoulders relaxing ever so slightly.

"I think that's wise," Colbert said as he sat across from Reid. "But before we discuss anything further, I want to be clear on who the new king will be."

"I'd like for Henrick to take over," Ackley said. "Gordon isn't ready for the responsibility, nor has he been groomed for anything other than leading soldiers."

"I'd like for my father to be king as well," Colbert said.

"Then that part is settled," Ackley said. "We kill Eldon, crown Henrick, and everyone lives happily ever after."

"There's only one problem," Dexter said as he sat next to his brother on the sofa. "My father doesn't want to be king."

"He may not have a choice," Ackley said. "Marsden needs a ruler. Henrick is the legitimate ruler whether he likes it or not."

"Do you think Prince Gordon would make a bid for the throne since he's Eldon's heir?" Colbert asked.

"I highly doubt it," Ackley responded.

"So we agree then?" Reid said. "Henrick will be the king?"

They all nodded.

"Since that's settled, tell me what you have planned," Ackley said.

Dexter rubbed his face. "Before we get to the planning part, I want to know what's going on between the two of you." He waved his hand, gesturing between Reid and Ackley. Reid could only gape at Dexter, stunned he cared more about discussing a relationship that didn't exist than planning the future of the kingdom.

"What do you mean?" Ackley asked.

"Please explain your relationship," Dexter said, carefully enunciating each word as if speaking to a daft child.

"What does that have to do with anything?" Ackley asked, cocking his head to the side, a sly smile on his lips.

Reid was about to answer that they were just friends when Dexter spoke again.

"Reid is my fiancée, and I care about her. Not only that, but if we're going to work together, I'd like to understand the nature of the relationship between you and her."

Ackley stretched his arms out along the back of the sofa, obviously trying to rile Dexter up. "I still don't know what it is you're asking."

"Like hell you don't," Colbert mumbled, shaking his head. "Is he always this difficult?" he asked Reid.

She rolled her eyes. "Always. And just so we're all clear, there's absolutely nothing going on between me and Ackley, especially of the romantic type. We're just friends."

"Friends?" Dexter repeated.

"Do you have a problem with that, cousin?" Ackley asked with a smirk.

"I don't like to make decisions when I don't have all the information," Dexter explained.

"If I didn't know any better, I'd say you're jealous."

"Maybe I am."

Jaw dropping at the admission, Reid decided to intervene. "He recruited me." She tapped the spot on her arm where her sleeve hid her tattoo. "Ackley is the brother I never had."

"That's good enough for me." Colbert looked to his brother for confirmation.

Dexter inclined his head. He took a deep breath, releasing the tension from his body. "Our preliminary plan is to assassinate the king on his journey to Axian. I want him dead before he reaches the City of Radella. There's a narrow stretch of road that's an easy place to set up an attack. I'm thinking of sending a group of fifty men. They'll hide in the hills. When the king arrives, they'll strike his carriage with special arrows I've had made. The carriage should catch fire. If the king steps out, attempting to get away, he'll be shot dead."

"Gordon is coming with five hundred men. How do you plan to handle the soldiers who attack the archers?"

Dexter smiled. "They won't be able to. For almost half a mile, on both sides of the road, the cliff is so steep no one will be able to climb it to reach my people."

"What about my family members?" Ackley asked.

"Tell them to travel ahead or behind the king, but not with him."

"Are Leigh and Idina coming?" Reid asked. She didn't think Ackley would want them anywhere near Eldon after he'd tried to kill them.

Ackley's eyes softened as he regarded her. "They're staying with Duke Ellington."

Ackley trusted Reid's father enough to leave his mother and sister in the duke's care? "Then it'll just be Gordon?"

"Gordon will ride with his men. Harlow and Dana will be in the carriage with Eldon."

Reid stood and started pacing behind the sofa. "I don't wish to kill either woman."

"Really?" Ackley asked, peering at her. "I thought you'd relish in the opportunity to kill that sorry excuse of a woman who's as plain as a piece of bread."

Reid whacked Ackley on the back of his head. "That was completely unnecessary."

"So was hitting me." He chuckled. "You can't tell me you don't fantasize about smashing her face into a table. I do. Regularly."

Leaning over the back of the sofa, she whispered in Ackley's ear, "I haven't thought about Gordon or Dana since I left northern Marsden."

Abruptly, Colbert stood. "I need to get back to work. Prince Ackley, do you approve of the plan?"

"Yes, although I want a few adjustments made to lessen the casualties."

"Agreed," Colbert answered. "Dexter and I will work to get a revised plan to you within twenty-four hours. Dex—are you heading to the training yard?"

"Yes."

"Good," Colbert said. "Take Prince Ackley with you. I think you both need to spar to work off some of your excess energy. Lady Reid, come with me. We have work to do."

Reid followed Colbert before Ackley or Dexter could argue otherwise. Once safely in the hallway, she thanked Colbert for his quick thinking.

"I actually want to talk to you about something personal." He led Reid to his office, where Finn was stretched across his dog bed, wagging his tail.

Reid bent to pat his side.

Colbert closed the door. "Have a seat."

Raising one eyebrow, she lifted her hands. "Where?" The sofa was covered with blankets and both chairs were piled high with books.

"Sorry." He grabbed the books off one chair, setting them on the floor.

"Be careful you don't hurt yourself," she said, taking a seat on the now-empty chair.

"I'm healed." As if to prove it, he touched his stomach where the wound had been.

"Care to tell me how that happened?"

"Not really." Sighing, he plunked onto his desk chair. "It was stupid of me." He drummed his fingers on the wooden surface. "Tell you what, I'll answer your question if you answer mine."

She studied him, trying to decide if it was worth it. "Deal."

"The incident happened on your first night here in the palace. While Dexter was escorting you here, I was monitoring a group of men who'd arrived a few weeks prior via a ship off our eastern coast."

"Men from Melenia?"

"I believe so."

"Why did you let them into Axian?"

"I wanted to see where the twenty-five men intended to go, so I had them followed. They'd been steadily traveling west toward the palace. When the group started to head north, the soldier I'd tasked with following them reported that one fell ill, so three were staying behind at an inn. That night, when Dexter arrived with you, I made the mistake of telling him this. Since the inn was only two hours east of here, he wanted to go see for himself. Even though it was the middle of the night, we jumped on horses and rode straight there. We found one man sick in bed, the other two drinking in the tavern. Dex approached the two in the tavern, trying to strike up a conversation. The foreigners had thick accents."

Colbert folded his hands together on top of the desk. "Dexter demanded to know why they were there. He pulled out a knife, pointing it at them. The ill man chose that moment to come downstairs. He saw the knife aimed at his friends, so he withdrew his own dagger and threw it. Dex never saw it coming. I jumped in front of the dagger."

"You could have been killed." Although Reid would have done the same thing for one of her sisters.

"I know. It was stupid. But all I could think about was that Axian needed Dex more than it needed me. I managed to turn just as the dagger hit me. It slid across my ribs instead of lodging in my flesh."

"You're one lucky man."

"I know."

"What happened to the foreigners?" She assumed Dexter would have done as Ackley would and slaughtered them.

"In the chaos, we lost them. Dexter was too worried about me to bother with them. The man I had watching them disappeared. I'm hoping he's still tracking them, although I can't be sure because he hasn't sent any reports since that night."

"He could be dead." Which would explain why they hadn't heard from him.

"Yes, that is a possibility." He leaned on the desk. "I've told you how I got hurt—which, by the way, you cannot mention to my mother—so now it's time for you to tell me what you can about Ackley."

"There's nothing to tell that you don't already know." Did Colbert think she hadn't been truthful with him and Dexter?

"He likes you."

"As a friend. That's all."

"No." Colbert shook his head. "He wouldn't tease you like he does if he didn't care for you."

If he cared for her, it was along the lines of a little sister. There had never been and would never be anything between her and Ackley. She felt no attraction to him in that way, and he'd made it perfectly clear he was married to his job. "It's a moot point," she said. "I am marrying your brother."

"I thought maybe there was something I didn't know."

She extended her arm across the desk, palm up. He took hold

of her hand. "There is nothing between Ackley and me. We are friends, that's all."

"Can I offer you a word of advice?"

"Of course."

"Talk with my brother. Assure him there's nothing between you and Ackley."

"I've already told him." Dexter's reaction to Ackley had seemed normal to her. After all, she'd felt threatened by Gytha even though Dexter had already ended things with the woman. And he hadn't talked to Reid about it, so she didn't know why she had to talk to him about this.

"And that, my dear Reid, is why I'm giving you advice. Please take it. I know my brother well. And, not to be rude, but you lack common sense when it comes to things of this nature."

Her face flushed, and she fidgeted. "Fine. I will have an awkward conversation with your brother. But I'm sure he won't care. He'll probably think me daft for even bringing it up."

"We'll see."

Reid entered the royal family's private sitting room. Gathered around the low table, Dexter, Colbert, and Ackley all spoke in hushed whispers. When she closed the door, all three turned her way.

"Don't stop on my account." She came in and sat down, glancing at the map on the table.

Dexter rolled it up. "The timing will be key. I'll go ahead and get my men into position." He stood, then headed to the door.

"Where are you going?" Reid asked.

"Colbert can fill you in." He left with the map in hand.

"I'm going to head out, too," Ackley said. "I should be back in about a week." He practically ran from the room.

"What am I missing?" Reid asked, bemused.

Colbert leaned back against the sofa, sighing. "Dex left to meet with our men who are going to carry out the mission."

"The men from the other night?"

He nodded.

"Are any of them soldiers in the army?" she asked.

"No. They're all citizens of Axian. They do not work at the palace and are not soldiers in the army." He pinched the bridge of his nose. "They are highly trained men and women who are not attached to the royal family in any way."

That made sense. "Are you okay?" She moved to sit next to him. The dark lines under his eyes made it appear as if he hadn't slept in days, and his skin seemed unnaturally pale.

"I'm fine. Just worried. The plan for assassinating the king is a solid one. But some factors have me concerned."

"Such as?"

"The men from Melenia. Where are they? Ackley thinks he knows, so he's leaving to investigate."

"Dexter isn't going with the group, is he?" She didn't know what to call them—rebels?

"No. He'll be back in a bit."

The door opened, and Nara entered. "Lady Reid, how are your ribs?"

"Much better." They were sore, and it still hurt to move too much. However, Reid couldn't sit around doing nothing any longer. Not when the king was on his way, an assassination plan was in the works, and she was getting married soon.

"I was hoping you'd say that. I need your help." Nara approached the narrow bookcase in the corner of the room.

"What are we doing?"

"You need to be able to exit the palace quickly in case something happens." She waved Reid over. "On the right side of this bookcase, there is a lever. Raise it, and it unlocks the door." There was a clicking sound, then Nara pulled the bookshelf toward her, revealing a dark corridor. "There are a series of hidden passageways between the walls. It's time you learn your way around here." She stepped into the darkness.

Reid spent the following week working alongside Nara. The princess wanted to make sure Reid knew her way around the palace—including the servants' hallways and the vast array of hidden corridors Reid hadn't known existed. Nara explained they'd been designed for a takeover. It not only allowed the royal family to quickly exit if need be, but it also allowed for their soldiers to infiltrate the palace. Once Reid could navigate the entire residence in the dark, Nara made her memorize what rooms the guests were staying in as well as where those rooms were located.

Nara didn't know about the assassination. Or, if she did, she pretended not to. Reid assumed the wedding would still take place even though the king would be dead. Regardless, they both went on as if everything were going according to plan.

Reid saw little of Henrick, Dexter, and Colbert. They were all busy making their own preparations for what was coming. Henrick spent most of his days bent over endless contracts and correspondence from the dukes and prominent families throughout the county. Dexter practically lived at the military compound, training and planning with his soldiers. Colbert rarely left his office.

After tossing and turning in bed for a few hours, Reid shoved her covers off and crawled out of bed. She padded across the room to her window. Pushing the curtain aside, she gazed out into the night at the beautiful city before her. Most windows were dark at this late hour, the moon just a sliver in the sky, and the stars bright and numerous.

For some reason, her mind whirled in a hundred different directions. The wedding, the assassination, the layout of the palace, the tension radiating from Nara, and the unknown all weighed heavily on Reid. She missed her home and her family. She missed knowing what each day would bring.

"You're awake," a deep voice said, startling Reid. Ackley stepped into her bedchamber.

"When did you get back?" She hadn't seen him since that morning a week ago.

"Just now." He joined her at the window, smelling of horse and sweat.

"What is it?" Something was wrong. Otherwise, he wouldn't have come to see her in the middle of the night.

He ran his hands through his hair. "If I hadn't seen it with my own eyes, I wouldn't have believed it."

A deep foreboding settled into Reid's stomach. "What is it?" she asked, not really wanting to know.

"Melenia soldiers. Hundreds of them."

Her legs went weak. She went over to her bed, leaning on the edge of it. "Where?"

"Just south of the Modig Mountains. With that many armed soldiers, they're about ten to twelve days away."

By bringing another kingdom into this, she feared Eldon planned on overthrowing the dukes. If he were bold enough to do something like that, he'd have total and complete control over Marsden. And Reid's flimsy ring and marriage to Dexter wouldn't save her. "What are we going to do?" They needed to inform the Knights. Even if the assassination went off without a hitch, the army would still be here.

"Everything was going according to plan," he mumbled. "Then my brother had to go and make a deal with Melenia. I did not see that one coming." He shook his head. "Let's go and wake the others. I'd say we should play dumb and confront the soldiers. However, they're carrying the king's banner. Attacking them would be the same as attacking the king."

226

She led the way to Dexter's suite, thinking about all Ackley had just revealed. After knocking, she waited.

The door opened a crack. "Reid?" a groggy Dexter asked.

"We have a problem."

He opened his door wider, glancing between Reid and Ackley. She quickly told him what Ackley had seen.

"I feared something like this would happen, and I already have a plan in place," he said. "Ackley, you look exhausted. Go get a few hours of sleep. In the morning, we'll tell the others before going to the military compound to move forward with the necessary preparations."

"I could use a little beauty sleep," Ackley said, pushing off the wall. "Reid, I'll walk you back to your room."

Dexter reached out, taking hold of Reid's arm. "I actually want to talk to Reid for a moment. I'll make sure she makes it safely back to her suite."

"That's probably for the best. I wouldn't want to accidentally fall asleep in Reid's bedchamber and get everyone in a tizzy." Whistling, Ackley strolled down the hallway.

Shaking her head at Ackley, Reid stepped inside Dexter's suite.

CHAPTER NINETEEN

Dexter led Reid over to a sofa where they sat next to one another. With the curtains pulled back, the stars provided a hint of light. Similar to Reid's suite, there was a door to the left leading to his bedchamber, and another to the right presumably to the bathing chamber and privy.

Reid twisted toward Dexter, then froze. He wore a robe, the front open to expose his chest. Making sure to keep her eyes on his face, she swallowed, not sure what to say. His hair stuck up in every direction, and Reid had the sudden urge to run her fingers through it. Instead, she folded her hands.

"Did you want to discuss something?" she asked. She'd been in such a hurry to warn him that she'd completely forgotten her robe. However, her nightgown covered her neck and arms. She hoped he couldn't see her chest through the thin material.

He scanned her body before quickly averting his eyes. When he rubbed the nape of his neck, Reid noticed the hint of scruff shadowing his jaw. A simmering desire started to build in the pit of her stomach.

"No," he replied, his gravelly voice sending a shiver through her. "I'll be honest—I just didn't want Ackley walking you to your room."

The conversation she'd had with Colbert replayed in her mind. He'd suggested she assure Dexter that her relationship with Ackley was platonic.

"Sorry," he mumbled. "That's probably not what you want to hear. You don't need some overprotective, jealous man around. I'm not usually like this. It's just that Ackley brings out this side of me." He reached forward, taking her hands in his. "I'm sorry."

"You're jealous of Ackley?" There was nothing to be jealous of.

He nodded. "You two are obviously friends. I'm jealous we don't have the same easy rapport with one another."

She was about to say she'd known Ackley longer. However, that wasn't the issue. "I feel comfortable around him," she admitted.

"And you don't with me?" he asked, a hint of hurt lacing his voice.

"When I first met you, you threatened to kill me."

He chuckled. "I wasn't serious."

"How was I supposed to know that?" Again, that wasn't the only reason she was awkward around him. In the semi-darkness, she couldn't see his eyes. It emboldened her. Taking a steadying breath, she said, "I've never been physically attracted to Ackley, so talking to him is always easy." She held her breath, awaiting his reaction.

His grip on her hands tightened, and he reared back ever so slightly. "Are you implying you're attracted to me?"

Her entire body warmed. Whether it was from her close proximity to Dexter, the fact he was holding her hands, or that she had a clear view of his chest and stomach muscles, she couldn't be sure. But holy hell, she needed some fresh air. She tried pulling her hands free, embarrassed she'd just admitted her attraction to him.

He gripped her hands even tighter. "Don't run away." He slid his hands up her forearms to her elbows, holding her in place. "This entire time, I thought the attraction was one-sided. I didn't think you wanted anything to do with me," he murmured, his hands gliding to her shoulders.

Was there a fire raging in the hearth she couldn't see? Maybe in his bedchamber? Something that gave off a tremendous amount of heat? Wait—did Dexter just admit he was attracted to her? Her eyes widened.

Reaching up, he gently trailed his fingers from her forehead down to her cheek. He pushed a lock of hair behind her ear. "Have you...ever been with a man before?"

She shook her head, not sure her voice would work right now. Obviously, she'd never had a gentleman court her since she'd been raised as a man. She'd never even had someone look at her the way Dexter was now. Her toes curled.

"I feel like I need to be honest with you," he said. "I've been with a few women before."

She tried scooting away from him, but his hands slid down her arms to her hands, holding on firmly.

"I've never been in love before," he continued. "And I've never been intimate with Gytha."

That admission surprised her since he'd had a relationship with the woman.

"I knew she cared for me, so I didn't want to encourage those feelings. The women I've been with haven't meant anything to me."

Reid needed to get out of his room so she could process all he'd revealed. She didn't know how any of it made her feel. For some reason, the most prominent feeling was utter embarrassment. It was difficult enough acting like a proper lady when she barely knew what to do. However, kissing or being intimate with a man? She knew even less about that. While her sisters had told her some of the basics, she'd never had an in-depth conversation about pleasing a man. At times like this, she wished her mother were still alive to guide her.

What she couldn't figure out was why they were having this conversation now. They wouldn't be married for another two weeks. And hadn't they decided not to share a bed right away so they could get to know each other before they slept together?

Why was it so hot in Dexter's room? "I should go back to my bedchamber," she blurted out. She'd almost forgotten that Melenia soldiers were on their way to the palace. In the morning, there would be a lot to do to prepare for the upcoming invasion.

"I'll walk you to your room." He took her hand and stood, pulling her up alongside him.

They exited his suite and headed to hers, neither speaking. When they reached her door, Dexter released her.

"I'll admit, you make me nervous," he said. "I never know how to act around you."

"Just be yourself." She didn't want him pretending to be someone he wasn't.

He shook his head. "What if I told you that, as myself, I want to shove you against this wall and kiss you?" He took a step closer to her. "What if I told you I want to join you in your room? That I want to slowly strip your nightgown off until your bare skin is revealed to me?"

Gasping, Reid's back hit the wall, her eyes widening in shock.

He chuckled. "See? I've scared you." He took a step away. "I never know whether I should be gentlemanly or not. If you'll appreciate that or take offense if I don't treat you as an equal. You're infuriating, confusing, beautiful, and intriguing. No one has challenged me the way you do, Reid Ellington. And since we're admitting things we shouldn't, I can't wait to marry you." He leaned down, gently placing a chaste kiss on her cheek. "Goodnight." He left Reid there.

Knees weak, she wasn't sure if she wanted to run and tackle him or slip into her bedchamber and lock the door. Maybe both.

The following morning, Reid dressed and exited her suite, about to head to the dining room when she came face to face with Gytha. "What are you doing here?"

"Funny, I ask that question about you all the time," Gytha replied.

Reid rolled her eyes.

Gytha sighed. "Prince Dexter assigned me to be your personal guard."

"I don't need to be protected."

"I told him the same thing. But neither you nor I have a choice in the matter."

Reid always had a choice. She headed to the dining room with Gytha on her heels. Thankfully, the woman remained outside when Reid entered. The entire family and Ackley were already eating.

"Dexter," Reid said as she took a seat at the table.

"Just humor me," he answered.

"Couldn't it be anyone else?"

"She's the best."

"I know. But she hates me."

"What are you two talking about?" Nara asked.

"Dexter assigned Gytha as my personal guard."

Colbert chuckled. Ackley's eyes narrowed. Henrick seemed confused.

"That's an excellent idea," Nara said. "With the king coming and this threat from Melenia, you should have a guard."

"Please," Dexter said. "As soon as Melenia is dealt with, you won't need a guard anymore."

Reid swallowed the ten nasty retorts on the tip of her tongue, knowing they wouldn't help her case. Because she couldn't say she was capable of defending herself in her condition. Until her ribs were fully healed, she was vulnerable. "Does anyone else in the family have a guard?"

"You're not familiar with the city and countryside like we are." Dexter set his fork down, leaning forward on his arms. "I don't know what Melenia intends to do. I may need to take my army out to stop them. I can't lead my men if I'm worried about you. Yes, you are perfectly capable of taking care of yourself and you probably don't need a guard, but I want you to have one. Please, do this for me."

"He's right," Ackley said. "You should have protection. A female guard is an excellent choice. And I've met Gytha." A wicked smile spread across his face. "I like her."

Of course he did. "I'd enjoy seeing the two of you fight," Reid said. "I'm not sure who'd win."

"I would," Gytha called from the other side of the door.

Reid groaned while everyone else laughed.

"Does this mean you'll cooperate?" Dexter asked.

She nodded and grabbed her fork, stabbing her eggs with more force than necessary.

As soon as she finished eating, Dexter asked her to accompany him to the military compound. He told Gytha she could have the next hour off since he would be with Reid. When they were by the lake with no one around, he informed her the king should have reached the pass yesterday where the assassination would occur.

"Does that mean King Eldon could already be dead?"

He nodded.

Walking beside Dexter, she tried to imagine what the assassination would have been like. Did the king suffer? Would anyone miss him? Reid wasn't sure the queen would care. "When will we have confirmation?"

"I was hoping we would have it before breakfast."

"Do you think something is wrong?"

"If I don't have word by supper, then yes, I will know something is wrong. I'm going to try not to worry until then."

She shivered, hoping everything went according to plan. With the king dead, would Melenia return to where they came from?

They entered the military compound, then went to Dexter's office. "I thought you should know we received a letter from your father. He said he won't sign the marriage contract until I'm named my father's heir."

Reid had figured as much. "Does your father know?"

"He does. Once the letter came, we showed it to Father, hoping he'd change his mind. He said he wanted to talk to Eldon first."

"If Eldon is dead, your father will have to change his heir."

"True. However, when Ackley told Father that Melenia is marching toward us and they are in league with Eldon to overthrow him, he signed the papers. I am officially my father's heir. He sent word this morning to your father."

"I imagine my father is already on his way for the wedding."

"Probably." Dexter sat on the edge of his desk. "My father also asked your father to have soldiers at the ready in case they're needed."

Reid started pacing. "Ironic we're preparing for a wedding *and* a war."

"The wedding was supposed to prevent the war."

Clearly, that wasn't going to happen. "Do you still think it wise to move forward with the wedding?"

"I do." He folded his arms. "With the king dead and the threat from Melenia neutralized, we'll need the dukes to be on board with crowning my father king. Our marriage and the support from Ellington will help ensure a peaceful transition."

Reid hoped Henrick lived a long, healthy life so Dexter wouldn't become king. The last thing she wanted was to be queen.

Ackley entered the office with Colbert.

"Markis is on his way up with a messenger," Colbert said, taking a seat.

Dexter moved around to the other side of his desk, shifting through some papers. "Excellent. Once we have confirmation, we can proceed with taking care of Melenia."

Ackley meandered around the room.

The door burst open. Markis entered with a man covered head to toe in gray. It looked like he was wearing some sort of skin suit that would blend in with rocky terrain.

"Thank you, Markis," Dexter said. "You may leave."

Once Markis shut the door, the man in gray said, "The king is alive. He had a decoy in his place. We killed the decoy."

Ackley swore. "And now Eldon knows someone's trying to kill him. Where's the king?"

"He was not with royal convoy," the man said.

"Blast it. We don't even know where he is." Ackley gripped the back of Reid's chair.

"We'll have to kill him here," Dexter said. "It'll be trickier and harder to keep our hands clean, but not impossible."

"What about Melenia?" Colbert asked.

"We can't do anything about them until the king is dead."

"I'm trying to figure out why my brother had a decoy in the first place," Ackley said, his words clipped. "He's never used one before."

"There are two options," Colbert said. "Either someone tipped him off or he had a clandestine meeting to attend and he didn't want anyone to know about it."

"I can assure you no one here tipped him off," Dexter said.

"Then we must assume he left the royal convoy to meet with the soldiers from Melenia," Colbert stated.

Reid couldn't believe they'd killed an innocent man pretending to be the king. Which meant she was going to have to see Eldon again. Unless he rode in with the Melenia soldiers and flat-out declared war. "How do you think the dukes will respond once they learn Melania soldiers are here?" She didn't think they would take the news well—even if the Melenia soldiers were there to help the dukes maintain control over Marsden.

"We must proceed as if we have no idea what just happened," Dexter said. "The king knows he can't use the Melenia soldiers without the dukes rising together to fight him. We have to assume he'll arrive and pretend to know nothing about the foreign soldiers. The wedding will take place. Then everyone will return home."

"I agree," Ackley said. "When everyone returns home, that's when Eldon will use the soldiers to take over Axian. Once he has control of Axian, he will invade northern Marsden." He cursed. "I should have seen his plan earlier." He resumed pacing. "I need to spar. Reid, where's your guard?"

"Gytha? She's around here somewhere."

Ackley stalked from the room without another word.

"Come," Colbert said to the man in gray. "I'll get you out of here without anyone seeing you."

Once Reid and Dexter were alone, Dexter went over to the window, staring outside. "I'm sorry," he mumbled.

"For what?"

"For not stopping the war."

She stood beside him. "It's not your fault." It was Eldon's. Placing her hand on Dexter's shoulder, she added, "And we don't know there's going to be a war. We still can prevent one."

He looked down at her. "I hate to ask this, but do you think the Knights can help?"

She'd been avoiding sending the Knights an update. "Possibly."

"Can you ask? Let them know what's going on to see if they'll provide any support?"

She could do that. But whose side would the Knights take? They had to know Melenia soldiers were here. So why hadn't they done something already? "I'll send them a message right now."

CHAPTER TWENTY

After visiting the bookstore, where Reid managed to slip a note to the Knights into the knitting book, she returned to the palace, Gytha on her heels the entire way. "Why must you walk behind me?"

"I can see better here."

When Reid craned to see over her shoulder, Gytha smirked, clearly enjoying her position as tormentor. "Can you at least walk beside me?" Then Reid wouldn't feel like an incompetent fool who had to be watched all the time.

"I think here is better." Gytha chuckled. "Ah, Lady Reid, you are far too easy to tease."

With her hands on her hips, Reid whirled on Gytha. "How would you feel if Dexter had someone following you around like a dog all day?"

"Did you just call me a dog?" Gytha asked, raising one eyebrow.

"No." Had Gytha missed the entire point Reid had tried to make?

The warrior woman patted Reid's shoulder. "If Prince Dexter assigned a guard to me, I'd be livid."

Exactly, so the woman knew how Reid felt.

"Which is why I am enjoying this so much."

Reid scowled before resuming her trek to the palace. The first wave of guests was due to arrive, and she needed to be there to greet them.

Two days later, they received word there'd been an attack on the royal convoy. Feigning shock, Dexter immediately sent a unit of soldiers to investigate and escort the convoy safely to the City of Radella. Given the size of the group, he expected them to arrive in seven days.

The following week passed in a blur. Guests trickled in, and Reid spent a lot of time greeting people. Most were eager to meet their future princess. Per Nara's request, Reid dressed the part of a fine northern lady, smiled a lot, and reiterated over and over again how happy she was to be in Axian, how much she looked forward to marrying Prince Dexter, and how thoroughly impressed she was with the prosperity of Axian under Prince Henrick's management.

For the first time, the palace sentries wore matching livery and the servants wore uniforms. The women Reid encountered had on dresses instead of pants. When she questioned Nara about it, the princess reminded Reid they had to abide by the law with the king due to arrive for the wedding.

That night, Reid tossed and turned, feeling like she was being sucked back into northern Marsden. As her freedoms were slowly stripped away, chains clamped around her wrists and ankles, shackling her to the stone flooring. She tried screaming for help...

"Reid," Ackley said, shaking her awake.

Her eyes flew open. It took but a moment to determine she was in her bedchamber in Axian—not in the king's castle. Sitting upright, she pushed her hair away from her face. "Bad dream."

"I figured."

"Did I wake you?" He shouldn't have heard her. His room was at the other end of this level, separated by sentries.

"I was coming to see you. When I heard you screaming, I entered without thinking." He patted her thigh. "I feared Eldon was in here squeezing your neck or he'd sent an assassin to murder you in your sleep."

The room was dark, the curtains closed, so Reid couldn't see Ackley's expression that well. "What did you need to see me about?"

"I was just leaving for a meeting with Dexter when word came that your father is here."

Her father had arrived in the middle of the night? She scrambled out of bed, searching for her robe.

A shadow moved by the door. "Did you not think me capable of doing my job?" Gytha demanded. "That I am so incompetent I couldn't protect Lady Reid?"

Reid had forgotten the woman was asleep in the sitting room. Had she heard Reid cry out in her dreams?

"Why didn't you wake Lady Reid from her nightmare?" Ackley asked Gytha.

"My job is to protect her from harm. A bad dream never hurt anyone."

Reid put her robe on, tying it.

"I managed to get by you and into Reid's bedchamber without you stopping me," he said.

"When you burst into the room, I was behind the door with a sword in hand. You are lucky I didn't kill you."

"Why didn't you?" He cocked his head to the side.

"I could tell it was you by your smell."

Reid chuckled. "Ackley smells?" She'd never noticed him having any particular aroma before. Unless they were sparring— then he stunk of sweat.

"His clothes have a hint of a leather smell to them," Gytha answered.

"Well," Reid said, because she had no idea what else to say. "I'd like to see my father." She exited her suite, Ackley and Gytha close behind, only to come face to face with Dexter, his hand raised to knock on her door. "What are you doing here?"

"I came to wake you." He scowled at Gytha and Ackley. "Apparently, I needn't have bothered." Still in his clothing from earlier in the day, he made a fine sight, even when rumpled.

"What time is it?" she asked.

"Well past midnight. Your father is in the stables. I told him we'd meet him in the sitting room. He didn't want to wake you. However, I knew you'd be mad if I didn't."

In the hallway, she paused, addressing Gytha and Ackley. "Neither of you need to come with me to see my father. Ackley, go to bed. Gytha, you can remain in my suite." She motioned to Dexter. "My fiancé will escort me back to my room." Without waiting for a response, she grabbed Dexter's arm and led him down the hallway toward the stairs. "I take it you've been working?"

"I have. There's a lot to do before the king or the foreign army arrive."

Suddenly, she froze.

He went down two steps before he realized she'd stopped. Shifting toward her, he said, "What's wrong?"

Their position on different steps made them eye level. "Nothing." This close, on the darkened staircase, she had the sudden urge to wrap her arms around his neck and kiss him. Instead, she whispered, "Make sure you're taking care of yourself. You need to sleep so you can be ready for whatever is coming."

Dexter wrapped his large hands around Reid's waist. Pulling her toward him, he leaned into her. "Are you worried about me?"

She couldn't answer. Not when he was this close. Not when

240

his lips hovered near hers. Without meaning to, she lifted her arms over his shoulders, her hands clasping behind his neck.

"Duke Ellington is waiting for Lady Reid in the sitting room." Nara's amused voice cut through their moment. "I hardly think now's the best time for such physical displays of affection. Wouldn't you agree?"

Reid wanted nothing more than to crawl under a rock and hide. Cheeks on fire, she scrambled away from Dexter.

"Goodnight, Mother," Dexter said, obviously frustrated at the interruption. Instead of seeming embarrassed, he took Reid's hand and tugged her to his side, escorting her down the staircase.

Nara, still dressed, made her way up the steps. "Goodnight, you two."

"Why is your mother up this late?" Reid asked. "Am I the only one who actually sleeps around here?"

When they entered the sitting room, Duke Ellington stood in front of the fireplace, a drink in hand.

"Where's everyone?" Reid asked, hurrying to wrap her father in a hug.

"It's just me." He kissed her forehead before pulling away.

"Kamden isn't even here?" While Reid hadn't expected her three eldest sisters to attend her wedding, she'd thought Kamden would at least.

"She is home tending to our guests," he whispered.

Reid had forgotten Leigh and Idina were hidden away in her father's castle.

"It's good to see you," Ellington murmured. "I was worried about you." When he saw she had the ring on, he smiled approvingly. "Glad to see it's on your finger where it belongs."

"How was your journey? How have you been?"

Ellington addressed Dexter. "The two of us need to talk."

Dexter nodded.

Then, to Reid, her father said, "I'll see you in a few days."

"What?" He'd just gotten there. "Won't I see you at

241

breakfast?" Reid wanted to spend the day with him so she could show him the palace, explore the city, and maybe go for a ride together.

Placing his hands on her shoulders, he looked into her eyes. "I plan to leave first thing in the morning. There are some things I need to do."

What could her father possibly have to do in Axian?

"I need to speak with Prince Dexter. Go to bed, Reid."

She tensed, not believing her father had dismissed her like a child.

When Dexter opened the door, a sentry entered. "Please escort Lady Reid to her suite," Dexter ordered. To Reid, he said, "I'll see you in the morning."

And just like that, she'd been dismissed by both her father and her fiancé. Tamping down her anger, she followed the sentry like a dutiful woman. Whatever was going on had to be of utmost importance. Otherwise, why wouldn't her father include her? She needed to trust her father and Dexter. Too bad trusting was so hard. She hated being left in the dark.

———

The following day, Duke Ellington didn't show up at breakfast. Since he'd arrived in the middle of the night, only a few sentries and the royal family knew he was in Axian. Had her father not traveled with a convoy of soldiers? There was no way he'd made the journey from his castle in Ellington all the way to the City of Radella alone.

Ackley leaned over to whisper in her ear. "You have family in Axian. It shouldn't be that difficult to figure out where your father might have gone."

And just like that, the anxious feeling she'd been dealing with evaporated. Of course he'd want to see his in-laws. Only, weren't they coming for the wedding? Maybe her father planned to escort them here himself.

Dexter set his goblet down with more force than necessary. Tilting his head to the side, he cracked his neck and blew out an annoyed breath.

"Problem?" Ackley drawled.

"I would appreciate it if you would refrain from whispering in my fiancée's ear, touching her, or playing with her hair." Dexter's glare bore into Ackley, his scowl harsh and foreboding.

When Dexter acted like this, it reminded Reid of when she'd first met him. A calm rage simmered below his surface, itching to break free.

"If my sister were here," Ackley replied coolly, "you'd see I treat her the same."

A sentry entered. He handed a letter to Dexter before leaving once more.

Before opening the letter, Dexter snapped, "I don't care if that's how you treat your sister. It bothers me. Therefore, I'd prefer you show enough respect to refrain from smothering Reid."

"Shouldn't we ask Reid if it bothers her?" Ackley countered.

Dexter mumbled something unintelligible. With jerky movements that betrayed his aggravation with Ackley, he ripped into the envelope and removed a slip of paper. After he read the letter, he placed it on the table, rubbing his forehead.

"What's wrong?" Reid asked.

"Soldiers have been spotted. Twenty miles from here."

"They're not holding their position in the open fields?" Ackley asked.

"No. They are marching directly toward the city. It appears the king is leading them, although the men are dressed in red, which is not the king's color." Shoving his chair away from the table, he rose. "Please excuse me. I must don my battle gear, then ride out to meet them before they get too close to the city."

When he left the room, panic flooded Reid. Why did Dexter

have to meet the soldiers? Resting her face against her hands, she breathed deeply, knowing how stupid it was to not want him to go. Dexter commanded the army. Therefore, he was doing what he must and what was right—even though Reid desperately wished he wouldn't put himself in harm's way.

Appetite gone, Reid pushed away from the table and left the dining room. In the corridor, Gytha followed right on Reid's heels, much too close. Reid momentarily paused, causing the warrior woman to collide into her, Gytha's boot scraping the back of Reid's foot. Her control suddenly snapped. Whirling around, she got right in the warrior woman's face. "What's your problem?"

Gytha leaned even closer, but Reid refused to retreat.

"I should be riding with my commander, not babysitting you," Gytha forced out between clenched teeth.

"I agree." Reid folded her arms, eyes narrowed.

"You do?" Gytha replied sharply.

"Yes! I'd rather you guard him than me. There are enough people in the palace to keep an eye on me. I'll be fine. Dexter, on the other hand, needs someone to watch his back."

Gytha straightened. "We agree?"

"We agree." But what could they do about it? "Let's go speak to Dexter." One of his best soldiers shouldn't be guarding Reid at the palace when he planned to leave to meet an army. "Where would he go to don his battle gear?"

"Ladies," Ackley said as he joined them. "What are you two scheming?"

"I should be with my commander, not Lady Reid," Gytha said.

"While I agree with you, someone must protect Lady Reid. If the army sends a unit of men ahead and attempts to take the palace by surprise, who will be here to make sure the royal family stays safe?"

Sentries were posted for events of that nature. However, Reid understood his point. "What if you went?" she suggested.

"Oh, I plan to. I just need to make sure I blend in with the soldiers so no one will recognize me." He winked, then continued his stroll down the hallway, whistling.

"What do you think?" Reid asked Gytha.

"We'll let Ackley accompany the soldiers. He won't even bother to ask permission—he'll just go. I am not at liberty to pick and choose what orders I do and do not obey."

Even knowing Dexter would have Ackley and Markis with him, Reid drifted through the day in a state of unease. She couldn't shake the fear something terrible would happen to him. Unable to take her pacing, Gytha dragged Reid to the military compound and forced her to do sword drills as a distraction.

Even though it was painful to go through the motions since her ribs hadn't fully healed, the physical activity drove the thoughts about Dexter, the foreign army, and her father's whereabouts to the back of her mind. All she could do was focus on the movements Gytha demanded of her. When Reid's arms were no longer capable of holding the wooden sword above her waist, she finally stopped for the day.

After a quick bath, she dressed, then joined the others for supper. When a servant placed a plate in front of her, Reid ate, though she was unable to recall what had been served before she'd even left the room. Now in her bedchamber, unable to sleep, she stood vigil at her window with Gytha by her side.

"Deep breath in and deep breath out," Nara instructed. "That's it."

Reid obeyed the princess's directions. "Tell me again why we're doing this?" she asked as they meandered through one of the interior courtyards. Dexter had been gone for three days, and they hadn't received a single word from him. The wedding was scheduled to take place in a week.

Nara rearranged the folds of her dress, seemingly

uncomfortable in the foreign attire. "We are doing this so we can control our anger and frustration when we must speak to the dukes from the north—instead of punching them in their faces as we'd rather do."

Reid snorted. "They're not all pigheaded."

"I know. But there's only so much of their backward thinking I can take. I don't know how you survived living in the north."

Reid had only survived because she'd been raised as a man.

A sentry approached. "Our soldiers are escorting the queen's party through the city. They are expected to arrive in the next five to ten minutes." He bowed, then left.

"You want to talk about backward, wait until you meet the queen," Reid said, smacking a hand to her forehead at the thought of having to deal with her. The woman never spoke her mind, did whatever Eldon told her to, and was as boring as a doorknob.

"Well, I suppose we should go to the front of the palace to greet them." Nara took Reid's hand. "Before we go, tell me how you're holding up."

The question embodied the sort of conversation Reid disliked having. While she didn't particularly care for Gytha, at least the woman never tried to get personal or talk about their feelings.

"It's okay to be worried," Nara said. "That doesn't mean you're weak."

"I don't like when things are out of my control," Reid admitted. And she hated relying on other people to take care of things. "Realistically, I understand I can't ride or fight beside Dexter." While she'd been taught to fight, she hadn't been trained in battle strategy or combat situations.

"But emotionally...you believe you'd handle this better if you could be at his side?"

"I do." Being involved in the action would help Reid regain control, making her feel wanted and important to the cause. Sitting around and taking orders wasn't something she was good at.

Nara wrapped an arm around Reid. "Did I ever tell you that you remind me of myself when I was your age?"

"Really?" Reid assumed Nara had always been a take-charge sort of person who knew what she wanted and had the utmost confidence in herself. Logically, Reid knew it probably wasn't true. Confidence in one's self was gained over time. But it was hard to remember that when faced with what Reid believed were her own shortcomings.

"Really."

They hurried to the front of the palace where Prince Henrick and Prince Colbert waited. Reid spotted Axian soldiers in the distance, escorting several carriages. For the first time, she realized she would soon come face to face with Gordon. If she were being honest, she'd been so wrapped up in her worry over Dexter's safety and the army's invasion that she'd completely forgotten Gordon even existed, much less spared a thought about seeing him again.

Three carriages stopped in front of the palace. The Axian soldiers continued around the side, out of sight. Only Marsden soldiers remained. One man dismounted, hurried over to the first carriage, and opened the door. Princess Dana emerged in a simple tan dress, her hair in a single braid. After a moment, Queen Harlow appeared and accepted the doorman's proffered hand, allowing him to help her out. In a sky-blue dress, her hair in soft waves around her face, the queen found her footing, then smoothed the folds of her gown.

Another man dismounted, barking out a few orders. The carriages and soldiers headed around the side of the palace, following the path the Axian soldiers had taken.

Reid scanned the three people at the foot of the steps—Prince Gordon, Princess Dana, and Queen Harlow. Henrick introduced himself before apologizing to the queen about the harrowing experience she'd endured when they'd been attacked on their journey.

"My wife, Princess Nara, will see you to your rooms. I'm sure you'd like to rest after such a long and trying journey. If you're up for it, we will see you at supper."

With a gracious smile, Nara stepped forward, inviting the queen and princess into the palace.

Once the women disappeared, Gordon approached.

"We're so sorry you were attacked," Colbert said. "We're currently investigating the situation."

"I'm glad. Thankfully, King Eldon wasn't with us," Gordon replied.

"Where is the king?" Henrick asked. "I'd hoped we'd have time for a talk."

"He'll be along shortly," was all Gordon would say.

After they entered the palace and exchanged a few more pleasantries, Colbert offered to escort Gordon to his room.

Prince Henrick excused himself. He'd arranged for the dukes to go hunting, and he was eager to join them.

Reid decided to go to the library to find Finn. She wanted to make sure he had food and water. Plus, she needed to ensure he didn't get into any trouble with all the strangers in the palace.

Gytha emerged from the shadows, joining her. "What's wrong with the queen? Doesn't she speak?"

"Women aren't encouraged to speak unless they are spoken to. And even then, they are expected to be demure."

Gytha shuddered. "It's a good thing you were raised as a man then."

A laugh escaped Reid.

"Lady Reid," Gordon called from down the hall.

A chill spread over her skin. What could he possibly have to say to her? She risked a glance at Gytha, whose eyebrows drew together in confusion.

"Yes, Prince Gordon?" Reid said, turning to face him.

He walked toward her, Colbert at his side. While Reid still

found Prince Gordon handsome, any pull she'd previously felt had vanished.

Smiling, he stopped a respectful distance away. "It's good to see you."

Reid chose not to respond. Instead, she merely inclined her head.

"Can we talk? Privately?" he asked.

"Lady Reid will not be going anywhere alone with you," Gytha cut in, eyeing him suspiciously.

Keeping his focus solely on Reid, he said, "The Reid I know would never let someone else dictate what she can or cannot do." He folded his arms, the challenge clear.

"And the Gordon I know would never let the king welcome soldiers from another kingdom into Marsden just to take over Axian." She watched his reaction closely, hoping to glean some knowledge.

Gordon stiffened.

It was all she needed to see. "Has the king been hiding things from you? His commander? His own brother?" Taking a step toward him, she whispered, "But that shouldn't surprise you. After all, he tried to kill your own mother with his bare hands."

He flinched, his face paling. "Who told you that? Ackley?"

"How can you support Eldon?"

"He's my king!"

"What about the foreign army?" she demanded.

"I've only heard rumors."

"Didn't you think to investigate?"

"There's only so much I can do."

Disappointment filled her at his cowardly answer. "I'm sorry to hear that." She turned and strode away from him, holding her head high even while her hands began to shake. Once she was safely around the corner, she slumped against the wall.

"What was that?" Gytha demanded.

"I don't want to talk about it."

"Don't take this the wrong way, Lady Reid, but you are one complicated individual."

"Dukes Willer, Tucker, Slader, and Lyndr brought fifty soldiers each. Dukes Ryder, Cartr, and Bridger each brought twenty," Gytha murmured into Reid's ear.

They were in the dining hall, everyone mingling since the food hadn't yet been served. "And my father?"

"No one has seen anyone wearing Ellington livery."

"That means, in addition to the Axian soldiers on hand, we have an extra two hundred and sixty men." *Such a paltry number,* Reid thought, fighting the despair threatening to rise within her.

"Lady Reid," Gordon said as he slid up next to her. "You're a difficult woman to talk to."

Because she'd purposefully been avoiding him all evening.

"I want to know where my brother is."

Disgusted, she glared at him. "You lost your king?"

"Not that brother. Ackley."

Oh. She hadn't even considered he might want to know where Ackley was. "He's busy," she said, purposefully being vague.

"With Ackley, I can never tell if that's a good thing or a bad thing."

"Depends on whose side you're on."

He eyed her. "Aren't we all on the same side?"

She shrugged, choosing to neither confirm nor deny her stance.

Gytha cleared her throat, nudging Reid.

"Prince Gordon, I don't think you've had the pleasure of meeting my dear friend and personal guard, Captain Gytha," Reid said, making the introduction Gytha clearly wanted.

"You're the commander of the king's army?" Gytha asked, eyebrow cocked.

"Yes."

"Is your army not very good?"

Gordon bristled. "Why would you think that?"

"Because the king recruited soldiers from Melenia," Gytha stated bluntly. "I must conclude that your men are incompetent. It's the only reason I can come to for why the king felt he had to look elsewhere to find men who could fight."

Gordon glanced around. The queen and Dana were on the other side of the room, far enough away they couldn't overhear. Most of the dukes conversed with either Prince Henrick or Queen Harlow.

"That's why it's important I speak to Ackley," Gordon mumbled. "He suspected Eldon was in communication with Melenia. Idina was investigating the matter."

Duke Ellington appeared, striding straight toward Reid. Relief washed through her. Her father was here, and he was okay. *Forget decorum.* She wrapped her arms around him, squeezing him tightly.

He held her at arm's length. Pretending he hadn't seen her in months, he twisted her this way and that as he examined her. "I can't believe my baby girl is finally getting married."

"I'm glad you're here."

"I wouldn't miss this for anything. Come, I want to introduce you to some of the dukes."

"Lady Reid," Gordon said. "I'm not done speaking with you."

Duke Ellington leveled him with a glare. "My daughter has no reason to speak with you." Wrapping his arm around her shoulders, her father escorted her over to where three dukes stood speaking to one another.

Reid found it interesting that all the northern dukes were in attendance; however, not a single one had brought his wife.

"Duke Tucker," Reid said, inclining her head in greeting. "It's good to see you again." While she'd welcomed him when he'd first arrived, she hadn't had a chance to speak with him since then.

"It is good to see you Lady Reid."

"This is Duke Willer and Duke Slader," Duke Ellington said, indicating the men on either side of Duke Tucker.

Duke Willer was in his eighties with solid white hair. He stood slightly hunched forward, a cane in hand. Duke Slader, on the other hand, looked to be about twenty. Sweat beaded on his forehead and his right hand slightly shook as he held a drink.

"We are discussing the letter Duke Axian sent," Duke Tucker stated.

Reid must have heard him wrong. Her grandfather wouldn't have sent a letter to the northern dukes.

"Do you believe him?" Duke Willer asked, his voice gravelly from old age.

"I do," Duke Slader whispered, his eyes moving back and forth as he watched to make sure no one could overhear them. "I believe Eldon is not the rightful heir. The king should either be Prince Gordon or Prince Henrick."

"I think it should be Henrick," Duke Ellington mumbled. "King Hudson didn't declare Prince Gordon his heir."

"I happen to agree with you," Duke Willer stated. "The problem will be that since your daughter here is marrying Prince Dexter, you have a vested interest in the outcome. Wouldn't you agree?"

"I side with the law," Duke Ellington said. "And, if the rumors are true, whoever is going to get this foreign army out of our kingdom."

Dukes Willer, Tucker, and Slader agreed.

Duke Lyndr weaseled his way over. "What are you discussing?" he asked, his crooked nose twitching as he observed the group.

"We were just saying what a lovely match your daughter and Prince Ackley will make," Duke Ellington replied.

Reid choked out a cough. "Excuse me, what did you say?"

Duke Lyndr smiled. "The king opened marriage negotiations between my youngest daughter, Eloise, and Prince Ackley."

Reid coughed again. No wonder Ackley had been in a foul mood.

"Are you okay?" Duke Ellington asked.

She nodded. "I'm just exhausted from all of the activities. If you'll excuse me, I am going to lie down." She hurried from the room before she could say something about how Ackley would never marry someone like Eloise.

———

Prince Henrick used the following days to take full advantage of the king's absence. Escorting the dukes around the city, he showed them how prosperous it could be to allow women to work alongside men. Demonstrations on how the people in his county traded with one another, ultimately increasing their wealth, were also given. Henrick reiterated his willingness to remain south of the Gast River, but he also stated he was open to trading with other counties if the king allowed it. In short, Prince Henrick tried to foster the dukes' loyalty by agreeing to adhere to the old ways while subtly introducing other, better ways to prosper—using the incentive of more wealth as one would use a shiny toy to attract a baby.

Reid was present for most of these events, remaining at her father's side as much as possible. She did sneak back to the bookstore every day, hoping to find a reply from the Knights. But the book of correspondence stayed empty. What did the Knights intend to do about the foreign army? Would they support the king or fight for the people?

Late one night, Reid entered her suite, Gytha at her side, exhausted from the dukes' constant chatter and their concern about including women in their business dealings.

"Tomorrow, we do something else," Gytha insisted. "I cannot guard you and listen to those pompous, arrogant, sorry excuses for men any longer. You have no idea how much restraint and willpower I exhibited today." She flopped on the sofa, then pounded her fist into the cushion.

"That's what I grew up in."

Gytha opened her mouth, about to respond, when the soldier in her suddenly snapped to attention. Reid froze, watching as Gytha whipped to the right and withdrew her dagger in one smooth move. "Who's there?" the warrior woman demanded.

The queen stepped out of the shadows, keeping her hands visible. "Lower your voice," she whispered. "No one can know I'm here."

Gytha sheathed her dagger, though her glare was openly hostile.

"I'd like a word with Lady Reid," the queen stated.

"I am not permitted to let Lady Reid out of my sight."

"Very well. Lady Reid, if you'll join me over here, away from the door?"

Reid was still in a state of shock that the queen was in her room. The young woman had always been so docile, Reid hadn't thought her capable of decision making. Curious, she joined the queen over by the windows. Not wanting anyone to see them, Reid closed the curtains.

Gytha remained on the sofa about twenty feet away, carefully watching them.

"Is there something I can do for you?" Reid asked. The room was fairly dark with only two candles lit, which left the corner the women conversed in shrouded in shadows.

"I see the way you look at me," Harlow started. "Like I'm a stupid, meek, incompetent fool."

Reid wanted to argue, but she bit her tongue. The queen was right—that was how Reid thought of Harlow.

"You, of all people, should know how deceiving appearances can be. Just because I act one way in front of most people doesn't mean I am always like that." Although she whispered, her voice held a hint of authority and confidence Reid had never noticed before.

Shame filled Reid for thinking so poorly of the queen. She should have taken the time to get to know the woman.

"I am here to warn you," the queen continued.

"Warn me? About the foreign army?" Did Queen Harlow know of the king's plans? Reid doubted he shared much with his wife. After all, he hated women and thought them subservient to men.

"I'm glad you know about them," she said. "But an army from at home or abroad is still an army. I'm sure you and the commander know how to deal with such threats." She pushed a lock of hair behind her ear. "But the real threat is the one no one ever sees coming."

Was the queen threatening Reid or trying to help her? She had no idea.

"Sometimes the quietest person in the room is the most dangerous."

"I'm not following," Reid said.

"My husband *thinks* he has the situation under control. He believes he knows which dukes support him. He also assumes the foreign army will not double cross him."

"What do you know?" Reid demanded. Did Harlow have connections no one knew about or had she been investigating on her own?

"I can't say too much. I shouldn't even be here talking to you. But know that while not everyone supports the king, they might not support the *removal* of the king, either. No one does anything without having an end goal in mind. Figure out the end goal, and you can circumvent their plans. If you don't understand what they're doing and why, you'll never be able to stop them."

Reid had no idea if Harlow meant herself, the king, the dukes, or the Knights. What she said could apply to anyone. Reid would have to think carefully about everything the queen had said and revealed to decipher the meaning.

"Navigate carefully, Lady Reid. Otherwise, you'll find yourself drowning with no one to help." After issuing that last warning —*threat?*—she touched the wall. A door sprang open. The queen left, the door closing and seamlessly blending in behind her.

"Did you know that was there?" Reid asked Gytha, gesturing at the invisible door.

"No, I didn't."

Neither had Reid. And she'd spent a week with Nara learning how to navigate through the servants' passageways and the subterranean tunnels. Not once had the princess said anything about this door being in Reid's suite.

"Did you hear anything the queen said?"

"I didn't hear a word. I was too busy making sure she didn't pull a knife and stab you."

Reid supposed she needed to discover Harlow's motives in order to figure out why the queen had felt the need to warn her. Once she did that, maybe the warning would make sense. For now, Reid wanted to crawl into bed. Her eyes were too heavy and her brain too foggy. In the morning, she would dissect her conversation with the queen.

Gytha shook Reid awake. "A letter from Dexter just arrived for you." She plopped on Reid's bed, handing her the letter.

Reid sat up, then rubbed her eyes. She opened the envelope, finding a single sheet of paper.

Eldon is leading the foreign army. He'll arrive in three or four days. Tell Gytha to prepare for a full-scale invasion.

Gytha cursed. She went over to the vanity, grabbing her weapons.

As Reid slid out of bed, she contemplated why Dexter had sent the letter to her instead of his mother or brother. Or even Gytha. Reid's conversation with the queen haunted her thoughts. What were Dexter's motivations?

"Let's go, Lady Reid." With one leg on a chair, Gytha strapped a dagger to her thigh.

"Where to?"

"The military compound."

"Let me change first." Reid removed her nightdress.

Gytha hissed. "You are still bruised up."

Reid examined her ribs. "It looks worse than it is. It's not as painful as it used to be."

"You shouldn't have done sword work with me. The commander should have told me you can't adequately defend yourself right now."

Grabbing pants and a tunic from the armoire, Reid decided not to argue with the woman. While she couldn't fight nearly as well as she would like to, she wasn't helpless. If it came to a life-or-death situation, she would push through the pain.

"No. Put a dress on."

"Why?" Now was hardly the time to wear something so impractical.

"The dukes need to see you as a lady. Ladies wear dresses. Not pants. Pants will intimidate those idiots."

Reid pulled on a simple lavender dress, wondering why it was acceptable for Gytha to wear pants. Granted, she was acting as a sentry and wore the uniform all sentries currently did.

The two women made their way out of the palace, across the lawn, and into the compound. After telling Reid not to leave her side, Gytha ran around barking orders to every soldier she encountered. Then she went to the top of the building, proceeding to blow a large horn three times. She waited ten minutes, then repeated the sequence, explaining to Reid it was a warning for the inhabitants of the city.

Next, they went to the armory. Gytha handed Reid several

daggers, along with sheathes to put them in. "You need one on each thigh, one on each arm, one on your back, and one on each calf."

Reid blinked. "If I were to need the one on my thigh, how do you suggest I obtain it given the fact I'm wearing a dress?" She put her hands on her hips, waiting for a response.

Gytha shrugged. "If you're alone in a room, you can get it. The point is, you'll have a weapon if you need one." Picking up a belt, she strapped it around her waist, securing a sword to it.

Reid attached the sheathes, then slid a dagger in each one.

"The compound is in the process of being locked down," Gytha said. "We need to get out of here before we're stuck."

They exited and headed back toward the palace, jogging across the lawn. Axian soldiers moved into position all around the palace. People with bags on their shoulders poured from buildings and made their way out of the city.

"Is that what they're supposed to do when they hear the horn?" Reid asked.

"Yes. They know to only grab what is necessary and to head south immediately."

A chill slid over Reid's skin. "I hope everyone gets out safely." At least they had a couple of days until the king and foreign army arrived.

"If they hurry, they should be able to get far enough."

"What are we going to do?" Reid asked. "Are we going to leave as well?"

"No. We're going to stay and face King Eldon."

Good. Because that was exactly what Reid wanted to do.

CHAPTER TWENTY-ONE

T he royal family informed the dukes a foreign army had been spotted heading directly for the palace, the king leading the soldiers.

"Why do you think it's a foreign army and not our own?" Duke Willer asked.

The dukes and royal family convened around a large dining table.

"They are dressed in solid red," Gordon stated. "That is not the uniform of Marsden soldiers."

"We cannot assume it's an act of war," Duke Ryder stated.

No surprise that Duke Ryder would side with the king. His daughter was Princess Dana—Gordon's wife.

"No," Gordon said. "We cannot. But I have men in position just in case. Until we know more, we will exercise caution."

Reid saw an opening, so took it. "Prince Gordon, do you think these foreign soldiers are the ones who tried to assassinate the king?"

"I don't know," he admitted. "When we were attacked, I didn't see anyone's face, nor did I see any sort of uniform."

Regardless, Reid had planted the seed, which was all she needed to do.

"Has the king been kidnapped?" Duke Ellington asked.

"I sent men to spy on the incoming army." Gordon shook his head. "It appears the king is riding with them in good spirits."

"I don't understand," Prince Colbert said. "Our king is in league with a foreign army?"

Everyone started talking at once.

Gordon raised his hand, capturing everyone's attention. "I don't know what's going on. However, since the king appears to be fine, we will assume the army means us no harm and the wedding will proceed as planned." He glanced at Reid, then quickly looked away. "If I find out the king is there against his will, we will retake our king, defeat the enemy, and Marsden will be victorious." With that, he strode out of the room.

"He is definitely a soldier," Gytha mumbled as she and Reid also exited. "He is not very eloquent with his speech."

While Reid agreed, she didn't say anything. Gordon was in a tough position—having sworn fealty to the king, being commander of the Marsden army, being the brother of the king, and having a keen love for his kingdom. If it came down to choosing between his king and kingdom, what would he do? Again, the queen's words came back to haunt Reid. What were Gordon's motivations? What did he want?

Two days later, the horn blew once, indicating the army had been spotted entering the city. Reid hoped they didn't destroy the beautiful buildings as they marched toward the palace. Some of these buildings were hundreds of years old. At least the people had made it safely out of the city.

Reid and Gytha made their way to the first floor, where they were supposed to meet the dukes. They'd decided they would all greet the king and army together. Many hoped the army would pose no threat.

As Reid headed along a corridor, Finn bounded toward her. She knew Colbert couldn't be far behind. Squatting, she rubbed Finn's head.

"We do not have time to pet the dog," Gytha said.

"Oh, I beg to differ," Colbert said as he stopped before them. "There's always time to pet Finn."

"Is the army flying the king's banner?" Gytha asked.

"Scouts are reporting the army is flying two banners—the king's banner and a red banner with a lion fanned in flames. I've never seen it before, so I am assuming it belongs to Melenia." He bent to attach a leash to Finn.

Reid had never seen the dog on leash before. She stood.

"I've been ordered to leave," Colbert explained. "That way, there will be at least one survivor should the king decide to slaughter you all." Although he tried to make a joke of it, the lines around his eyes revealed how tense he was. "Don't look so panicked," he said, placing a hand on Reid's arm. "Markis just arrived. He and a handful of Axian soldiers are going with me."

"Where to?" she asked. Obviously, it would be somewhere out of the city. However, with the army less than a mile away, he wouldn't have much of a head start should soldiers pursue him.

"There's a place," Gytha said. "He'll be safe. Don't worry."

Reid couldn't help but worry. There were too many people she cared about in harm's way and too many things that could go wrong. Everything was a big unknown, and she hated it.

Markis came running down the corridor. "They're in the city proper," he said. "Let's go." He grabbed Colbert by the sleeve, dragging him down the hallway, Finn dutifully following.

Since Markis was here, Dexter and Ackley had to be as well.

Gytha pulled Reid into one of the rooms. "When we get to the front of the palace, do not show shock, fear, or any other emotion —no matter what happens. Understand?"

Reid nodded.

"Are you armed?"

"Yes." Even though Reid knew she'd strapped the daggers to her arms and legs, she patted them to reassure herself.

When they reached the front door, Gytha told Reid she'd be out of sight but still nearby. Gytha didn't want the king to be able to easily identify her as Reid's guard.

Wishing she could hide out of sight as well, Reid exited the palace. Henrick stood at the top of the steps, Nara at his side. The dukes had spread out on the lower steps, all wearing tunics embroidered with their family's crest.

Reid spotted her father among them.

Gordon strode out of the palace with both Dana and Harlow. The queen stood next to Henrick, Gordon and Dana on her other side. Reid decided to stand beside Nara.

"Has anyone heard from Prince Ackley?" Gordon asked.

"I'm right here, brother," Ackley said, pulling the sleeves of his shirt down over his arms as he exited the palace. He stood next to his brother.

Since Ackley was here, didn't that mean Dexter had to be here as well? Peering at Ackley, Reid searched for any kind of signal from him, but he didn't even look her way. Folding her hands, she faced the lawn, waiting for the king and army to arrive.

Soldiers were stationed around the perimeter of the palace and the rooftop. All wore crisp, matching uniforms.

Reid felt a strong, warm presence behind her. Turning, she watched Dexter exit the palace, relief almost choking her at the sight. He wore a plain black tunic, similar to his father's, which bore the Winston family crest on the front. The same symbol as the king, only smaller and less ostentatious.

He came up next to her, not once meeting her eyes. "What?" he whispered.

"Nothing." She'd just never seen him dressed so demurely before. Normally, he wore military attire, which exposed his muscular arms. The man beside her looked like a subdued duke or prince—which was what she assumed he was going for. He almost didn't look or feel like her Dexter.

A low, rumbling sound reverberated through the ground.

"Here they come," Dexter murmured, taking a deliberate step away from Reid.

Soldiers appeared. Rows and rows of men dressed in solid red with a lion stitched on the front of their uniforms. They kept coming. Hundreds of them. They lined up on the front lawn, leaving a space in the middle leading directly to the palace entrance. Then the horses appeared. There were probably thirty or so carrying men dressed in a variation of the red uniform. Reid assumed they were the officers. They rode down the aisle to the steps of the palace. When they fanned out, she realized the king was among them.

Reid examined the soldiers noting they all had a similar look to them—wide-shouldered, muscled arms, short hair. They resembled the three groups of assassins she'd encountered as well as the miners from Bridger, confirming her suspicions that the men weren't assassins or miners, but soldiers from another kingdom.

Eldon dismounted, moving to stand before Henrick. Everyone bowed or curtsied. "Rise," Eldon commanded as he scanned those present on the steps.

Reid glanced between Henrick and Eldon—father and son. What were they each thinking?

"Welcome," Henrick said. "We are pleased and honored you traveled here for the wedding. Please come inside for some refreshments."

Wasn't he going to ask about the hundreds of soldiers in formation on the lawn?

Gordon's hands balled into fists, but he didn't question his brother.

Was no one going to demand to know what was going on?

Were they all supposed to pretend as if nothing were amiss? Reid wanted to shake sense into everybody.

Dexter took a step forward, garnering the king's shrewd attention. Reid wanted to throw her body in front of the prince to protect him from the king. Instead, she held her position.

"May I inquire as to why soldiers from Melenia are here in the kingdom of Marsden?" Dexter asked.

Swirling inside Reid was a combination of relief that someone had finally asked what was going on, mixed with a cold fear of what the answer would be.

"Someone tried to assassinate me," the king said.

"Forgive me, cousin" Dexter replied, "but I was informed the attack happened last week. Is that correct?"

"Yes."

A chill slid over Reid. Dexter had called Eldon *cousin* for a reason. To everyone here, they were cousins. However, Reid knew the truth. These two men were half brothers. They had the same father, different mothers. And their father stood two feet away from them, his face drawn.

Dexter tilted his head, observing Eldon. "If the attack happened last week, how did you manage to send a message to another kingdom, procure some sort of alliance, get the soldiers to travel here by ship—a journey that takes two weeks—and then have said soldiers trek across Axian? All in under one week?"

The king's eyes narrowed. "That was not the attack I was referring to."

Henrick stepped between Eldon and Dexter. "King Eldon, perhaps we should have these soldiers set up camp just outside the city? I fear we do not have the appropriate accommodations for so many here." He spread his hands out, indicating the palace lawn.

"You do not need to concern yourself with these soldiers," the king replied. "Commander Beck," he barked, glancing over his shoulder. One of the men who'd ridden in on a horse stepped forward. "You know what to do." Then, to everyone on the steps, the king ordered, "Let's head inside."

The dukes, all the royal family members, the king, and a handful of the king's soldiers followed Nara into the palace. She led everyone into a grand sitting room that was two stories tall and opened to a courtyard. A handful of servants carrying trays filled with food and drinks entered, handing out the refreshments.

"I can assure you that our palace is safe," Henrick said, eyeing the soldiers. "You don't need to worry about security while you're here."

"That is good to hear since I intend to stay for a while."

The fake smile on Reid's face froze. Before the king arrived, Reid had known he was coming here to take over Axian. Regardless, the shock of so many soldiers and the reality of it actually happening was hard to stomach. She sat on a chair close to the window, her father not far away. Gytha was nowhere to be seen. Dexter made a point of standing near his mother, closer to the king. Dexter never once looked in Reid's direction. It was as if he couldn't care less about her. At the other end of the room, Gordon paced back and forth. Ackley finally went and put his arm around Gordon, forcing him to remain in place while he whispered in his ear.

"After the wedding tomorrow," Nara said to the king, "we would be happy to show you around Axian."

"Ah, yes. The wedding." Eldon motioned for one of his soldiers to step forward. When the soldier produced a decanter of fine alcohol, a servant rushed into the room with a tray of goblets. The king poured a small amount into each goblet, then distributed them to the dukes and princes. Not one woman received a drink. Normally, it would have offended Reid. However, she had no desire to accept anything the king had to offer.

Duke Ellington took the goblet handed to him, then came to stand directly behind Reid.

"I'd like to make a toast," King Eldon said. "To Prince Dexter and Lady Reid." When he lifted his goblet, everyone copied the gesture. "To a long and healthy marriage. Why are the two of you so far apart? You're getting married tomorrow." A slow smile spread across his face. "Come now—you should be happy."

Dexter didn't even glance in Reid's direction.

"They are still getting to know one another," Duke Ellington commented.

"Well," the king drawled, lifting his goblet higher, "to the happy couple!"

Everyone took a drink. When Ellington set his aside, Reid noticed the same amount of alcohol remained. He hadn't drunk a drop. Relief filled her.

People started to eat the food the servants had brought, and conversations sprang up.

Duke Ellington leaned down. "Do you know which room I'm staying in?" he murmured.

Reid nodded.

"Wait five minutes, then leave and meet me there." He meandered around the room, talking to people here and there, before he slipped out the side door.

Even though people were talking, Reid found it to be useless chatter about the weather or the harvest. Several people spoke a little louder than necessary. She assumed everyone was nervous. Ackley and Gordon were side by side. The dukes remained close to the king. However, no one dared ask anything substantial—like what Eldon intended to do with the foreign army.

Since no one was paying her any attention, she made her way over to the sentry standing guard near the door. "Which way to the privy?" she asked.

"I don't know," he replied.

It was only natural he wouldn't know, seeing as he was a soldier from northern Marsden. Reid had only asked the question so if the king inquired after her, the soldier would relay she'd needed to relieve herself.

She exited the room. Five steps down the hallway, Gytha suddenly appeared at Reid's side. Silently, they made their way to Duke Ellington's chambers. Not bothering to knock, Reid entered with Gytha. Her father continued to shove clothes into a travel bag without looking up.

"Where are you going?" Reid asked.

He tied the bag, then studied Reid, his hands on his hips. "To speak with the person in charge of the Knights."

Reid had never seen a tattoo on her father's wrist, so she knew he wasn't a Knight. "You know about them?" She glanced at Gytha, who stood quietly by the door.

"I do," he replied.

Had Ackley told him? Or had he found out some other way? "I already sent them a message. They know a foreign army is here." And she hadn't heard a word about what they wanted her or Ackley to do. Weren't the Knights supposed to be protectors of the kingdom?

"I can't sit around when we are on the brink of war. I must do something." He slung his bag over his shoulder. "I won't be back in time for the wedding—if the wedding even takes place." He went over to the window, peering outside. The lawn was still full of soldiers. "You have a choice."

He'd never given her a choice before.

"You can come with me now or you can stay here. There are pros and cons to each decision. However, I must leave before the king has a chance to stop me."

"What do you hope to accomplish?"

"We need to show this army that we are not to be trifled with. We will send them back to wherever it is they're from."

Reid agreed with his end goal. However, she wasn't sure how to go about accomplishing it. If she went with her father, she'd be running away. It might keep her safe and out of harm's way. Yet, the thought of leaving Dexter here to fend for himself didn't sit well with her. Not only that, but if she left, she'd also be turning

267

her back on her wedding. On the other hand, this was Reid's chance to get out of it. However, no matter how she looked at it, the idea of running away and not marrying Dexter felt wrong. "I'll stay."

The duke nodded. He approached Reid, then kissed her forehead. "Be smart, stay safe." On his way out of the room, he mumbled something to Gytha before disappearing.

"Now what?" Reid asked, having no desire to return to the sitting room where the king was.

"That is a good question," Gytha replied. Going over to the window, she peered outside. "I don't like any of this. Why are there only men in this so-called army from Melenia? Where *is* Melenia?"

A knock sounded, and Ackley entered. "King Eldon hereby requests the honor of your presence tonight for supper in the great hall." His eyes were vacant, his voice bland and monotone.

"He's made you the errand boy again?" Reid teased, trying to lighten the mood and get some sort of reaction from Ackley.

He didn't laugh.

Reid waved him over.

"What?" He folded his arms.

"You could kill him right now."

"I could. But I'm afraid that if something happens to him, those soldiers have orders to attack. We need to tread carefully. I'd like those soldiers to go home before we kill Eldon."

"We might not get another shot," she pointed out.

"I hate to sound like Prince Henrick, but we need to consider what's going to happen to our citizens. I can't let thousands of innocent people die simply because we want Eldon gone."

"Thousands of people may die regardless."

"True."

"In that case, what's our next move?"

"It depends on the king's next move." He winked. "See you at supper."

The dukes and the royal family attended supper that evening to honor the king. A feast was spread from one end of the table to the other. King Eldon sat at the head of the table, speaking cordially to those around him. He appeared to be a kind, considerate man, asking questions about wives, children, and harvests. If Reid had to pick a word to describe him, she'd say he was personable.

Watching him, she realized he always appeared that way since he was soft spoken. His easy manner hid his evil intentions. If Reid hadn't seen his cruel side for herself—if she didn't know he'd tried to kill his siblings—she'd believe he was simply here for the wedding and the soldiers were for his protection. Because Eldon didn't look evil. He didn't act evil. How could he be so cunning and ruthless underneath the façade? It was the perfect cover—one even she'd bought when she'd first met him.

"I'd like to make a toast," Eldon said, raising his goblet. "To the happy couple! I look forward to your wedding tomorrow."

Everyone murmured *cheers*, then took a sip of their wine.

"Speaking of which, where is Duke Ellington?" Eldon asked.

Reid set her goblet on the table. "He said he was working on something special for my wedding," she replied, forcing a smile.

"Did he say anything about missing supper?"

"No. However, he did go into the city. Maybe he is simply held up?" She took a bite of her food, hoping Eldon couldn't read the lie on her face.

After an uncomfortable minute, he smiled. Addressing everyone present, but keeping a keen eye on Reid, he said, "My brother, Prince Gordon, has an announcement."

Reid wondered what Gordon could have to say. He sat directly across from her, Dana at his side.

Gordon's focus remained on his plate as he cleared his throat. "Princess Dana and I are expecting our first child."

269

A round of applause rippled through the room. Someone made a toast, congratulating the parents-to-be.

The news surprised Reid. While Gordon didn't care for Dana, they'd managed to make a child together. Which meant they'd been intimate. She couldn't imagine Gordon sleeping with Dana.

"Try to wipe that horrified look off your face," Ackley murmured. "I know it's shocking to imagine Dana performing such duties, but it must have happened. At least once." He took a drink of his wine, waggling his eyebrows.

Reid tried not to laugh.

"Father, are you all right?" Dexter asked.

A sheen of sweat covered Henrick's forehead. "I'm fine," he said. "Although, I do think I'm going to retire for the night. We have a big day ahead of us tomorrow." He'd been fine earlier, and Reid had only seen him eat a few bites of his food.

Nara stood. "I'll go with you." They exited the room, Nara glancing over her shoulder once, worry evident in her creased brow.

"I hope Prince Henrick isn't too sick to attend the wedding tomorrow," Eldon said. "It would be a shame if something happened to him."

Fear and anger boiled inside Reid. If Eldon did something to harm Henrick in any way, she'd assassinate him herself.

"Lady Reid," Gytha said, stepping away from the wall where the personal guards were stationed for the evening. "The seamstress wishes to see you. I assume it is to make sure your dress is ready for tomorrow."

Gytha was lying. Reid's completed dress already hung in her bedchamber. "Of course." After Reid stood, she gracefully exited the room, her hands shaking at her sides.

"Sorry," Gytha mumbled once they were alone. "I had to get you out of there. If you could have seen the expression on your face..."

270

"Don't apologize. I don't think I could have been around the king another moment."

They went directly to Henrick's bedchamber. He was already in bed, Nara at his side.

"How is he?" Reid asked.

Nara shook her head. "I don't know. I sent for a healer."

"Is he actually sick or is this Eldon's doing?" Gytha demanded.

"Eldon is my son," Henrick wheezed. "He wouldn't hurt me. I'm sure this is just a cold. It will pass."

Nara pushed his hair back off his forehead. "You're right," she said. "Your own flesh and blood could never do something so evil."

Reid spotted a single tear slide down Nara's face.

CHAPTER TWENTY-TWO

R eid awoke. Today was her wedding day. A dozen emotions swirled within her. However, trepidation seemed to be the dominant one. She slid out of bed and stretched. Gytha was nowhere to be seen.

Reid padded into the sitting room, thinking Gytha may have fallen asleep in there. Instead of the warrior woman, Ackley lounged on the sofa as if he didn't have a care in the world.

"What are you doing here?"

"Good morning, princess."

"Where's Gytha?"

"Helping Prince Dexter."

"Is everything all right?"

He raised a single eyebrow.

"Never mind," Reid mumbled. "Don't bother answering that."

Ackley rose to peer outside. "On a positive note, Dexter managed to get most of the foreign army to set up camp just outside the city."

Reid stood at his side, observing the two dozen or so men who remained on the lawn. "Even their tents are different." Instead of the typical squared tent, theirs were rounded.

"I'm guessing that's a squad of officers," Ackley mused. "Gordon was going to try to talk to their leader." He yawned. "I'll doubt he'll glean any new information."

"Why are you so tired?"

"I've been up all night."

Examining him, she noted the dark circles under his eyes. "What's Gytha doing with Dexter?"

"Some guy named Seb arrived last night with five wagons full of weapons. Last I saw her, she was busy helping Dexter smuggle the weapons into the military compound without the king or the foreign army seeing."

Reid recalled Dexter ordering arrowheads from Seb when he'd visited the man's homestead in the woods. "Do we have a plan?"

"Several, but I don't know if any will work."

"Why are you here?" Didn't he have better things to do than babysit her?

"Gytha asked me to watch you."

Reid eyed him, wondering if he was smitten with the warrior woman.

The door flew open, and Gytha entered. "Prince Dexter just received word Prince Henrick has worsened." After closing the door, she plopped on a chair, rubbing her eyes. "Princess Nara wants to proceed as if nothing is amiss."

A sick foreboding filled Reid. She suspected Eldon had somehow poisoned Henrick.

"Prince Henrick is meeting with each duke individually," Gytha said. "He is making sure they all know Prince Dexter is his heir."

Ackley turned to Gytha, clearly impressed. "That's smart."

Gytha rested her head against the back of the sofa, briefly closing her eyes. "Prince Henrick said we must learn from the mistakes of the past."

"Are you done helping Dexter?" he asked.

"I am. I officially release you of your duty to watch over and protect Lady Reid," she said, sitting straighter.

Ackley gave a curt nod before heading to the door. "Excellent. I have a few things I need to do before the wedding."

Once he left, Reid eyed Gytha. "How are we supposed to proceed as if nothing is amiss?" Henrick was bedridden, a foreign army lurked nearby, and the king was here.

Gytha shrugged. "I guess you get ready for your wedding."

"Do you want to help me, or should I call for Joce?"

The warrior woman snorted. "All servants were evacuated. Only soldiers remain in the palace, so you're stuck with me. I need to warn you, though—I don't know how to do hair or makeup."

That could be problematic since Reid also didn't know how to do either. Oh well, how hard could it be?

As she bathed and dressed, she couldn't help but wonder what life with Dexter would be like. Up until now, she'd refused to think about it. But with the wedding only hours away, she had to face it. He'd said they wouldn't share a marriage bed right away. However, what if the king wanted proof of consummation? What then? Her nerves started to flutter.

"Let's apply your makeup," Gytha said once Reid had managed to get the dress on and fastened correctly. "You are too pale."

As Gytha applied powder to Reid's face, Reid said, "When I first met you, I hated you."

"Trust me, the feeling was mutual."

"I'm sorry for coming into Axian and taking Dexter."

Gytha lowered the brush, observing Reid. "I won't pretend to not be hurt over it," she admitted. "However, I understand. Just make sure you protect Dexter and Axian. That's all that matters."

Once Gytha finished Reid's makeup and hair, Reid examined herself in the mirror. The simple yet elegant dress had been made from heavy, cream-colored silk, the scooped neckline embroidered with thick gold thread. A golden velvet mantle hung from Reid's shoulders down to the hem of her dress. Gytha had braided a portion of Reid's hair, but she'd left the rest to fall in soft waves around her shoulders. A crown rested atop her head, the braid coiled above it to keep it in place.

"Do you need to change?" Reid asked Gytha.

"Yes. Prince Dexter wants me to look like your attendant instead of a soldier." When she rolled her eyes, Reid laughed.

After Gytha readied herself, they headed to Prince Henrick's suite. He still remained in bed, Nara at his side.

Reid took his hand and squeezed it. "Has the healer been here?"

"She has," Nara answered. "She suspects he's been poisoned." Her eyes filled with tears. "She administered a few potions, but none have worked."

Reid sank onto the bed. Henrick's eyes were glazed, his skin blotchy, and his body cold to touch.

"You...look...beautiful," he wheezed. "I wish I could be there to see you marry my son today."

"I wish you could be there, too."

"I want to tell you something." He clutched Reid's fingers. "I was wrong."

"About what?" she asked.

"My son, Eldon. He is just like his uncle, Hudson. Both have an evil streak. I was blind to only see the good and to hope for the best."

"You had no way of knowing."

"He did this to me." He took a shaky breath. "I want you to promise me you will help my wife and sons protect this county. I failed in my duties. Now you all must fix this for me. I am so sorry."

"I promise." Reid would do everything in her power to take care of the people of Axian.

"Thank you." Henrick closed his eyes, his breaths coming out short and loud.

"Has Dexter been to see him?" Reid asked Nara.

"He has. Henrick made Dexter promise the same thing." Nara

275

wiped her eyes. "You better go. It's almost time for the wedding to start."

Nara escorted Reid and Gytha out of the room. Before closing the door, Nara lowered her voice. "I don't know what the king has planned. Be on guard."

"We will," Gytha said.

Nara handed Reid a dagger. "This is mine. Slide it up your sleeve. Just in case."

Reid nodded and took the weapon, doing as instructed.

"Good luck," Nara whispered, then closed the door.

"I cannot believe the king would do something so dishonorable as to poison Prince Henrick," Gytha fumed as they headed down the hallway.

"I agree." It was one of the main reasons Reid supported the assassination of the king. Except now, she didn't know how they would manage to pull it off.

When they reached the antechamber, they went inside, waiting while the guests took their seats in the great hall. Too concerned about Henrick, Reid didn't dwell on the upcoming ceremony or the fact that not a single one of her family members would be there to witness the event—not even her grandparents.

Ackley slipped into the small room. "It's time. With the exception of your father, all the dukes are here. Are you ready?"

Suddenly nervous, Reid clutched her shaking arms. "Yes."

Ackley placed a hand on each of Reid's shoulders, squeezing tightly. "You look beautiful." He smirked. "Just focus on Prince Dexter and ignore the king."

"Easier said than done." Reid took a deep breath, releasing it slowly.

"Since a married man must walk you down the aisle—and neither your father nor your grandfather is here, and Henrick is still sick in bed—Gordon has offered to escort you. Is that okay?"

She shrugged, unable to find her voice. This was it.

"I'll see you in there," Gytha said as she left the room.

"Come on." Ackley took Reid's arm. "I'll walk you to the doors, then Gordon will take over." They exited the antechamber, then headed down the hallway to the front of the great hall.

At the doors, Gordon waited for her. Ackley kissed her cheek and gave her shoulder a reassuring squeeze before he went inside.

"I'm sorry your father isn't here," Gordon said. "Do you know where he is?"

She took his offered arm. "Are you asking out of concern or did your brother put you up to it?"

"Concern. For you."

Reid nodded. "You are aware Eldon has a foreign army here, right?"

He flinched, body tensing.

"How can you stand by and support him?" she demanded.

"He is my brother and king."

"He's going to destroy the kingdom. Have you considered the possibility that once Eldon has eliminated all contenders for the throne, the Melenia army will turn on him and take over Marsden?"

"We shouldn't be having this conversation right now," Gordon whispered.

"When the time comes, I hope you make the right choice—to stand with us instead of against us."

The doors swung open, revealing a packed room.

"And who is *us*?" he asked, cocking his head. "You?"

"*Us* is the kingdom. The entire kingdom."

Gordon gingerly took the first step, escorting Reid down the aisle toward the dais where the ceremony would take place. Dexter waited for her at the end of the aisle. In full uniform, he appeared bold and commanding. When she smiled at him, he grinned back.

At the end of the aisle, Gordon handed her over to Dexter. Reid and Dexter took their places, standing side by side. Instead of the marriage binder coming forward, the king moved to stand before them.

"And here I thought this was going to be a punishment," the king muttered so only Reid and Dexter could hear. "But you two appear far too familiar with one another. This will never do." He *tsked*, the sound mocking and almost evil. It caused Reid's blood to run cold.

Out of the corner of her eye, Reid realized Nara wasn't in the front row where she was supposed to be.

An Axian soldier entered from the side door near the dais, coming to stand beside the king. He held out a piece of paper. Eldon took the message and dismissed the soldier.

After reading the paper, he folded it and sighed. "Ladies and gentlemen, thank you for coming to celebrate the marriage of Prince Dexter and Lady Reid. However, I've just received some tragic news." He lifted the letter as proof. "It is with a grave heart that I inform you of the untimely passing of Prince Henrick."

A collective gasp spread across the room. Dexter jerked, shocked by the news.

"In light of this unfortunate event, I cannot marry such a lovely couple on this day. Today must be reserved as a day of mourning, not celebration."

A ringing sound reverberated in Reid's ears. Henrick was dead.

Sliding the paper under his cape, Eldon cleared his throat. "It is also with great sadness that I reveal the second part of my message." When he raised his right arm, soldiers began to march into the hall, closing and locking the doors.

Apprehension filled Reid. What did the king intend to do? Would he slaughter them all? Her hands shook, fear swirling low in her gut.

Harlow stood behind Eldon, off to the side against the wall, not saying a word or showing an ounce of emotion on her expressionless face.

"A secret organization known as the Knights of the Realm is

responsible for Prince Henrick's death. I have proof that the Knights assassinated the prince." Shaking his head, he moved to sit on the throne chair.

A ripple of whispers whipped across the room.

"What's worse," the king said, his voice trembling, as if he were on the verge of crying, "is that my own brother, Prince Ackley, has been linked to this murderous organization."

Blackness hovered around the edges of Reid's vision. This could not be happening. The king was pinning Henrick's death on Ackley and the Knights?

"Any person—man or woman—with a tattoo of a rose and dagger is to be killed on sight. I will give a substantial reward to anyone who brings me a person with the tattoo—either dead or alive."

How did the king know about the Knights? As far as Reid was aware, Ackley had told Idina and Gordon. Had one of them told Eldon? It seemed unlikely. Did Leigh know? Would she have told her son?

The king remained seated on the throne chair. A dozen soldiers lined up on the dais. Since they wore the king's colors, Reid assumed they were the king's Shields. Soldiers from the foreign army lined the perimeter of the room, blocking all the exits. Reid caught sight of Seb, who was dressed as a Melenia soldier. Had Dexter somehow managed to infiltrate the army with his own men? It was the first glimmer of hope that there might be a plan in place.

"Prince Ackley," Eldon said, his voice sounding weak. "Come here."

Two of the king's men stepped forward, grabbed Ackley's arms, and shoved him to his knees before Eldon. One yanked Ackley's sleeve up, exposing his tattoo. Two additional soldiers withdrew their swords, pointing them at Ackley.

"Prince Ackley. You are hereby stripped of your title and considered a traitor to the crown."

Reid almost laughed. Ackley could easily dispatch all four soldiers in under twenty seconds. However, he remained kneeling on the floor, staring at his brother. The queen's words rushed back to Reid—what were Ackley's motives for behaving so submissively? If he acted like a crazed assassin, everyone would believe the king. However, if he seemed like a non-threatening brother whom the king simply wanted to get out of the way, then people might begin to doubt the king.

"Kill him," the king ordered.

Without thought, Reid lunged forward to help Ackley. However, Dexter caught her, pressing three fingers into her back. He wanted her to move on the count of three. She slid Nara's dagger from her sleeve, palming it as she prepared to attack. Using three fingers, Dexter then touched four spots on her back, indicating the four soldiers surrounding Ackley. Then he tapped the lower right spot, meaning he needed her to strike the soldier closest to her. He touched one finger, the second, and then the third.

With every ounce of strength she possessed, Reid threw her dagger at the soldier closest to her. It embedded deep into his back. He stumbled, falling forward.

The soldier holding the sword to Ackley's neck raised his arm high, preparing to strike. Dexter withdrew his own sword, slicing into the soldier's arm before he could kill Ackley.

The soldier who held the second sword on Ackley met with the same fate, thanks to Gordon.

Grunting, Gytha threw a dagger at the fourth soldier's chest. He crumpled to the floor.

All four soldiers had been injured or killed in less than five seconds. Heaving in deep breaths, her wedding dress now splattered with blood, Reid stood tall, wondering what they were going to do now. The king remained frozen, his eyes wide with shocked fury.

An odd groaning sound reverberated, then the floor beneath

Ackley opened. Still on his hands and knees, Ackley fell straight down, disappearing from sight.

Dexter shoved Reid. She yelped as she went flying into the hole, tumbling onto the hard, dusty floor. Chaos reigned above her. She scrambled out of the way just as Dexter landed on his feet next to her.

"Run," Dexter commanded.

Instantly, Reid sprang to her feet, ignoring the pain in her ribs and her scratched hands. A long hallway stretched out before her, Ackley already running along it. She sprinted after him. The king shouted at his soldiers to attack. Screams rang through the air.

The hallway ended in a small empty room. Ackley waved her forward, then pushed her out of the way. Dexter came in right behind her, Gordon soon after.

Gytha sprinted toward them, sword in hand. Two soldiers gave chase, mere feet behind her. "Shut the door," she yelled as she turned to fight.

"No!" Reid cried, moving to help her friend.

Ackley yanked her back as Dexter slammed the door shut. He slid a metal bar across it, sending them into complete darkness.

"We have to help her!" Panic and horror consumed Reid. She couldn't let her friend die.

There was a rubbing sound, then a torch flared to life. Dexter held it up, blinking away tears. "Let Gytha do her job," he said. "She will be furious if we don't follow protocol and listen."

"What will they do to her?" Horrified, Reid's mind started working overtime. Would they take Gytha as a prisoner? Would they torture her to get information about the royal family's whereabouts? Would they kill her?

"When I shut this door, it closed the trap door. She should only have to deal with the soldiers stupid enough to chase her. Once she disposes of them, she'll have to figure a way out."

"Is there a way out?" Ackley asked, his voice barely audible.

"This palace has been here for centuries. It was built for

situations such as this one. Stop worrying about Captain Gytha. Let's get moving." Dexter hurried over to one of the walls, feeling around with his free hand. He pushed on a brick, and a door swung open as he did so. "There's a network of underground tunnels designed for this very thing." He led the way down a dark tunnel. "I just never thought I'd actually have to use them."

They traversed through tunnel after tunnel until Reid feared they'd lost their way. However, Dexter never hesitated as he led them with a torch in hand. After at least a mile of twists and turns, they ascended a wooden staircase and exited into a windowless room.

"Where are we?" Gordon asked.

"The military compound." Dexter doused the torch.

CHAPTER TWENTY-THREE

Reid froze, unable to move. She couldn't even see her own hand in front of her face. A moment later, a door creaked open and Dexter ushered them into a brightly lit hallway. They ran through corridor after corridor until they came to one of the interior courtyards. Dexter barked out a series of orders, and soldiers scrambled to comply.

"What are we doing?" Reid asked. Everything had happened so quickly she hadn't had time to sort through what was going on.

"We're going to a safe location to plan," Dexter replied. "Then we'll retake the palace and kill King Eldon." He said it so simply— as if they weren't facing several seemingly impossible tasks.

Horses were brought forward, along with handfuls of clothes. Dexter ordered everyone to change. Reid removed her wedding dress, then put on a plain brown tunic and pants. Someone handed her a hat to cover her hair. When she finished, she realized everyone else had dressed similarly.

"Let's go," Dexter said as he mounted.

Reid climbed on one of the smaller horses. Once she was situated, a soldier placed a heavy cape over her shoulders. Realizing chainmail lined it, she pulled it closer, thankful it would protect her body and the horse's backside from arrows. Gordon, Ackley, and Dexter received similar capes.

"How are we going to get out of the city without the king's soldiers spotting us?" Reid inquired.

"Those are not the king's soldiers," Gordon snapped.

"Why are you coming with us?" Reid asked.

Gordon pressed the palm of his hand to his forehead. "Eldon is conspiring with a foreign army. He has taken my soldiers and tossed them aside in favor of Melenia's. I have to stop him before we lose Marsden."

"What about Dana?"

"She's pregnant. Eldon already named my firstborn son as his heir. He won't hurt Dana. He needs her."

With Gordon now on their side, Reid felt more confident in their quest to retake the kingdom.

A large door built into the side of the wall swung open. "We have to start out slow," Dexter said, heading toward the darkened corridor. "It's steep."

A soldier handed him a torch. He entered the corridor, revealing a ramp descending into a tunnel. Reid followed behind him, her horse not hesitating in the confined space. Once Gordon and Ackley made it inside, the door slammed shut.

"They have orders to blow the tunnel if enemy soldiers breach the compound," Dexter explained.

Not wanting to think about that scenario, Reid followed Dexter down the ramp. The ground eventually leveled out, and they were able to ride a bit faster. No one spoke. After a solid hour, they headed up an incline. Dexter dismounted, then fumbled with a door. It took him a few tries until it finally opened. Once they were out in the bright sunlight, Dexter closed and locked the door, which had been built into the side of a rocky mountain covered with vines. After making sure the entrance remained concealed, he mounted and led the way through the dense forest.

They rode until they came to a narrow dirt path. Then they

pushed the horses faster, no one speaking as they covered as much ground as possible before it became too dark to travel any farther. When they could barely see, Dexter led them off the trail and into the cover of the forest.

"Sleep. As soon as there's enough light, we'll continue."

Too exhausted to think about the past twenty-four hours, Reid tied her horse to a tree, removed her cape, and stretched out on the ground. She heard the men mumbling about finding water for the horses. But she didn't care. She closed her eyes, immediately falling asleep.

Someone shook Reid awake. When she opened her eyes, she saw Dexter kneeling beside her. "It's time to go," he whispered.

"Wait." She grabbed his hand before he could stand. "I'm sorry."

"This isn't your fault."

Reid scrambled to her knees. "No." How could she explain it so he would understand? "I'm sorry your father is dead." She wished there were a nicer, kinder way to say it, but there wasn't.

He closed his eyes, nodding once.

Sliding her hands on either side of his face, Reid waited until he'd opened his eyes and focused on her. "We'll deal with this together." Eldon, retaking the kingdom, Henrick's death—all of it. She would stand by Dexter's side to right all the wrongs.

He let out a shaky breath, then quickly hugged her before they rose.

"Time to head out?" Gordon asked as he stood and stretched.

Dexter nodded. "We need to get moving in case Melenia soldiers are trying to track us."

There was barely enough light to see since the sun hadn't risen yet. A light fog coated the ground. Reid put her cape on, then mounted her horse.

Dexter led them back to the dirt road. Once again, they pushed their horses as fast as they could. Come late afternoon, Reid realized some of the terrain looked familiar.

"Why are we going to my grandparents' house?" she asked.

"That's where I was told to go if there ever was a problem," Dexter answered.

The four of them made their way to the front of the manor. When Reid dismounted, the front door opened. She expected to see her grandmother standing there. However, Duke Ellington exited, followed by Colbert. Finn shoved past Colbert's legs, barreling down the steps to greet Reid. She handed her horse's reins to Ackley before kneeling to pet the dog.

"What are you doing here?" Reid asked her father. "I thought you said you were going to speak with the person in charge of the Knights?"

He shoved his hands in his pockets, pursing his lips. "That is exactly what I'm doing."

Anna exited the house. "Hello, Reid."

What was Anna doing here? How did Duke Ellington know her?

Reid stood, trying to put the pieces of the puzzle together. Anna raised her eyebrows, as if waiting for something from Reid. In that moment, Anna had an uncanny resemblance to Reid's sister, Kamden.

Reid took a step back. This was the woman from the portrait in her grandparents' dining room. Shock rolled through her as she made the connection. "You're my mother."

End of Book Two

Hidden Knights
Knights of the Realm, Book 3

This is the stunning conclusion to the
Knights of the Realm series!

ABOUT THE AUTHOR

Jennifer Anne Davis graduated from the University of San Diego with a degree in English and a teaching credential. She is currently a full-time writer and mother of three kids. She is happily married to her high school sweetheart and lives in the San Diego area.

Jennifer is the recipient of the San Diego Book Awards Best Published Young Adult Novel (2013), winner of the Kindle Book Awards (2018), a finalist in the USA Best Book Awards (2014), and a finalist in the Next Generation Indie Book Awards (2014).

Visit Jennifer at:
www.JenniferAnneDavis.com

facebook.com/AuthorJenniferAnneDavis
twitter.com/authorjennifer
instagram.com/authorjennifer
pinterest.com/authorjennifer
goodreads.com/jenniferannedavis
bookbub.com/authors/jennifer-anne-davis